From the Pages of
Journey to the Center of the Earth

Otto Lidenbrock had no mischief in him, I readily admit that; but unless he changes in unlikely ways, he will die a confirmed original.
(page 3)

My uncle went on working, his imagination went off rambling into the ideal world of combinations; he lived far away from earth, and genuinely beyond earthly needs.
(page 26)

"All the theories of science demonstrate that such a feat is impossible!"
(page 32)

Large though it is, that asylum is not big enough to contain all Professor Lidenbrock's madness!
(page 44)

We traveled around the enormous base of the volcano. The professor hardly took his eyes off it; he gesticulated, he seemed to challenge it and say: "Here's the giant that I'll tame!"
(page 76)

The crater of Snaefells resembled an inverted cone, whose opening might have been half a league in diameter. Its depth appeared to be about two thousand feet. Imagine the aspect of such a container when it filled with thunder and flames. The bottom of the funnel was about 250 feet in circumference, so that its rather gentle slopes allowed its lower brim to be reached without difficulty. Involuntarily I compared the whole crater to an enormous hollow grenade launcher, and the comparison frightened me.
(page 89)

My hair stood on end with terror. The feeling of emptiness overcame me. I felt the center of gravity shifting in me, and vertigo rising up to my brain like drunkenness. There is nothing more treacherous than this attraction toward the abyss.
(page 94)

"To Hell with your calculations!" replied my uncle in a fit of rage. "To Hell with your hypotheses!" (page 131)

If the 'average' number of difficulties did not increase, we could not fail to reach our goal. And then, what glory! I had come around to reasoning in this way, quite like a Lidenbrock. Seriously. Was this due to the strange environment in which I was living? Perhaps. (page 133)

Impossible to get away. The reptiles approach; they wheel around our little raft at a speed that express trains could not match; they swim concentric circles around it. I've gripped my rifle. But what can a bullet do against the scales that cover the bodies of these animals? (page 168)

Ah! the descent of this electric sphere has magnetized all the iron on board; the instruments, the tools, the weapons, move about and clash with a sharp jangle; the nails in my shoes cling tenaciously to a plate of iron set into the wood. I cannot pull my foot away! (pages 180–181)

"As long as the heart beats, as long as the flesh pulsates, I can't admit that any creature endowed with willpower needs to be overwhelmed by despair." (page 215)

Ah! What a journey! What a wonderful journey! Having entered through one volcano, we had exited through another, and that other one was more than twelve hundred leagues away from Snaefells, and from that barren landscape of Iceland at the edge of the world! (pages 228–229)

From that day on, the professor was the happiest of scholars, and I was the happiest of men, for my pretty Virland girl, resigning her place as ward, took up position in the house on the Königstrasse in the double capacity of niece and wife. No need to add that her uncle was the illustrious Otto Lidenbrock, corresponding member of all the scientific, geographical, and mineralogical societies on the five continents of the earth. (page 232)

JOURNEY TO THE CENTER OF THE EARTH

Jules Verne

*With an Introduction and Notes
by Ursula K. Heise*

Translated by Frederick Amadeus Malleson

*Translation revised by Ursula K. Heise
Illustrations by Rachel Perkins*

George Stade
Consulting Editorial Director

ℬ
BARNES & NOBLE CLASSICS
NEW YORK

ℬ
BARNES & NOBLE CLASSICS
NEW YORK

Published by Barnes & Noble Books
122 Fifth Avenue
New York, NY 10011

www.barnesandnoble.com/classics

Le Voyage au centre de la Terre was first published in 1864. Frederick Amadeus Malleson's English translation (1877) has been thoroughly revised by Ursula K. Heise for this edition of *Journey to the Center of the Earth*.

Published in 2005 by Barnes & Noble Classics with new Biography, Chronology, Introduction, A Note on the Translation, A Note on Measurements, Notes, Comments & Questions, and For Further Reading.

Journey to the Center of the Earth
ISBN-10: 1-59308-252-5
ISBN-13: 978-1-59308-252-9
LC Control Number 2005923983

Produced and published in conjunction with:
Fine Creative Media, Inc.
322 Eighth Avenue
New York, NY 10001

Michael J. Fine, President and Publisher

Printed in the United States of America
QM
1 3 5 7 9 10 8 6 4 2
FIRST PRINTING

Jules Verne

The creator of the *roman scientifique*, the popular literary genre known today as science fiction, Jules Gabriel Verne was born in the port town of Nantes, France, in 1828. His father, Pierre, was a prominent lawyer, and his mother, Sophie, was from a successful ship-building family. Despite his father's wish that he pursue law, young Jules was fascinated by the sea and all things foreign and adventurous. Legend holds that at age eleven he ran away from school to work aboard a ship bound for the West Indies but was caught by his father shortly after leaving port.

Jules developed an abiding love of science and language from a young age. He studied geology, Latin, and Greek in secondary school, and frequently visited factories, where he observed the workings of industrial machines. These visits likely inspired his desire for scientific plausibility in his writing and perhaps informed his depictions of the submarine *Nautilus* and the other seemingly fantastical inventions he described.

After completing secondary school, Jules studied law in Paris, as his father had before him. However, during the two years he spent earning his degree, he developed more consuming interests. Through family connections, he entered Parisian literary circles and met many of the distinguished writers of the day. Inspired in particular by novelists Victor Hugo and Alexandre Dumas (father and son), Verne began writing his own works. His poetry, plays, and short fiction achieved moderate success, and in 1852 he became secretary of the Théâtre lyrique.

In 1857 he married Honorine Morel, a young widow with two children. Seeking greater financial security, he took a position as a stockbroker with the Paris firm Eggly and Company. However, he reserved his mornings for writing. Baudelaire's recently published French translation of the works of Edgar Allan Poe, as well as the days Verne spent researching points of science in the library, inspired him to write a new sort of novel: the *roman scientifique*. His first such novel, *Five Weeks in a Balloon*, was an immediate success and earned him a publishing contract with the important editor Pierre-Jules Hetzel.

For the rest of his life, Verne published an average of two novels a year; the fifty-four volumes published during his lifetime, collectively known as *Voyages Extraordinaires*, include his best-known works, *Journey to the Center of the Earth*, *Around the World in Eighty Days*, and *Twenty Thousand Leagues Under the Sea*.

In 1872 Verne settled in Amiens with his family. During the next several years he traveled extensively on his yachts, visiting such locales as North Africa, Gibraltar, Scotland, and Ireland. In 1886 Verne's mentally ill nephew shot him in the leg, and the author was lame thereafter. This incident, as well as the tumultuous political climate in Europe, marked a change in Verne's perspective on science, exploration, and industry. Although not as popular as his early novels, Verne's later works are in many ways as prescient. Touching on such subjects as the ill effects of the oil industry, the negative influence of missionaries in the South Seas, and the extinction of animal species, they speak to concerns that remain urgent in our own time.

Verne continued writing actively throughout his life, despite failing health, the loss of family members, and financial troubles. At his death in 1905 his desk drawers contained the manuscripts of several new novels. Jules Verne is buried in the Madeleine Cemetery in Amiens.

Table of Contents

List of Illustrations
viii

The World of Jules Verne and
Journey to the Center of the Earth
ix

Introduction by Ursula K. Heise
xv

A Note on the Translation
xxxi

A Note on Measurements
xxxiii

JOURNEY TO THE
CENTER OF THE EARTH
1

Endnotes
233

Inspired by Journey to the Center of the Earth
237

Comments & Questions
241

For Further Reading
247

List of Illustrations

My uncle pounced on this shred with understandable eagerness. . . .10

Ragged clouds drifted over my head. 47

The little horse, bending his knees, crawled out from under the professor's legs. 70

We could see the two peaks boldly projected against the dark grey sky. 84

It softly brushed the edge of the middle chimney. 92

In the walls were distinct impressions of fucus and lycopods. 107

A jet of water spurted out of the rock and hit the opposite wall. . . .123

"Perhaps at this very moment there's a storm unleashed above." . .130

These were white mushrooms thirty to forty feet tall. 153

Two monsters disrupt the surface of the ocean. 170

The complete history of animal life was piled up. 191

A human being watched over this countless herd of mastodons! . .200

It floated on the flood of lava, amidst a hail of ashes. 223

I could feel the heaving of the mountain. .227

The World of Jules Verne and
Journey to the Center of the Earth

1828 Jules Gabriel Verne is born in the port city of Nantes, France, the first of the five children who will be born to Pierre and Sophie Allotte Verne. His father, an attorney, will encourage young Jules to pursue a career in law. His mother, from a ship-building family, instills in him a love of the sea.

1831 Victor Hugo's *Notre-Dame de Paris* (*The Hunchback of Notre Dame*) is published.

1833 George Sand's novel *Lélia* is published by the well-known publisher Pierre-Jules Hetzel, who later will publish Verne's novels.

1834 Jules begins attending secondary school. During his years at school, he excels in geology, Latin, and Greek. Also greatly interested in machinery, he makes frequent visits to nearby factories.

1839 It is said that the adventurous boy tries to run away to sea aboard a ship bound for the West Indies but is apprehended by his father before reaching open waters.

1843 Tahiti becomes a French protectorate.

1844 Alexandre Dumas's *Le Comte de Monte Cristo* (*The Count of Monte Cristo*) is published.

1847 Jules begins studying law in Paris; he will receive his degree in two years. In Paris, family friends introduce him to some of France's most distinguished writers, including Victor Hugo. Jules begins writing to supplement his meager allowance. Several of his plays are well received in theaters; his fiction appears in the Parisian magazine *Musée des familles*.

1852 Louis-Napoléon becomes emperor of France as Napoléon III. Novelists Alexandre Dumas (père and fils) secure Verne a position as secretary of the Théâtre lyrique.

1853   French administrator Georges-Eugène Haussmann begins alterations and municipal improvements in Paris, including the construction of the wide boulevards that distinguish the city to this day. The Crimean War begins, pitting Russia against France, England, and the Ottoman Turks.

1854   French poet Charles Baudelaire's translation of the works of Edgar Allan Poe captivates Verne and initiates his lifelong admiration of the American author.

1857   Verne marries the widow Honorine de Viane Morel, whom he had met the previous year. Quitting his position at the Théâtre lyrique, he embarks on a career as a stockbroker at Eggly and Company, although he continues to devote his mornings to writing. Charles Baudelaire's volume of poems *Les fleurs du mal* (*The Flowers of Evil*) and Gustave Flaubert's novel *Madame Bovary* are published.

1859   Verne spends hours in the library gaining the scientific knowledge that will inform his fiction. He travels to England and Scotland. English naturalist Charles Darwin's *On the Origin of Species by Means of Natural Selection* is published. Work begins on the Suez Canal.

1861   Verne travels to Norway and Denmark. His son and only child, Michel, is born. He meets the legendary photographer Nadar.

1862   Verne's manuscript *Cinq semaines en ballon* (*Five Weeks in a Balloon*) is accepted by Hetzel for publication. Until his death, Verne will publish an average of two books a year with Hetzel, forming the cumulative series known as *Voyages Extraordinaires* (*Extraordinary Voyages*). Hugo's *Les Misérables* appears.

1863   *Five Weeks in a Balloon* is published to great success.

1864   *Voyage au centre de la Terre* (*Journey to the Center of the Earth*) is published. Verne writes an article on Poe for *Musée des familles*.

1865   *De la Terre à la Lune* (*From the Earth to the Moon*) appears. English writer Lewis Carroll's *Alice's Adventures in Wonderland* is published.

1866   *Voyages et aventures du capitaine Hatteras* (*The Adventures of Captain Hatteras*) is published.

1867   Verne travels with his brother Paul to New York aboard the

Great Eastern. Les enfants du capitaine Grant (*The Children of Captain Grant*) is published.

1868   He purchases his first yacht, the *Saint-Michel*, named for his only son.

1869   *Vingt mille lieues sous les mers* (*Twenty Thousand Leagues Under the Sea*) is published in two volumes (1869–1870). Its depiction of the submarine *Nautilus* (named after the first submarine, invented around 1800 by American engineer Robert Fulton) predates the construction of the first submarine by twenty-five years.

1870   The Franco-Prussian War breaks out; Verne serves in the Coast Guard.

1871   *Une ville flottante* (*A Floating City*), partly inspired by a trip to Niagara Falls, New York, is published. Verne's father dies. The Franco-Prussian War ends.

1872   The Verne family moves to Amiens, where Verne will reside the rest of his life.

1873   Another Verne masterpiece, *Le tour du monde en quatre-vingts jours* (*Around the World in Eighty Days*), is published. French poet Arthur Rimbaud's confessional autobiography *Une Saison en Enfer* (*A Season in Hell*) is published.

1874   *Le Docteur Ox* (*Dr. Ox's Experiment and Other Stories*) appears, along with *L'Île mystérieuse* (*The Mysterious Island*). *Around the World in Eighty Days* is adapted for the stage. Verne purchases a new yacht, the *Saint-Michel II*.

1875   *Le Chancellor* (*The Chancellor*) is published.

1876   *Michel Strogoff* is published.

1877   *Les Indes noires* (*The Child of the Cavern*) and *Hector Servadac* are published. Verne buys his last yacht, the *Saint-Michel III*.

1878   A leisurely cruise aboard the *Saint-Michel III* takes Verne and his brother to North Africa, Portugal, and Gibraltar.

1879   *Les Cinq cents millions de la Bégum* (*The Begum's Fortune*) and *Les tribulations d'un Chinois en Chine* (*The Tribulations of a Chinaman in China*) are published.

1880   Verne cruises to Scotland and Ireland. *La Maison à vapeur* (*The Steam House*) is published.

1881   Verne cruises to Holland, Denmark, and Germany. *La Jan-gada* (*The Giant Raft*) is published.

1882   Verne moves his family to a larger house in Amiens with a circular tower; today it is a well-known Verne landmark and the headquarters of the Jules Verne Society in Amiens.

1883   Scottish writer Robert Louis Stevenson's novel *Treasure Island* is published. War in Indochina breaks out.

1884   Verne voyages to Italy, where Pope Leo XIII personally blesses his work.

1885   Victor Hugo dies. English novelist Henry Rider Haggard publishes *King Solomon's Mines*.

1886   Verne's deranged nephew, Gaston, shoots him in the leg, laming him for life. This personal disaster, and his growing cynicism about industrialization, marks a turn toward pessimism in Verne's outlook and writing. His longtime publisher, Hetzel, dies. Verne sells the *Saint-Michel III* because of financial concerns. Robert Louis Stevenson publishes *Dr. Jekyll and Mr. Hyde*.

1887   Verne's mother dies.

1888   Verne is elected to the municipal council of Amiens, where he will serve for fifteen years.

1889   *Sans dessus dessous* (*Topsy-Turvy*) appears, which contains notably negative views on the potential of technology. His later novels will take on various forms of social injustice, from the plight of orphans to the corrupting power of missionaries in foreign lands.

1895   English novelist H. G. Wells's *The Time Machine* is published.

1897   *Le Sphinx des glaces* (*The Ice Sphinx*), written as a sequel to Poe's 1838 novel *The Narrative of Arthur Gordon Pym*, is published. Flagging health plagues Verne. His brother Paul dies. English writer Rudyard Kipling's *Captains Courageous* and Edmond Rostand's play *Cyrano de Bergerac* are published.

1899   Verne's *Le testament d'un excentrique* (*The Will of an Eccentric*) deals with the oil industry's ravages of the environment.

1905   Leaving a drawer filled with manuscripts, and with his family gathered at his bedside, Jules Verne dies of complications from diabetes. He is buried in Madeleine Cemetery in Amiens. His posthumously published novels, altered considerably by his son, Michel, remain a source of scholarly debate and interest.

Introduction

Traveling to the center of the Earth would involve a downward trip of about 4,000 miles that would cut through the Earth's crust and its mostly solid, rocky mantle into a liquid core of iron alloy, then end at a solid inner core of iron and nickel. Pressure and temperature would rise with increasing depth, and temperatures would reach about 10,300 degrees Fahrenheit at the Earth's center—hardly a climate that many geo-tourists would enjoy! Much of this knowledge about the geophysical structure of the Earth was acquired in the course of the twentieth century, long after Jules Verne published *Journey to the Center of the Earth*. In 1864, when the book appeared, different hypotheses about the nature of the Earth competed with each other. Even then, though, in light of any of the contemporary scientific theories, a journey to the Earth's core belonged to the realm of the fantastic. Why then did Verne, who was intensely interested in the science and technology of his day, choose this idea as the founding assumption of what was to become one of his most famous novels? And why is this journey undertaken not by a dreamer or a madman, but by a hard-core scientist, a professor of mineralogy and geology who is thoroughly familiar with the scientific debates of his time?

For a reader who first encounters *Journey to the Center of the Earth* at the beginning of the twenty-first century, the enthusiasm of Professor Otto Lidenbrock, his nephew Axel, and even Lidenbrock's goddaughter Graüben for mineralogical specimens and geological theories may seem nothing short of eccentric. After Alfred Wegener's theory of continental drift—originally proposed in the 1920s—had been generally accepted in the 1960s, geology disappeared from public awareness as a science that could bring about exciting new discoveries and theories. But in the middle of the nineteenth century, geology was a brand-new branch of knowledge rife with the opposing theories and opinions of some of the best minds of the day. Far from being an arcane branch of scientific knowledge of mostly academic interest, it touched upon the most basic questions of the origin of life and human beings and the nature of the very soil they walk upon. Not just scholars but public and religious authorities believed they had a vital stake in the outcome of geological controversies.

As a scientific discipline, geology had in fact only come into being in the first half of the nineteenth century. Before that, mineralogists had been just about the only scientists to study the inanimate environment, conducting their investigation of the Earth most frequently in the context of French and German mining schools. Their study consisted of a mix of natural philosophy, theology, and the beginnings of empirical observation, without the benefit of an established academic framework. Abraham Gottlob Werner, a German professor at the Mining School of Freiberg in the late eighteenth century, combined the study of rock formations with the biblical account of Genesis. The Scottish naturalist, chemist, and geologist James Hutton opposed Werner's theories and grounded his own account of the development of the Earth on observable processes and on the principle of uniformitarianism—that is, the idea that the processes that had gone into the shaping of the Earth over immensely long periods of time had not fundamentally changed and could still account for geological development. Hutton's work was followed by that of Scottish geologist Charles Lyell, whose classic book *Principles of Geology*, published in 1830, laid down the foundations of a new, empirically based science of the Earth.

But the Earth is so vast and all-encompassing that it often appeared complicated to infer its general operating principles from the processes observable in one particular place. Indeed, huge areas of geology—the 70 percent of the Earth's surface that is under water, as well as its interior—are simply inaccessible to direct human observation. (Lyell once joked that an amphibious observer who could inhabit both land and sea would be a more suitable geologist than a human being.) For these reasons, divergent theories about the nature of the Earth continued to rage throughout the nineteenth century. While some scholars argued that the interior of the Earth had to be mostly liquid, with the solid ground a mere thin crust not unlike ice on lake water, others replied that on mathematical grounds the Earth could not be anything but for the most part solid. The age of the Earth was similarly subject to vastly divergent estimations, and this issue became part of the violent controversy over Darwin's theory of evolution in the 1850s and 1860s. Biological evolution occurs over immense periods of time, and in general, the development of the physical structure of the Earth over hundreds of thousands or even millions of years contradicts creationist accounts of a much shorter time span for the origins of the Earth.

In Verne's day, therefore, geological theories about the origin and gradual shaping of the Earth, along with biological insights into the evolution of life, were what genetic engineering and nanotechnology are for us today: innovative and exciting areas of scientific research that have a profound bearing on the way we think about our own identity and experience our everyday lives. Verne's familiarity with these debates shows up in every chapter of *Journey to the Center of the Earth*, which abounds in references to the leading scientific minds of his day, from naturalists and geologists such as Georges Cuvier to explorers such as Alexander von Humboldt and archaeologists such as Jacques Boucher de Perthes. Caught up in the evolving plot, a contemporary reader's attention might easily slide over such references unawares. But their presence is the equivalent of mentions of James Watson and Francis Crick, Stephen Hawking, or Bill Gates in a novel written today.

Verne's editor, Pierre-Jules Hetzel, claimed in a preface he wrote in 1866—just two years after the first publication of *Journey to the Center of the Earth*—that Verne's novels were finally making a place for science in the domain of literature, and that Verne would eventually present all the knowledge of geography, geology, physics, and astronomy that modern science had accumulated. Verne himself once remarked to the French novelist Alexandre Dumas père, "Just as you are the great chronicler of history, I shall become the chronicler of geography." It is not hard to see why an integration of scientific knowledge with compelling literary characters and plots would have proved an attractive mix both to the audience of Verne's own day and those of subsequent periods: It combines the heady excitement of techno-scientific innovation with the pleasures of narrative storytelling and the free flight of the imagination.

This combination of science and fantasy may explain why Verne did not stick with the serious scientific theories of his day, but included marginal and controversial notions, too, such as that of a hollow Earth. English astronomer Edmund Halley proposed the idea that the Earth is hollow in the late seventeenth century. Swiss mathematician Leonhard Euler pursued the theory in the eighteenth century, as did Americans John Cleves Symmes and Jeremiah Reynolds and Scottish mathematician Sir John Leslie in the nineteenth century. (Axel alludes to Symmes in chapter XXIX, mistakenly identifying him as English rather than American.) Such theories influenced not only Verne, but also other writers and were sporadically revived until the early twentieth century. Edgar Allan Poe's "Manuscript Found in a Bottle" and *Narrative of Arthur Gordon Pym* and Edgar Rice Burroughs's *At the Earth's Core* and *Pellucidar* are other examples. Yet by the time Verne published *Journey to the Center of the Earth* in 1864, hollow-Earth theories, while not entirely disproved, were not a central topic of debate among leading scientists.

Verne, famous for his extensive and meticulous note taking, was surely not unaware of this fact; what led him to use the idea of a hollow Earth as the foundation for his novel was no doubt the way in which the notion allowed him to tie scientific exploration into some of the oldest and most significant motifs of the Western literary tradition. On the surface, the plot of *Journey to the Center of the Earth* seems relatively straightforward: Lidenbrock and his nephew by sheer coincidence discover an ancient cryptogram that points to the bottom of an Icelandic volcano as the entryway to a passage that will eventually lead to the Earth's core. Axel prefers the safety of life above ground and is reluctant to leave his fiancée, the professor's goddaughter Graüben, but Lidenbrock becomes obsessed with the idea of retracing the steps of his illustrious predecessor, the sixteenth-century Icelandic scholar Arne Saknussemm, [. . .] to the center of the Earth. Lidenbrock, Axel, and their Icelandic guide Hans penetrate deep beneath the Earth's crust, where they discover an alternative world of plants, animals, and even human beings that have long gone extinct on the surface, and return to ground level through another volcano. Although this plot may at first appear to be quite linear, it derives much of its narrative force from the way in which it invokes some of the founding stories of Western culture: the quest narrative, the descent to the underworld, and the initiatory voyage.

Professor Otto Lidenbrock is without any doubt a prime example of a hero on a quest so urgent that no one and nothing can stop it.

His obstinacy in reaching the center of the Earth in spite of seemingly insurmountable obstacles puts him in the company of other literary figures whom we remember principally because of their overriding obsession with a single project: Jules Verne's own Captain Nemo from *Twenty Thousand Leagues under the Sea* and Phileas Fogg from *Around the World in Eighty Days* provide the most obvious parallels, but one is also reminded of Captain Ahab, the protagonist of Herman Melville's *Moby-Dick*. While these may well be more complex characters, Lidenbrock shares with them their stubborn single-mindedness, their iron determination, and the reckless imposition of their will on others who have no desire to take part in the pursuit but are dragged along regardless. Even seen through Axel's reluctant eyes, however, Uncle Lidenbrock remains likable: His personal foibles, which Axel dwells on with a mix of gentle malice and affection, make him a more human figure than Nemo or Ahab, and the novel leaves us in no doubt that Lidenbrock is genuinely attached to his nephew and his ward Graüben—though his concern for them will never in the end deter him from his quest for knowledge.

While there is no doubt something clichéd about this portrait of the fierce scientist with the warm heart under his crust of social brusqueness, it is Lidenbrock's enthusiasm and determination in the pursuit of science that gives the novel much of its propulsive energy (as literary critics have pointed out, his temper is compared to volcanic eruptions and electric discharges long before his expedition actually encounters these phenomena in their literal shape). Yet it is curious that Lidenbrock's scientific obsession is not presented as a quest for genuine innovation and original discovery, but rather as the repetition of a project that was already executed by someone else centuries earlier. The discovery of sixteenth-century scholar Arne Saknussemm's manuscript certainly strikes a familiar note, as ancient books or maps and lost manuscripts written in secret codes play a crucial role in many nineteenth- and twentieth-century adventure romances. But here, the discovery turns the journey into the realm of the unknown into a simultaneous quest for the traces left by the historic predecessor; the search for the new combines with an attempt to reconnect with the past. These two time vectors in Lidenbrock's voyage point to two quite different conceptions of history: on one hand, the idea of progress and its association with the increase of scientific knowledge, and on the other hand, the idea of a heroic past in which great men accomplished tasks that are difficult to repeat for ordinary individuals of the modern age. The ultimate outcome of Lidenbrock's quest should be seen in light of this tension between different perspectives on the relationship of modern society to its past and future.

But whatever the philosophical implications of the professor's expedition into the unknown may be, the reader's attraction to following the journey lies above all in the abundance of physical detail that Verne provides. Whether the expedition's goal is reached or not soon seems less important than the marvelous details that unfold before the travelers' eyes. As the famous science-fiction writer Isaac Asimov has shrewdly noted, the scientific implausibility of humans penetrating deep into the Earth's mantle despite increasing heat and pressure is compensated by Verne's emphasis on precise details. From the meticulous attention paid to the tools and instruments the expedition requires to the narrator's lovingly detailed descriptions of the physical features of each geological layer they encounter, Verne's writing bewitches the reader with its insistence on the wonders of sheer materiality. He writes of the ingenuity of Ruhmkorff lamps with as much devotion as he describes the colored striations of marble in underground tunnels and the festive scintillations of light falling on thousands of bits of crystal and quartz embedded in walls and vaults of rock. Of course, this intense physical presence of nature is not always inviting for the characters: Steep vertical slopes, regions without a drop of water, heat, fierce storms, and darkness so absolute as to be almost palpable endanger the travelers, just as the primeval magnificence of the subterranean landscapes delights them. But whether it is splendid or menacing, the physicality of the environment in Verne's novel holds the reader spellbound.

At the same time, Verne associates the materiality of the Earth with symbolic and metaphoric dimensions that may be quite familiar to the reader. Some of the most influential texts of the Western cultural tradition, from Homer's *Odyssey* and Virgil's *Aeneid* to Dante's *Divine Comedy*, prominently feature the protagonist's descent into the underworld, the realm of the dead, as an important part of his social and spiritual development. Usually, the point of this voyage to the underworld is to confront deceased individuals whom he used to know: parents, lovers, friends, or public figures from his own era, whose manner of death and afterlife are significant for his own course of life and contribute to a deeper understanding of his past and present. In *Journey to the Center of the Earth*, this confrontation with death and desolation starts long before the protagonists descend into the crater of the Snaefells volcano; fully a third of the novel is taken up with the description of their journey toward and across Iceland. This part of the trip takes the expedition through a magnificently portrayed wasteland of cold, solitude, and poverty where plants, animals, and humans are barely able to survive and shadowy lepers scurry away at the travelers' approach. The impoverished Icelanders, portrayed as almost congenitally prone to silence and stolid acceptance of extreme adversity, sometimes seem to form part of an all-encompassing landscape of rock, ice, and steam more than of human society as we usually conceive it. All of these elements already suggest that the protagonists have entered a netherworld that will confront them with the bare essentials of their own existence.

Once the travelers start descending below the surface of the Earth and move outside the boundaries of human society, their exploration turns into a temporal as much as a geographical journey. They discover a prehistoric world of gigantically sized plants and mushrooms, a realm not only of fossils and bones but also of living, breathing, and battling dinosaurs and other animals long extinct on the planet's surface. In large segments of two chapters (XXXVIII and XXXIX) that were not part of the novel when it was published in 1864, they even encounter predecessors of the human species itself. Verne added them in 1867 as a direct fictional transplantation of discoveries about Stone Age humans that the French archaeologist Jacques Boucher de Perthes made in the 1830s and 1840s, but which were only generally accepted in the late 1850s and early 1860s. They were the basis for his claim, revolutionary at the time, that not only fauna and flora but human beings themselves have a history that counts in the hundreds of thousands of years. When the members of the Lidenbrock expedition encounter such long-extinct humans living in a prehistoric natural environment, they are confronted not just with a personal or social past, but with ecological and biological history. Geological layers, therefore, function in the novel as metaphors for both collective cultural and scientific memory, and traversing these layers implies traveling back in time.

As a precursor of such present-day imaginary encounters with prehistoric flora and fauna as Steven Spielberg's film *Jurassic Park*, Verne's *Journey* invites us to ask questions about how we remember, reconstruct, and invent the past and present of our biological surroundings. But while *Jurassic Park*, with its rampaging, man-eating dinosaurs, is ultimately intended as a warning about the excessive manipulation of nature by science and consumerism, the point in *Journey to the Center of the Earth* is quite different. Professor Lidenbrock and his nephew also encounter dangerous dinosaurs—but they end up battling each other, not the intruding humans, and in fact don't even seem to notice them. Verne does not mean to show us a natural world pushed beyond its limits by humans and taking its revenge on them. Rather, he invites us to compare this visceral confrontation with a primeval natural world in the middle pages of the novel to the very different encounter with the natural that takes place at the beginning of the story, in the description of Professor Lidenbrock's scientific lectures and his work on carefully classified mineralogical samples in his study.

Lab work and field work, abstract taxonomies and concrete perception, analytical distance and lived immersion, the attempt to master nature intellectually and the way in which nature always offers more marvelous panoramas than the human mind can grasp—these are the juxtapositions upon which the novel hinges. It doesn't seem that Verne wants his readers to value one over the other. Verne has quite a bit of fun at Professor Lidenbrock's expense, through narrator Axel's bemused and sometimes sarcastic comments about his pedantry, but the more visceral encounter with nature would never have taken place were it not for Lidenbrock's passion for abstruse old books and manuscripts, by means of which he discovers the passage into the interior of the globe. *Journey to the Center of the Earth* highlights both dimensions of the scientific enterprise, emphasizing their tensions but also their inevitable conjunction in the quest for more and better knowledge.

So the journey to the underworld, while it breathes new life into an ancient literary motif, also serves as a framework for reflection on the much more recent problems of a scientific approach to the natural world and its history. In addition, it contrasts this scientific perspective of relentless inquisitorial rigor, which is exemplified by

Professor Lidenbrock, with the more emotional, irrational, and sometimes visionary dimensions that his nephew Axel represents in the narrative. While Axel is a devoted scientist in his own right, he initially cares nothing about his uncle's expedition; his thoughts are more taken up with his love for Graüben than with the possible scientific benefits such a mission might bring. Younger, less experienced, and physically more frail than his uncle, Axel often reacts with dismay or despair to difficult situations that Lidenbrock and the Icelander Hans face with stolidity and optimism.

Yet it should be noted that it is Axel, not his uncle, who is able to solve the two intellectual puzzles that bookend the novel. At the beginning, Axel finds the key that breaks the code in Arne Saknussemm's cryptogram, and at the end, Axel discovers why the compass stopped functioning properly during the underground voyage. Clearly, then, there are scientific insights that are foreclosed to Professor Lidenbrock, not because of any intellectual weakness but because of his social and emotional ineptitude—his impatience, his eruptive temper, his disregard for erotic relations. Arriving at scientific truths, the novel seems to signal, requires not only technical expertise, which Lidenbrock certainly possesses, but also the kind of emotional warmth and visionary talent at which his nephew excels. Axel discovers the solution to Saknussemm's textual puzzle during a hallucinatory state of mind; and it is again during a hallucination that he has the most sweeping and most lyrical vision of time travel that the novel offers:

> I take up the telescope and scan the ocean. . . . I gaze upward in the air. Why should not some of the birds restored by the immortal Cuvier again flap their wings in these heavy atmospheric layers? The fish would provide them with sufficient food. I survey the whole space, but the air is as uninhabited as the shore. . . .
>
> Wide awake, I dream. I think I see enormous chelonians on the surface of the water, antediluvian turtles that resemble floating islands. Across the dimly lit beach walk the huge mammals of the first ages of the world, the leptotherium found in the caverns of Brazil, the mericotherium from the icy regions of Siberia. Farther on, the pachydermatous lophiodon, a giant tapir, hides behind the rocks, ready to fight for its prey with the anoplotherium, a strange animal that resembles

the rhinoceros, the horse, the hippopotamus and the camel, as if the Creator, in too much of a hurry in the first hours of the world, had combined several animals into one. The giant mastodon curls his trunk, and smashes rocks on the shore with his tusks, while the megatherium, resting on its enormous paws, digs through the soil, its roars echoing sonorously off the granite rocks. Higher up, the protopithecus—the first monkey that appeared on the globe—climbs up the steep summits. Higher yet, the pterodactyl with its winged hand glides on the dense air like a large bat. In the uppermost layers, finally, immense birds, more powerful than the cassowary and larger than the ostrich, spread their vast wings and are about to strike their heads against the granite vault.

All this fossil world is born again in my imagination. I travel back to the biblical age of the world, long before the advent of man, when the unfinished world was as yet insufficient to sustain him. My dream then goes back farther to the ages before the advent of living beings. The mammals disappear, then the birds, then the reptiles of the Secondary period, and finally the fish, the crustaceans, mollusks, and articulated beings. The zoophytes of the Transition period also return to nothingness. All the world's life is concentrated in me, and my heart is the only one that beats in this depopulated world. There are no more seasons; climates are no more; the heat of the globe continually increases and neutralizes that of the radiant star. Vegetation grows excessively. I glide like a shade amongst arborescent ferns, treading with unsteady feet the iridescent clay and the multicolored sand; I lean against the trunks of immense conifers; I lie in the shade of sphenophylla, asterophylla, and lycopods, a hundred feet tall.

Centuries pass by like days! I move back through the series of terrestrial transformations. Plants disappear; granite rocks lose their purity; solids give way to liquids under the impact of increasing heat; water covers the surface of the globe; it boils, evaporates; steam envelops the earth, which gradually dissolves into a gaseous mass, white-hot, as large and radiant as the sun!

In the midst of this nebula, fourteen hundred thousand times more voluminous than this globe that it will one day become, I am carried into planetary spaces! My body subtilizes, sublimates itself in its turn and, like an imponderable atom, mingles with these immense vapors that follow their flaming orbits through infinite space.

What a dream! Where is it carrying me? My feverish hand
sketches the strange details out on paper! I have forgotten everything,
the professor, the guide, and the raft! A hallucination possesses my
spirit (pp. 162–163).

It is, of course, noteworthy that this journey to the beginnings of the
cosmos fictionalizes, in reverse time sequence, some of the chief scientific findings of Verne's era—the discovery of the enormous age of
the Earth and Darwin's theory of evolution, which was published in
1859, just five years prior to *Journey to the Center of the Earth*. It is
also remarkable that Axel, in the throes of a properly scientific hallucination, loses the analytical distance that usually characterizes
scientific work, and gradually shifts from normal scientific observation with a telescope to a visual imagination of nonexistent natural
objects. He then places himself physically among these objects (leaning against the trunks of imaginary trees) and finally feels his body
merge with the elementary forces of the cosmos in a climactic moment of transcendence. That such visionary states clearly cannot be
sustained for long (Axel almost falls off the expedition's raft because
of his hallucination!) does not diminish their importance for science as Verne represents it. Otto Lidenbrock, a man who pulls the
leaves of plant seedlings to speed along their growth, is clearly incapable of the kind of surrender to nature that is spelled out in his
nephew's vision, and this capability, in the novel, is an indispensable
ingredient for a truly inspired and innovative scientific perspective.

The enormous lyrical power of Axel's vision arises not only from
what it tells us about Verne's understanding of science and its relationship to the natural world. It is also gripping because it forms
part of what is clearly the initiation voyage of a young man who has
still to learn how to occupy his position in the social and scientific
realms. The vision occurs after Axel has already suffered two near-
death experiences—he almost dies from thirst, and he gets lost and
spends agonizing hours alone in complete darkness and despair.
Axel's vision includes two very different bodily experiences: first, a
concentration of all the biological life forces of the world in his body
and the beating of his heart, then a complete dissolution of his body
in its merger with the inanimate physical forces of the universe.
Both, clearly, form part of an initiatory process during which the

descent into the realm of death gradually metamorphoses into a physical, social, and perhaps spiritual rebirth.

The journey upward to the mouth of the volcanic crater that delivers the Lidenbrock expedition back to the world above ground amid an eruption of liquid rock is portrayed as a metaphorical rebirth that will in the end enable Axel to return home and marry the woman he has desired from the beginning of the novel. The superbly intelligent but stubborn and narrow-minded Lidenbrock, with his iron determination and implacable leadership, and the Icelandic guide Hans, with his loyalty, courage, and stoic acceptance of hardships and deprivations, serve as two different models of masculinity in relation to which Axel has to define his own identity—without, of course, merely becoming a replica of either.

What makes Verne's *Journey to the Center of the Earth* such a complex, fascinating, and influential work of literature, then, is its distinctive combination of the most advanced science of its day with more speculative approaches to knowledge and literary figures and plots that have had a long tradition and far-reaching influence in the Western tradition. This combination is characteristic of many of Verne's works. He developed this hallmark brand of narrative after studying law and spending his early years as an unsuccessful playwright—a dramatic legacy that is still obvious in the extended, skillfully handled dialogues between Lidenbrock and his nephew in *Journey to the Center of the Earth*. Verne is remembered principally as one of the two nineteenth-century fathers of the science-fiction genre, along with the British author H. G. Wells—even though we should keep in mind that the term "science fiction" did not exist in Verne's and Wells's day. The term was coined in the 1920s, in the United States. The kind of novel Verne and Wells wrote in Europe in the late nineteenth century would have been called "scientific romance."

Yet, in many ways, Verne's novels are quite unlike the genre that evolved out of his work in the twentieth century. While much twentieth-century science fiction focuses on the exploration of outer space, Verne wrote only two novels that take his characters away from the Earth, on trips to the moon. With few exceptions, the plots of his novels are set in the present or recent past rather than in the future—*Journey* is set in the resolutely contemporary year of 1863. (One of the exceptions to this rule is *Paris in the Twentieth*

Century, a text that was long lost but then rediscovered in the 1980s and finally published in 1994). And while many Verne novels explore human interaction with technology and machines, not all of them do, and some are more focused on scientific knowledge itself rather than on the technological apparatus that dominates so much science fiction after him. The kind of technology that appears in Verne's novels, at any rate, is generally based on that of his own day, with little or no projection into the future.

But Verne's novels do create alternative worlds, some of them entirely imaginary even though they are set in remote parts of our own very real planet, and his protagonists explore them with some of the tools of modern science and technology. For a nineteenth-century reader, Verne's narratives would have had clear affinities with other romances of adventure, as well as with certain kinds of travel writing—they may have seemed only a step or two beyond the strange tales of faraway lands and different cultures that colonial officers, explorers, traders, and adventurers brought back to Europe. Modern literary scholars often associate Verne's writings with those of other novelists who combined adventure stories with issues of science and technology, such as Mary Shelley, Edgar Allan Poe, and H. G. Wells. Verne himself gave his novels the general title *Voyages extraordinaires: Les mondes connus et inconnus* (*Extraordinary Journeys: Known and Unknown Worlds*). In an age of colonial expansion and geographical exploration all over the world, the blank spaces on Europeans' maps of the globe were shrinking fast. Verne's novels look forward to a time when exotic countries will be too familiar to warrant further exploration, and turn instead to other unknown realms and other kinds of exploratory journey in the air, under water, inside the Earth, or in outer space. Verne's distinctive combination of extant methods and tools of exploration and imaginary realms and landscapes exerted a shaping influence on the emergent genre of the scientific romance and, later, of science fiction.

Jules Verne's career, after his years as a minor playwright, took a decisive turn in the 1860s when the publisher Pierre-Jules Hetzel accepted his novel *Five Weeks in a Balloon* for publication, and made him into one of the regular contributors to the *Magasin d'éducation et de récréation* (*Magazine for Education and Entertainment*). Over the subsequent four decades, many of Verne's novels were first published in this magazine, in serial form. In fact, *Journey to the Center of the Earth* is unusual among Verne's works in that it was published in book form rather than serially, in 1864, just before Hetzel's magazine got off the ground. Because Hetzel's magazine was designed to appeal to younger readers, Jules Verne's writings are sometimes still considered to be adventure reading for youngsters rather than serious literature. Yet Verne's enormous influence on writers inside and outside of science fiction, as well as the in-depth attention he has received even from literary critics of a decidedly high-theoretical bent—prominent names such as Roland Barthes, Pierre Macherey, and Michel Serres come to mind—prove that the colorful surface of adventure and exploration in his writing hides conceptual depths that only a more mature and careful reading will unearth.

Nineteenth-century translations that substantially rewrote and distorted the text of many of Verne's novels and were reprinted again and again throughout the twentieth century have made it difficult for readers who cannot access the original to perceive the complexity of the author's work. Neither have the film versions through which many contemporary readers first encounter Jules Verne contributed anything to a better understanding of his novels. *Journey to the Center of the Earth* has been made into motion pictures several times, including the well-known 1959 version directed by Henry Levin, which features James Mason and Pat Boone in the leading roles, and a 1999 made-for-television version directed by George Miller. Neither bears much resemblance to Jules Verne's text, since both fundamentally alter the basic set of characters and the development of the plot. First-time readers of the novel are therefore likely to be surprised by the sophistication of its thought and language.

But even a more faithful film version would surely have difficulty capturing the novel's fascination with spoken and written language. Perhaps most obviously, Verne loves to take scientific language and display its lyrical and dramatic potential. From the mineral specimens in Professor Lidenbrock's study to the numerous prehistoric animals Axel imagines in the underground landscape, scientific vocabulary pervades the novel and yet is evoked with so much energy, excitement, and playfulness that it never smacks of pedantry and cold abstraction. When scientific pedantry is on display, as it sometimes is in the sparrings between Axel and his uncle about the physical, chemical, and climatic details on which the success of their mission hinges, it is always within a context of dramatic dialogue that makes it part of fast, precise, and often quite witty repartees that would no doubt play well on a stage. Verne's abundant use of semicolons and exclamation marks in the novel, in addition, helps to convey the sense of breathless excitement that often grips his characters when they are on the trail of an important discovery or conclusion.

Speech and writing also play an important part in the plot of *Journey to the Center of the Earth*. Otto Lidenbrock regularly becomes a butt of his students' jokes, because he stumbles over polysyllabic scientific terms in his lectures and then rains down a hail of swearwords on his audience, the very antithesis of rational, scientific discourse. In spite of this impediment, however, Lidenbrock is an accomplished polyglot who can converse in multiple languages, an arena from which his less multilingual nephew is excluded. Axel and Otto Lidenbrock's tendency to speak often and at length, in turn, is contrasted throughout the novel with their guide Hans's—and, more generally, the Icelanders'—preference for monosyllabic utterances and extended silences. Each of these ways of handling language is explored in its relation to the kind of mastery of the physical world it enables.

Written texts similarly open up varying and intricate perspectives on the characters. Lidenbrock is a confirmed bibliophile, and the plot starts out from the purchase of an antiquarian book and the discovery of a manuscript note it contains. But in spite of his knowledge of books and languages, Lidenbrock cannot decipher the cryptogram, while his nephew, much less expert in both areas, discovers the key. Both Lidenbrock and his nephew keep extensive notebooks and diaries during their journey, and both of these seem to survive the journey. Axel alludes to the publications Lidenbrock has prepared on the basis of the scientific data he collected during his journey, and he gives us his account of some of the most dramatic moments in the form of a log he kept at the time. Yet how Axel could have written anything under the life-threatening circumstances he describes is mysterious, and how his or his uncle's notes could have survived the final trip through erupting lava is more elusive still.

If the novel, otherwise meticulous in its attention to physical possibilities and impossibilities, does not provide an answer to such riddles, it is not because of carelessness on Verne's part. In a narrative that is so intensely concerned with questions of origins—cosmological, geological, evolutionary, and anthropological—the riddle of the surviving notes points us to the novel's own perhaps inexplicable origin at the intersection of empirical observation, scientific theorizing, philosophical speculation, and different kinds of storytelling. Complexities such as these underneath the surface of a gripping adventure tale make Verne's *Journey to the Center of the Earth* a compelling read almost a century and a half after its first publication, and have turned the novel into one of the paradigmatic stories of the modern age.

Acknowledgments

Grateful acknowledgments are made to William Butcher and Daniel Compère, whose detailed work on Jules Verne's novels in general and *Journey to the Center of the Earth* in particular was very helpful in preparing this edition. Heather Sullivan of Trinity University provided useful references on the history of geology in the nineteenth century.

Ursula K. Heise is Professor of English and Comparative Literature at Stanford University. Her book *Chronoschisms: Time, Narrative, and Postmodernism* appeared from Cambridge University Press in 1997. She has published numerous articles on contemporary American and European literature in its relation to science, ecology and new media. She is currently completing a book manuscript entitled *World Wide Webs: Global Ecology and the Cultural Imagination.*

A Note on the Translation

This edition of *Journey to the Center of the Earth* is based on the translation of Frederick Amadeus Malleson, which appeared in 1877. Malleson's translation is more faithful than an earlier one that had appeared in 1872, but it renders Verne's brisk and variable prose in a distinctly Victorian English that makes the text sound more dated in the translation than it is in the original.

Malleson also took other liberties with the text: He added chapter headings that did not exist in the original text, added explanatory notes, condensed dialogue that he considered too lengthy, and, being a clergyman, added religious diction in some places and elided or amended phrases of Verne's that seemed to imply what he considered to be slight disregard for Christian theology and scripture. Malleson's translation has been comprehensively revised for the present edition so as to bring the English text back into closer correspondence with Verne's original: The chapter titles have been eliminated, Verne's dialogues and original wording have been restored in full, and the syntax and vocabulary of the English text have been updated to reflect Verne's lively, engaged and often witty style as closely as possible.

—Ursula K. Heise

A Note on Measurements

Temperatures in the novel are given in degrees Celsius, not Fahrenheit, as is customary in continental Europe.

Verne gives measures of length in units, such as leagues and fathoms, that were used in France in the eighteenth century, prior to the introduction of the metric system; those that appear frequently in the text include:

    1 league = approx. 4 kilometers = approx. 2.5 statute miles
    1 fathom = 2 meters = approx. 2.2 yards
    1 Danish mile = 7.3 kilometers = 4.6 statute miles

JOURNEY TO
THE CENTER OF
THE EARTH

I

ON MAY 24, 1863, a Sunday, my uncle, Professor Lidenbrock, rushed back to his little house located at No. 19 Königstrasse, one of the most ancient streets in the old town of Hamburg.

Martha, the maid, must have believed that she was far behind schedule, for the dinner had only just begun to cook on the kitchen range.

"Well," I said to myself, "if my uncle, the most impatient of men, is hungry, he will cry out in dismay."

"Mr. Lidenbrock so soon!" the good Martha exclaimed in amazement, half opening the dining-room door.

"Yes, Martha; but very likely the dinner is not half cooked, for it's not two yet. Saint Michael's clock has only just struck half-past one."

"Then why is Mr. Lidenbrock coming home so soon?"

"He'll probably tell us himself."

"Here he is; I'll stay out of the way, Mr. Axel, while you argue with him."

And the good Martha retreated to her culinary laboratory.

I was left alone. But arguing with the most irascible of professors was out of the question for someone of my somewhat undecided turn of mind. Just as I was cautiously retreating to my handsome room upstairs, the street door squeaked on its hinges. Large feet made the wooden staircase creak, and the master of the house rushed through the dining-room immediately to his study.

But during his swift passage, he had flung his hazel walking stick into a corner, his rough broad brim hat on the table, and these emphatic words at his nephew:

"Axel, follow me!"

I had scarcely had time to move when the professor already exclaimed in a tone of utter impatience:

"Well! You aren't here yet?"

I rushed into my redoubtable master's study.

Otto Lidenbrock had no mischief in him, I readily admit that; but unless he changes in unlikely ways, he will die a confirmed original.

He was professor at the Johanneum* and taught a course on mineralogy, in the course of which he invariably broke into a rage once or twice each session. Not that he was at all concerned about having diligent students in his class, or about the degree of attention with which they listened to him, or the success they would eventually achieve; such details never bothered him. His teaching was "subjective," as German philosophy calls it; it was meant for himself, not others. He was a learned egotist, a well of science whose pulleys creaked when you wanted to draw anything out of it: in a word, a miser.

There are quite a few professors of this sort in Germany.

Unfortunately, my uncle was not gifted with great skill of delivery, if not in private, then at least when he spoke in public, and this is a deplorable shortfall in a speaker. Indeed, during his lectures at the Johanneum, the professor often came to a complete standstill; he struggled with a reluctant word that did not want to pass his lips, one of those words that resist, expand and finally slip out in the quite unscientific form of an oath. Hence his intense rage.

Now in mineralogy there are many half-Greek and half-Latin terms that are hard to pronounce, rough words that would injure the lips of a poet. I don't want to speak ill of this science. Far from it. But when one faces rhombohedral crystals, retinasphaltic resins, gehlenites, fassaites, molybdenites, tungstates of manganese, and titanite of zirconium, even the most skilled tongue may slip.

In the city, therefore, my uncle's forgivable weakness was well-known, and it was exploited, and it was expected at the more dangerous moments, and he broke out in a rage, and there was laughter, which is not in good taste, not even for Germans. And if there was always a full audience at the Lidenbrock lectures, how many came regularly to be entertained by the professor's wonderful fury!

Nevertheless, my uncle, I must emphasize, was a genuine scholar. Even though he sometimes broke his specimens by handling them too roughly, he combined the geologist's genius with the mineralogist's keen eye. Armed with his hammer, his steel pointer, his magnetic needles, his blowpipe, and his bottle of nitric acid, he was a very powerful man. By assessing the fracture, the appearance, the

---

*Famous school in Hamburg.

hardness, the fusibility, the sonorousness, the smell, and the taste of any mineral, he was able to classify it unhesitatingly among the six hundred substances known to science today.

The name of Lidenbrock was therefore mentioned with respect in colleges and learned societies. Humphry Davy, Humboldt, and Captains Franklin and Sabine never failed to call on him on their way through Hamburg. Becquerel, Ebelman, Brewster, Dumas, Milne-Edwards, Saint-Claire Deville[1] consulted him about the most difficult problems in chemistry. This discipline was indebted to him for quite remarkable discoveries, and in 1853 *A Treaty of Transcendental Crystallography* by Professor Otto Lidenbrock had appeared in Leipzig, a large folio with illustrations which, however, did not cover its expenses.

Add to all this that my uncle was curator of the museum of mineralogy established by Mr. Struve, the Russian ambassador, a valuable collection whose reputation is known throughout Europe.

This, then, was the person who called me with such impatience. Imagine a tall, slender man, of an iron constitution, and with a fair complexion which made him look a good ten years younger than his fifty. His large eyes moved incessantly behind his full-sized spectacles; his long, thin nose looked like a knife blade; mischievous tongues have even claimed that it was magnetic and attracted iron filings. Sheer calumny: it attracted nothing except snuff, but that, to be honest, in great quantities.

When I add that my uncle walked in mathematical strides of half a fathom, and if I point out that in walking he kept his fists firmly clenched, a sure sign of an irritable temperament, it will be clear enough that his company was something less than desirable.

He lived in his little house in the Königstrasse, a building made half of brick and half of wood, with a stepped gable; it overlooked one of those winding canals that intersect in the middle of Hamburg's old town, which the great fire of 1842 had fortunately spared.

The old house leaned a little, admittedly, and bulged out towards the street; its roof sloped a little to one side, like the cap over the ear of a Tugendbund student;* its verticality left something to be

---

*Literally, "League of Virtue"; a civic association in early-nineteenth-century Germany.

desired; but overall, it held up well, thanks to an old elm which buttressed it in front, and which in spring pushed its flowering branches through the window panes.

My uncle was reasonably well off for a German professor. The house was all his own, container and contents. The contents consisted of his god-daughter Graüben,[2] a seventeen-year-old from Virland,* Martha, and myself. As his nephew and an orphan, I became his laboratory assistant.

I admit that I plunged eagerly into the geological sciences; I had the blood of a mineralogist in my veins, and never got bored in the company of my precious rocks.

In a word, one could live happily in the little house in the Königstrasse, in spite of the impatience of its master, for even though he showed it in a somewhat rough fashion, he was nevertheless very fond of me. But that man was unable to wait, and nature herself was too slow for him.

In April, after he had planted seedlings of mignonette and morning glory in the clay pots in his living-room, he would go every morning and tug them by their leaves to accelerate their growth.

Faced with such a character, one could do nothing other than obey. I therefore rushed after him into his study.

_____

*Town and province in modern Estonia.

THIS STUDY WAS A genuine museum. Specimens of everything known in mineralogy lay there labeled in the most perfect order, according to the great divisions into inflammable, metallic, and lithoid minerals.

How well I knew all these bits of mineralogical science! How many times, instead of enjoying the company of boys of my own age, had I enjoyed dusting these graphites, anthracites, coals, lignites, and peats! And the bitumens, resins, organic salts that needed to be protected from the least atom of dust! And these metals, from iron to gold, whose current value disappeared in the absolute equality of scientific specimens! And all these stones, enough to rebuild the house in the Königstrasse, even with a handsome additional room, which would have suited me admirably!

But on entering this study, I barely thought of all these wonders. My uncle alone filled my thoughts. He had thrown himself into an armchair covered with Utrecht velvet, and held in his hands a book that he contemplated with the profoundest admiration.

"What a book! What a book!" he exclaimed.

This exclamation reminded me that my uncle was also a bibliophile in his moments of leisure; but an old book had no value in his eyes unless it was very difficult to find or at least illegible.

"Well!" he said to me, "don't you see? Why, this is a priceless treasure that I found this morning browsing in Hevelius the Jew's shop."

"Magnificent!" I replied, with an enthusiasm made to order.

But actually, what was the point of all this fuss about an old quarto, apparently bound in rough calfskin, a yellowish volume with a faded seal hanging from it?

Nonetheless, there was no end to the professor's admiring exclamations.

"Look," he went on, both asking the questions and supplying the answers. "Isn't it a beauty? Yes; admirable! Did you ever see such a binding? Doesn't this book open easily? Yes, because it remains open anywhere. But does it shut equally well? Yes, because the binding and the leaves are flush, all in a straight line, with no gaps or separations anywhere. And look at this spine, which doesn't show a single crack even after seven hundred years! Why, Bozerian, Closs, or Purgold* might have been proud of such a binding!"

As he was speaking, my uncle kept opening and shutting the old tome. I really could do no less than ask a question about its contents, although it did not interest me in the least.

"And so what's the title of this marvelous work?" I asked with an eagerness so pronounced that it had to be fake.

"This work," replied my uncle with renewed enthusiasm, "is the *Heims Kringla* of Snorre Turleson, the famous Icelandic author of the twelfth century![†] It's the chronicle of the Norwegian princes who ruled in Iceland."

"Really!" I exclaimed, with my best effort, "and of course it's a German translation?"

"What!" replied the professor sharply, "a translation! And what would I do with a translation? Who cares about a translation? This is the original work in Icelandic, that magnificent language, rich and simple at the same time, which allows for an infinite variety of grammatical combinations and multiple word modifications!"

"Like German," I skillfully remarked.

"Yes," replied my uncle, shrugging his shoulders; "but in addition Icelandic has three genders like Greek, and declensions of nouns like Latin."

"Ah!" I said, a little shaken in my indifference; "and is the typeface beautiful?"

"Typeface! What do you mean by typeface, wretched Axel? Type! As if it were a matter of typeface! Ah! do you think this a printed book? But, ignorant fool, this is a manuscript, and a Runic[‡] manuscript at that!"

---

*Nineteenth-century bookbinders.

†Snorri Sturluson (1179–1241) was an Icelandic poet, historian, and leader; his work *Heimskringla* is a collection of sagas.

‡The runic alphabet was used by Germanic peoples in Britain, northern Europe, and Iceland from approximately the third century to the sixteenth century.

"Runic?"

"Yes! Are you going to ask me now to explain that word to you?"

"Of course not," I replied in the tone of a man whose self-esteem has been hurt.

But my uncle persevered anyway, and told me, against my will, about things that I did not care to know.

"Runes," he explained, "were characters once used in Iceland, and according to legend, they were invented by Odin himself. So look at this, impious young man, and admire these letters created by the imagination of a god!"

Well, not knowing what to say, I was going to prostrate myself before this wonderful book, a way of answering equally pleasing to gods and kings, because it has the advantage of never giving them any embarrassment, when a little incident happened to turn the conversation into another direction.

It was the appearance of a dirty slip of parchment which slipped out of the volume and fell to the floor.

My uncle pounced on this shred with understandable eagerness. An old document, hidden for time immemorial in an old book, inevitably had an immeasurable value for him.

"What's this?" he exclaimed.

And at the same time, he carefully spread on the table a piece of parchment, five inches by three, which was covered with horizontal lines of illegible characters.

Here is the exact facsimile. It is important to me to let these bizarre signs be publicly known, for they incited Professor Lidenbrock and his nephew to undertake the strangest expedition of the nineteenth century.

My uncle pounced on this shred with
understandable eagerness.

The professor mused a few moments over this series of characters; then he said, raising his spectacles:

"These are Runic letters; they are identical to those of Snorre Turleson's manuscript. But what could they possibly mean?"

Since Runic letters seemed to me an invention of the learned to mystify this poor world, I was not sorry to see that my uncle did not understand them. At least, it seemed that way to me, judging from the movement of his fingers, which began to tremble violently.

"But it's certainly old Icelandic!" he muttered between his teeth.

And Professor Lidenbrock should know, for he was considered a genuine polyglot. Not that he could speak all two thousand languages and four thousand dialects which are spoken on the earth, but he did know his share of them.

And so, faced with this difficulty, he was going to give way to all the impetuosity of his character, and I was anticipating a violent outbreak, when two o'clock struck on the little timepiece over the fireplace.

Immediately, the housekeeper Martha opened the study door and said:

"Dinner is ready!"

"To hell with dinner!" shouted my uncle, "and the one who prepared it, and those who will eat it!"

Martha fled. I followed her, and hardly knowing how I got there, I found myself seated at my usual place in the dining-room.

I waited a few moments. The professor did not come. This was, to my knowledge, the first time he had ever missed the ritual of dinner. And yet what a dinner it was! Parsley soup, ham omelet garnished with spiced sorrel, fillet of veal with compote of prunes, and for dessert, sugared shrimp, the whole washed down with a nice Moselle wine.

All this my uncle was going to sacrifice to a bit of old paper. Well, as a devoted nephew I considered it my duty to eat for him as well as for myself. That I did conscientiously.

"I've never seen such a thing," said Martha the housekeeper. "Mr. Lidenbrock not at table!"

"Who could believe it?"

"This means something serious is going to happen," said the old servant, shaking her head.

In my opinion, it meant nothing more serious than an awful scene when my uncle discovered that his dinner had been devoured.

I had come to my last shrimp when a stentorian voice tore me away from the pleasures of dessert. With one leap I bounded out of the dining-room into the study.

III

"It's obviously Runic," said the professor, knitting his brows. "But there's a secret here, and I'll discover it, or else . . ."

A violent gesture finished his thought.

"Sit there," he added, pointing with his fist at the table, "and write."

I was ready in an instant.

"Now I'll dictate to you every letter of our alphabet which corresponds with one of these Icelandic characters. We'll see what that will give us. But, by St. Michael! Take care that you don't make mistakes!"

The dictation began. I did my best. Every letter was called out one after the other, and resulted in the unintelligible sequence of the following words:

mm.rnlls	esreuel	seecJde
sgtssmf	unteief	niedrke
kt,samn	atrateS	Saodrrn
emtnaeI	nuaect	rrilSa
Atvaar	.nscrc	ieaabs
ccdrmi	eeutul	frntu
dt,iac	oseibo	KediiY

When this work was ended, my uncle quickly took the paper on which I had been writing, and examined it attentively for a long time.

"What does this mean?" he kept repeating mechanically.

On my honor, I could not have enlightened him. Besides he did not question me, and went on talking to himself.

"This is what we call a cryptogram," he said, "where the meaning is hidden under deliberately scrambled letters, which in their proper order would result in an intelligible sentence. When I think that there's perhaps the explanation or clue to some great discovery here!"

As far as I was concerned, there was absolutely nothing in it, but of course, I took care not to reveal my opinion.

Then the professor took the book and the parchment, and compared them with one another.

"These two writings are not by the same hand," he said; "the cryptogram is of a later date than the book, and I see one irrefutable proof of that. The first letter is actually a double m, a letter which can't be found in Turleson's book because it was only added to the Icelandic alphabet in the fourteenth century. So there are at least two hundred years between the manuscript and the document."

This, I admit, seemed pretty logical to me.

"I'm therefore led to believe," continued my uncle, "that one of the owners of this book wrote these mysterious letters. But who the devil was that owner? Didn't he put his name somewhere on the manuscript?"

My uncle raised his spectacles, took up a strong magnifying glass, and carefully examined the first pages of the book. On the back of the second one, the half-title page, he discovered a sort of stain which looked like an ink blot. But in looking at it very closely one could distinguish some half-erased letters. My uncle understood that this was the interesting part; so he focused on the stain, and with the help of his big magnifying glass, he ended up identifying the following symbols, Runic characters that he read without hesitation.

ᛏᛌᛘᛁ   ᛌᛏᚱᚾᛊᛊᛏᛉ

"Arne Saknussemm!" he exclaimed in a tone of triumph. "Now *that* is a name, and an Icelandic name at that, the name of a sixteenth-century scholar, a famous alchemist!"[3]

I looked at my uncle with a certain admiration.

"Those alchemists," he resumed, "Avicenna, Bacon, Lully, Paracelsus,[4] were the real and only scholars of their time. They made discoveries at which we may rightfully be astonished. Why wouldn't this Saknussemm have hidden some surprising invention in this incomprehensible cryptogram? It must be so. It is so."

The Professor's imagination caught fire at this hypothesis.

"No doubt," I ventured to reply, "but what interest would this scholar have had in hiding a marvelous discovery in this way?"

"Why? Why? How would I know? Didn't Galileo do the same by Saturn?* Besides, we'll see. I'll get at the secret of this document, and I'll neither sleep nor eat until I've found it out."

"Oh!" I thought.

"Nor you either, Axel," he added.

"The devil!" I said to myself, "then it's lucky that I've eaten dinner for two!"

"First of all," said my uncle, "we must find out the language of this 'cipher'; that can't be too difficult."

At these words I quickly raised my head. My uncle continued his soliloquy.

"Nothing's easier. There are a hundred and thirty-two letters in this document, seventy-seven consonants and fifty-five vowels. Now the words of southern languages approximately match this distribution, whereas northern tongues are infinitely richer in consonants. Therefore this must be a southern language."

These conclusions were very appropriate.

"But what language is it?"

I expected scholarship in response, but was confronted with in-depth analysis instead.

"This Saknussemm," he went on, "was an educated man; now since he wasn't writing in his own mother tongue, he would naturally select the language that was used by the cultivated minds of the sixteenth century, I mean Latin. If I'm mistaken, I can try Spanish, French, Italian, Greek, or Hebrew. But the scholars of the sixteenth century generally wrote in Latin. I'm therefore entitled to declare a priori: this is Latin."

I jumped up from my chair. My memories of Latin rebelled against the assumption that this sequence of baroque words could belong to the sweet language of Virgil.

---

*Galileo discovered the rings of Saturn with a primitive telescope in 1610 but misinterpreted the unclear images he perceived as being those of a triple planet system.

"Yes, it's Latin," my uncle continued, "but scrambled Latin."

"Good luck!" I thought. "If you can unscramble this, my uncle, you're a clever man."

"Let's examine it carefully," he said, taking the sheet on which I had written. "Here is a series of one hundred and thirty-two letters in apparent disorder. There are words that consist only of consonants, like the first one, *mm.rnlls*; others where vowels predominate, as for instance the fifth one, *unteief*, or the next-to-last one, *oseibo*. Now, this arrangement was obviously not planned: it came about *mathematically* as a consequence of the unknown rule which determined the order of these letters. It seems certain to me that the original sentence was written normally, then scrambled according to a rule that we have to discover. Whoever has the key to this cipher can read it fluently. But what is that key? Axel, do you have this key?"

I said not a word in answer to this question, for a very good reason. My eyes had fallen on a charming picture on the wall, a portrait of Graüben. My uncle's ward was at that time in Altona,* staying with a relative, and her absence made me very sad because, I may confess it now, the pretty Virland girl and the professor's nephew loved each other with entirely German patience and tranquility. We had become engaged unbeknownst to my uncle, who was too much of a geologist to understand such feelings. Graüben was a charming blue-eyed blonde, rather given to gravity and seriousness; but that did not prevent her from loving me sincerely. As for me, I adored her, if there is such a word in the German language! So the picture of my pretty Virland girl instantaneously shifted me out of the world of realities into that of imagination and memory.

I saw the faithful companion of my labors and my pleasures again. Every day she helped me put my uncle's precious rocks in order; she labeled them with me. She was a very accomplished mineralogist, Miss Graüben! She could have taught a scholar a few things. She was fond of investigating abstruse scientific questions. What sweet hours had we spent studying together! and how much I envied the luck of those insensible stones that she handled with her charming hands!

---

*District of Hamburg.

Then, when our leisure hours came, we used to go out together, we walked along the shady avenues by the Alster, and went together up to the tar-covered old windmill that looks so handsome by the side of the lake; on the way, we chatted and held hands. I told her things that made her laugh heartily. And so we reached the banks of the Elbe,* and after having said goodnight to the swans that float among the big white water lilies, we returned to the quay on the steamer.

This is as far as I had gotten in my dream when my uncle brought me violently back to reality by banging his hand on the table.

"Let's see," he said, "the first idea that must come to mind to scramble the letters of a sentence is, I think, to write the words vertically instead of horizontally."

"Indeed!" I thought.

"Now we must see what the result would be. Axel, write any sentence on this piece of paper, but instead of arranging the letters one after the other, place them successively into vertical columns, so as to group them together in five or six lines."

I understood what he was after, and immediately I wrote from top to bottom:

I	y	r	h	i	G	e
l	o	y	,	t	r	n
o	u	m	m	t	a	!
v	v	u	y	l	ü	
e	e	c	l	e	b	

"Good," said the professor, without reading them. "Now write out those words in a horizontal line."

I obeyed, and ended up with the following sentence:

IyrhiGe loy,trn oummta! vvuylü eecleb

"Perfect!" said my uncle, tearing the paper out of my hands. "This already resembles the ancient document: vowels and consonants are

---

*The two principal rivers flowing through Hamburg.

in the same disorder. There are even capitals in the middle of words, and commas too, just as in Saknussemm's parchment."

I couldn't help but find these observations very ingenious.

"Now," said my uncle, looking straight at me, "to read the sentence you've just written, and which I don't know, all I have to do is take the first letter of each word, then the second, then the third, and so forth."

And my uncle, to his great astonishment, and above all my own, read out:

"I love you very much, my little Graüben!"

"What!" said the professor.

Yes, without being aware of it, like a clumsy lover, I had written down this compromising sentence!

"Aha! you're in love with Graüben?" he said in the tone of a guardian.

"Yes . . . no . . ." I stammered.

"Aha! You love Graüben," he mechanically repeated. "Well, let's apply the process to the document in question."

My uncle, falling back into his all-absorbing contemplation, had already forgotten my careless words. I say merely "careless," for the mind of the scholar could not understand these affairs of the heart. But fortunately, the business of the document won out.

At the moment of his major experiment, Professor Lidenbrock's eyes flashed right through his spectacles. His fingers trembled as he took up the old parchment again. He was seriously moved. At last he coughed loudly, and with a grave voice, calling out the first, then the second letter of each word one after the other, he dictated me the following series:

> mmessunkaSenrA.icefdoK.segnittamurtn
> ecertserrette,rotaivsadua,ednecsedsadne
> lacartniiiluJsiratracSarbmutabiledmek
> meretarcsilucoYsleffenSnI.

When I came to the end, I must admit that I was excited; these letters, pronounced one by one, had conveyed no meaning to my mind. I expected, therefore, that the professor would let a magnificent Latin phrase roll majestically from his tongue.

But who could have foreseen it! A violent bang of the fist shook the table. The ink spilled and the pen dropped from my fingers.

"That's not it!" my uncle shouted, "this makes no sense!"

Then, crossing the study like a cannonball, descending the staircase like an avalanche, he rushed into the Königstrasse and ran away at full speed.

IV

"HE's GONE?" EXCLAIMED MARTHA, running out of her kitchen at the noise of the violent slamming of doors.

"Yes," I replied, "completely gone!"

"Well; and how about his lunch?" said the old servant.

"He won't have any."

"And his dinner?"

"He won't have any."

"What?" exclaimed Martha, with clasped hands.

"No, dear Martha, he won't eat any more, and no one else in the house either! Uncle Lidenbrock is going to make us all fast until he succeeds in deciphering an old scrawl that is absolutely undecipherable!"

"Oh, my dear! must we then all die of hunger?"

I hardly dared to confess that, with so absolute a ruler as my uncle, that fate was inevitable.

The old servant, seriously alarmed, returned to the kitchen moaning.

When I was alone, I thought I would go and tell Graüben all about it. But how would I be able to escape from the house? The Professor might return at any moment. And suppose he called me? And suppose he tackled me again with this deciphering work, which not even old Oedipus could have solved! And if I did not answer his call, what would happen?

The wisest thing was to remain where I was. A mineralogist at Besançon had just sent us a collection of siliceous nodules, which I had to classify. So I set to work. I sorted, labeled, and arranged all these hollow rocks, in each of which grew little crystals, in their display case.

But this work did not absorb all my attention. The business of the old document kept working in my brain. My head throbbed with excitement, and I felt a vague uneasiness. I had a premonition of an incipient disaster.

In an hour my nodules were all arranged in good order. Then I dropped down into the old velvet armchair, my arms hanging down and my head thrown back. I lit my long crooked pipe, whose head was sculpted to look like an idly resting naiad; then I entertained myself by watching the carbonization that gradually turned my naiad into a real negress. Now and then I listened whether a well-known step sounded on the stairs. But no. Where could my uncle be at that moment? I imagined him running under the beautiful trees which line the road to Altona, gesticulating, hitting the wall with his cane, violently thrashing the grass, cutting the heads off the thistles, and disturbing the solitary storks in their rest.

Would he return in triumph or discouraged? Which would get the upper hand, he or the secret? I was asking myself these questions, and mechanically took between my fingers the sheet of paper with the incomprehensible succession of letters I had written down; and I repeated to myself:

"What does it mean?"

I tried to group the letters so as to form words. Quite impossible! When I put them together by twos, threes, fives or sixes, nothing came of it but nonsense. To be sure, the fourteenth, fifteenth and sixteenth letters made the English word 'ice'; the eighty-fourth, eighty-fifth and eighty-sixth made up the word 'sir.' In the midst of the document, in the third line, I noticed the Latin words "rota," "mutabile," "ira," "nec," "atra."

"Devil," I thought, "these words seem to justify my uncle's view about the language of the document. In the fourth line I see the word 'luco,' which translates as 'sacred wood.' It is true that in the third line there's the word "tabiled", which looks like perfect Hebrew, and in the last the words 'mer,' 'arc,' 'mère,' which are purely French."

All this was enough to drive a poor fellow crazy. Four different languages in this ridiculous sentence! What connection could there possibly be between such words as ice, sir, anger, cruel, sacred wood, changeable, mother, bow, and sea? The first and the last might have something to do with each other; it was not at all surprising that in a document written in Iceland there should be mention of a sea of ice; but it was quite another thing to get to the end of this cryptogram with so small a clue.

So I struggled with an insurmountable difficulty; my brain heated up, my eyes became blinked at that sheet of paper; its hundred and thirty-two letters fluttered around me like those silver teardrops which float in the air around our heads when the blood has rushed toward it.

I was in the grip of a kind of hallucination; I was suffocating; I needed air. Mechanically, I fanned myself with the piece of paper, the back and front of which came successively before my eyes.

What was my surprise when, in one of those rapid turns, at the moment when the back was turned to me, I thought I caught sight of the Latin words "craterem" and "terrestre," among others!

A sudden light burst in on me; these hints alone gave me the first glimpse of the truth; I had discovered the key to the cipher. To read the document, it would not even be necessary to read it with the paper turned upside down. Such as it was, just as it had been dictated to me, so it might be spelled out with ease. All the professor's ingenious combinations were coming into their own. He was right as to the arrangement of the letters; he was right as to the language. He had been within a hair's breadth of reading this Latin document from end to end; but that hair's breadth, chance had given it to me!

You will understand if I was excited! My eyes glazed over. I could barely use them. I had spread the paper out on the table. It was enough to take one look at it to grasp the secret.

At last I calmed down. I forced myself to walk twice round the room quietly and settle my nerves, and then I sank again into the huge armchair.

"Let's read it," I exclaimed, after having filled my lungs with air.

I leaned over the table; I laid my finger successively on every letter; and without a pause, without one moment's hesitation, I read off the whole sentence aloud.

But what amazement, what terror came over me! I sat overwhelmed as if struck by a sudden deadly blow. What! that which I read had actually, really been done! A mortal man had had the audacity to penetrate! . . .

"Ah!" I exclaimed, jumping up. "But no! no! My uncle will never know it. He'd insist on doing it too. He'd want to know all about it. Nothing could stop him! Such a determined geologist! He'd go, he would, in spite of everything and everybody, and he'd take me with him, and we'd never get back. Never! never!"

My overexcitement was beyond all description.

"No! no! it can't be," I declared energetically; "and as it's in my power to prevent the knowledge of it coming into the mind of my tyrant, I'll do it. By dint of turning this document round and round, he too might discover the key. I'll destroy it."

There was a little fire left in the fireplace. I seized not only the paper but Saknussemm's parchment; with a feverish hand I was about to fling it all on the coals and annihilate this dangerous secret when the study door opened. My uncle appeared.

V

I HAD ONLY JUST time to replace the unfortunate document on the table.

Professor Lidenbrock seemed to be greatly abstracted.

His main concern gave him no rest. Evidently he had gone deeply into the matter, analytically and with profound scrutiny. He had brought all the resources of his mind to bear on it during his walk, and he had come back to try out some new combination.

He sat in his armchair, and pen in hand he began with what looked very much like an algebraic calculation: I followed his trembling hand with my eyes; not one of his movements was lost on me. Might not some unhoped-for result come of it? I trembled, too, very unnecessarily, since the true key was in my hands, and no other would open the secret.

For three long hours my uncle worked on without a word, without lifting his head; erasing, starting over, then erasing again, and so on a hundred times.

I knew very well that if he succeeded in setting down these letters in every possible relative position, the sentence would come out. But I also knew that twenty letters alone could form two quintillion, four hundred and thirty-two quadrillion, nine hundred and two trillion, eight billion, a hundred and seventy-six million, six hundred and forty thousand combinations. Now there were a hundred and thirty-two letters in this sentence, and these hundred and thirty-two letters would yield a number of different sentences, each made up of at least a hundred and thirty-three figures, a number almost impossible to calculate or conceive.

So I felt reassured about this heroic method of solving the problem.

But time passed; night came on; the street noises ceased; my uncle, bending over his task, noticed nothing, not even Martha half opening the door; he heard not a sound, not even this noble servant saying:

"Will Professor Lidenbrock not have any dinner tonight?"

Poor Martha had to go away unanswered. As for me, after long resistance, I was overcome by sleep, and fell asleep at one end of the sofa, while Uncle Lidenbrock went on calculating and erasing his calculations.

When I awoke the next morning that indefatigable worker was still at his task. His red eyes, his pale complexion, his hair tangled in his feverish hand, the red spots on his cheeks, said enough about his desperate struggle with the impossible, and with what weariness of spirit and exhaustion of the brain the hours must have passed for him.

In truth, I felt sorry for him. In spite of the reproaches which I thought I had a right to make him, a certain feeling of compassion began to take hold of me. The poor man was so entirely taken up with his one idea that he had even forgotten how to get angry. All his vital forces were concentrated on a single point, and because their usual vent was closed, it was to be feared that their pent-up tension might lead to an explosion any moment.

I could have loosened the steel vice that was crushing his brain with one gesture, with just one word! But I did nothing.

Yet I was not an ill-natured fellow. Why did I remain silent in such a crisis? In my uncle's own interest.

"No, no," I repeated, "no, I won't speak! He'd insist on going, I know him; nothing on earth could stop him. He has a volcanic imagination, and would risk his life to do what other geologists have never done. I'll keep silent. I'll keep the secret that chance has revealed to me. To reveal it would be to kill Professor Lidenbrock! Let him find it out himself if he can. I don't want to have to reproach myself some day that I led him to his destruction."

Having made this resolution, I folded my arms and waited. But I had not anticipated a little incident which occurred a few hours later.

When the maid Martha wanted to go to the market, she found the door locked. The big key was gone. Who could have taken it out? Assuredly, it was my uncle, when he returned the night before from his hurried walk.

Was this done on purpose? Or was it a mistake? Did he want to expose us to hunger? This seemed like going rather too far! What! should Martha and I be victims of a situation that did not concern us in the least? It was a fact that a few years before this, while my uncle was working on his great classification of minerals, he went for forty-eight hours without eating, and all his household was obliged to share in this scientific fast. As for me, what I remember is that I got severe stomach cramps, which hardly suited the constitution of a hungry, growing lad.

Now it seemed to me as if breakfast was going to be lacking, just as dinner had been the night before. Yet I resolved to be a hero, and not to be conquered by the pangs of hunger. Martha took it very seriously, and, poor woman, was very much distressed. As for me, the impossibility of leaving the house worried me even more, and for good reason. You understand me.

My uncle went on working, his imagination went off rambling into the ideal world of combinations; he lived far away from earth, and genuinely beyond earthly needs.

At about noon, hunger began to sting me severely. Martha had, without thinking any harm, cleared out the larder the night before, so that now there was nothing left in the house. Still I held out; I made it a point of honor.

Two o'clock struck. This was becoming ridiculous; worse than that, unbearable. I opened my eyes wide. I began to say to myself that I was exaggerating the importance of the document; that my uncle would surely not believe in it, that he would set it down as a mere puzzle; that if it came to the worst, we would restrain him in spite of himself if he wanted to undertake the adventure; that, after all, he might discover the key of the cipher by himself, and that I would then have suffered abstinence for nothing.

These reasons seemed excellent to me, though on the night before I would have rejected them with indignation; I even found it completely absurd to have waited so long, and made a decision to say it all.

I was looking for a way of bringing up the matter that was not too abrupt when the professor jumped up, put on his hat, and prepared to go out.

What! Going out again, and locking us in once more? Never.

"Uncle!" I said.

He seemed not to hear me.

"Uncle Lidenbrock?" I repeated, speaking more loudly.

"What?" he said like a man suddenly waking up.

"Well! The key?"

"What key? The door key?"

"But no!" I exclaimed. "The key to the document!"

The Professor stared at me over his spectacles; no doubt he saw something unusual in physiognomy, for he seized my arm, and questioned me with his eyes without being able to speak. Nonetheless, never was a question more forcibly put.

I nodded my head up and down.

He shook his pityingly, as if he was dealing with a lunatic.

I made a more affirmative gesture.

His eyes sparkled with live fire, his hand threatened me.

This mute conversation would, under the circumstances, have interested even the most indifferent spectator. And the truth is that I did not dare to speak out any more, so much did I fear that my uncle would smother me in his joyful embraces. But he became so urgent that I was at last compelled to answer.

"Yes, that key, chance—"

"What are you saying?" he shouted with indescribable emotion.

"There, read that!" I said, giving him the sheet of paper on which I had written.

"But this doesn't mean anything," he answered, crumpling up the paper.

"No, not when you start to read from the beginning, but from the end . . ."

I had not finished my sentence when the professor broke out into a cry, more than a cry, a real roar! A new revelation took place in his mind. He was transfigured.

"Aha, ingenious Saknussemm!" he exclaimed, "so you first wrote out your sentence backwards?"

And throwing himself on the paper, eyes dimmed and voice choked, he read the entire document from the last letter to the first.

It was phrased as follows:

In Sneffels Yoculis craterem kem delibat
umbra Scartaris Julii intra calendas descende,
audas viator, et terrestre centrum attinges.
Kod feci. Arne Saknussemm.

Which bad Latin may be translated like this:

> Descend into the crater of Snaefells Jökull, which the shadow of Scartaris touches before the calends* of July, bold traveler, and you will reach the center of the earth. I did it. Arne Saknussemm.

In reading this, my uncle jumped up as if he had inadvertently touched a Leyden jar.† His audacity, his joy, and his conviction were magnificent to see. He came and he went; he gripped his head with both his hands; he pushed the chairs out of their places, he piled up his books; incredible as it may seem, he juggled his precious geodes; he sent a kick here, a thump there. At last his nerves calmed down, and like a man exhausted by too great an expenditure of vital power, he sank back into his armchair.

"What time is it?" he asked after a few moments of silence.

"Three o'clock," I replied.

"Really? The dinner has passed quickly. I'm starving. Let's eat. And then . . ."

"Well?"

"After dinner, pack my suitcase."

"What!" I exclaimed.

"And yours!" replied the merciless professor and entered into the dining-room.

---

*First day of the month in the Roman calendar.
†Device that stores static electricity.

VI

AT THESE WORDS A cold shiver ran through me. Yet I controlled myself; I even decided to put a good face on it. Scientific arguments alone could have any weight with Professor Lidenbrock. Now there were good ones against the practicability of such a journey. Go to the center of the earth! What nonsense! But I kept my dialectics in reserve for a suitable opportunity, and focused on dinner.

It is no use to tell of the rage and imprecations of my uncle before the empty table. Explanations were given, Martha was set at liberty, ran off to the market, and did her part so well that an hour afterwards my hunger was appeased, and I returned to the gravity of the situation.

During the dinner, my uncle was almost merry; he indulged in some of those learned jokes which never do anybody any harm. Dessert over, he signaled to me to follow him to his study.

I obeyed; he sat at one end of his table, I at the other.

"Axel," he said very mildly; "you're a very ingenious lad, you've done me a splendid service, at a moment when I, tired of the struggle, was going to abandon the combinations. Where would I have lost myself? Impossible to know! Never, my lad, will I forget it; and you'll have your share in the glory to which your discovery will lead."

"Oh, come!" I thought, "he is in a good mood. Now's the time for discussing this glory."

"Before anything else," my uncle resumed, "I recommend that you keep absolute secrecy, you understand? There are not a few in the scientific world who envy my success, and many would be ready to undertake this enterprise who'll only find out about it at our return."

"Do you really think there are many people bold enough?"

"Certainly; who would hesitate to acquire such fame? If that document were divulged, a whole army of geologists would be ready to rush into the footsteps of Arne Saknussemm."

"That's something I'm not convinced of, Uncle, because we have no proof of the authenticity of this document."

"What! And the book inside which we discovered it?"

"Granted. I admit that Saknussemm may have written these lines. But does it follow that he's really carried out such a journey? Couldn't this old parchment be misleading?"

I almost regretted uttering this last, somewhat daring word. The professor knitted his thick brows, and I feared I had seriously compromised my own safety. Happily no great harm came of it. A kind of smile sketched itself on the lips of my severe interlocutor, and he answered:

"That is what we'll see."

"Ah!" I said, a bit offended. "But allow me to exhaust all the possible objections against this document."

"Speak, my boy, don't be afraid. You're quite at liberty to express your opinions. You're no longer my nephew only, but my colleague. Go ahead."

"Well, in the first place, I'd like to ask what are this Jökull, this Snaefells, and this Scartaris, names which I've never heard before?"

"Nothing's easier. I received a map from my friend Augustus Petermann* at Leipzig not long ago; it could not have come at a better time. Take down the third atlas on the second shelf in the large bookcase, series Z, plate 4."

I rose, and with the help of such precise instructions could not fail to find the required atlas. My uncle opened it and said:

"Here's one of the best maps of Iceland, that of Handerson, and it'll solve all our difficulties."

I bent over the map.

"Look at this volcanic island," said the professor; "and observe that all of them are called Jökulls. This word which means 'glacier' in Icelandic, and because of Iceland's high latitude, almost all the eruptions break through layers of ice. Hence this term of Jökull is applied to all the island's volcanoes."

"Very good," I said; "but what of Snaefells?"

I was hoping that this question would be unanswerable; but I was mistaken. My uncle replied:

"Follow my finger along the west coast of Iceland. Do you see

---

*Perhaps a reference to the German geographer August Heinrich Petermann (1822–1878), a specialist on Africa and the Arctic.

Reykjavik, the capital? Yes. Good. Go up the innumerable fjords* on those shores eaten away by the sea, and stop just under 65° latitude. What do you see there?"

"A kind of peninsula looking like a bare bone with an enormous knee cap at the end."

"A fair comparison, my boy. Now do you see anything on that knee cap?"

"Yes; a mountain that seems to have grown out of the sea."

"Right. That's Snaefells."

"Snaefells?"

"It is. It is a mountain of five thousand feet, one of the most remarkable ones on the island and certainly the most famous one in the whole world if its crater leads down to the center of the earth."

"But that's impossible!" I exclaimed, shrugging my shoulders, and put off by such a ridiculous assumption.

"Impossible?" replied the professor severely. "Why?"

"Because this crater is obviously filled with lava and burning rocks, and therefore . . ."

"But suppose it's an extinct volcano?"

"Extinct?"

"Yes; the number of active volcanoes on the surface of the globe is currently only about three hundred. But there's a much larger quantity of extinct ones. Now, Snaefells is one of these, and since historic times it's had only one eruption, that of 1219; from that time on, it has quieted down more and more, and now it is no longer counted among active volcanoes."

To such definitive statements I could make no reply. I therefore took refuge in other dark passages of the document.

"What's the meaning of this word Scartaris, and what have the calends of July to do with it?"

My uncle stopped to think for a few moments. I had a minute of hope, but only one, because he soon answered me as follows:

"What is darkness to you is light to me. This proves the ingenious care with which Saknussemm wanted to indicate his discovery. Snaefells has several craters. So it was necessary to point out which

---

*Name given to narrow gulfs in the Scandinavian countries (author's note).

one of these leads to the center of the globe. What did the Icelandic scholar do? He observed that at the approach of the calends of July, that's to say in the last days of June, one of the peaks, called Scartaris, throws its shadow down the mouth of that particular crater, and he committed that fact to his document. Could there possibly have been a more exact guide? As soon as we arrive at the summit of Snaefells we'll have no hesitation as to the proper road to take."

Decidedly, my uncle had answered every one of my objections. I saw that his position on the old parchment was impregnable. I therefore ceased to press him on that part of the subject, and as above all things he had to be convinced, I passed on to scientific objections, which in my opinion were far more serious.

"Well, then," I said, "I'm forced to agree that Saknussemm's sentence is clear, and leaves no room for doubt. I even admit that the document looks perfectly authentic. That learned scholar did go to the bottom of Snaefells; he saw the shadow of Scartaris touch the edge of the crater before the calends of July; he even heard the legendary stories of his time about that crater leading to the center of the world; but as reaching it himself, as for carrying out the journey and returning, if he ever went, no, a hundred times no!"

"And your reason?" said my uncle in an especially mocking tone of voice.

"It's that all the theories of science demonstrate that such a feat is impossible!"

"All the theories say that, do they?" replied the professor in a jovial tone. "Oh! evil theories! How they will bother us, those poor theories!"

I saw that he was mocking me, but I continued all the same.

"Yes; it's perfectly well known that the interior temperature rises one degree for every 70 feet in depth; now if this proportion to be constant and the radius of the earth is fifteen hundred leagues, the temperature at the core must be more than 200,000°C. Therefore all the substances in the interior of the earth are in a state of incandescent gas, because the metals, gold, platinum, the hardest rocks, can't resist such heat. So I have the right to ask whether it's possible to enter into such an environment!"

"So, Axel, it's the heat that troubles you?"

"Of course it is. If we reach a depth of only ten leagues we'll have arrived at the limit of the terrestrial crust, for there the temperature will be more than 1,300°C."

"And are you afraid of melting?"

"I'll leave it up to you to decide that question," I answered rather sullenly.

"This is my decision," replied Professor Lidenbrock, putting on one of his grandest airs. "Neither you nor anybody else knows with any certainty what's going on in the interior of this globe, since not the twelve thousandth part of its radius is known; science is eminently perfectible, and every theory is constantly put in question by a newer one. Wasn't it believed until Fourier* that the temperature of the interplanetary spaces was constantly decreasing? And don't we know today that the greatest cold of the ethereal regions never goes beyond 40 or 50°C below zero? Why wouldn't it be the same with the interior heat? Why wouldn't it, at a certain depth, reach an upper limit instead of rising to the point where it melts the most resistant metals?"

Since my uncle was now moving the question to the terrain of theories, I had no answer.

"Well, I'll tell you that true scholars, amongst them Poisson,† have demonstrated that if a heat of 200,000°C existed in the interior of the globe, the white-hot gases from the molten matter would expand so much that the crust of the earth could not resist, and it would explode like the sides of a boiler under steam."

"That's Poisson's opinion, Uncle, nothing more."

"Granted, but other distinguished geologists also hold the opinion that the interior of the globe is neither gas nor water, nor any of the heaviest minerals known, for in that case, the earth would weigh less than it does."

"Oh, with numbers you can prove anything!"

"But is it the same with facts, my boy? Is it not known that the number of volcanoes has considerably diminished since the first

---

*Jean-Baptiste-Joseph Fourier (1768–1830), French mathematician who became famous through his work *The Analytical Theory of Heat* (1822).

†Siméon-Denis Poisson (1781–1840), French mathematician who wrote extensively on the application of mathematics to such areas of physics as electricity and mechanics. Lidenbrock is referring to his *Mathematical Theory of Heat* (1835).

days of creation? And if there is heat at the core, can we not therefore conclude that it's decreasing?"

"Uncle, if you enter into the domain of speculations, I have nothing further to discuss."

"But I have to tell you that my opinion is supported by those of very competent people. Do you remember a visit that the celebrated chemist Humphry Davy paid to me in 1825?"

"Not at all, for I wasn't born until nineteen years later."[5]

"Well, Humphry Davy did call on me on his way through Hamburg. We discussed for a long time, among other problems, the theory of the liquidity of the earth's inner core. We agreed that it couldn't be liquid, for a reason which science has never been able to refute."

"What reason?" I said, a bit astonished.

"Because this liquid mass would be subject, like the ocean, to the attraction of the moon, and therefore there would be interior tides twice a day that would push up the terrestrial crust and cause periodical earthquakes!"

"Yet it's evident that the surface of the globe has been subject to combustion," I replied, "and it's quite reasonable to suppose that the external crust cooled down first, while the heat gathered at the center."

"A mistake," my uncle answered. "The earth has been heated by combustion on its surface, not the other way around. Its surface was composed of a great number of metals, such as potassium and sodium, which have the property of igniting at mere contact with air and water; these metals kindled when atmospheric steam fell on the soil as rain; and by and by, when the waters penetrated into the fissures of the earth's crust, they caused more fires with explosions and eruptions. Hence the numerous volcanoes during the first ages of the earth."

"What an ingenious theory!" I exclaimed, a little in spite of myself.

"Which Humphry Davy demonstrated to me by a simple experiment. He made a ball of the metals that I've mentioned, which was a very fair representation of our globe; whenever he made a fine dew fall on its surface, it swelled up, oxidized and formed a little hill; a crater opened at its summit; the eruption took place, and spread such heat to the entire ball that it became impossible to hold it in one's hand."

In truth, I was beginning to be shaken by the professor's arguments; besides, he proposed them with his usual passion and enthusiasm.

"You see, Axel," he added, "the condition of the nucleus has given rise to various theories among geologists; there's no proof at all for this interior heat; my opinion is that there's no such thing, there cannot be; at any rate, we'll see for ourselves, and like Arne Saknussemm, we'll know exactly what the fact of the matter is concerning this big question."

"Very well, we'll see," I replied, warming to his enthusiasm. "Yes, we'll see, that is, if it's possible to see anything there."

"And why not? Can we not depend on electric phenomena to give us light, and even on the atmosphere, which might become luminous due to its pressure as we approach the center?"

"Yes," I said, "yes! That's possible, after all."

"It's certain," answered my uncle in a tone of triumph. "But silence, do you hear me? silence on the whole subject, so that no one gets the idea of discovering the center of the earth before us."

VII

Thus ended this memorable session. This conversation threw me into a fever. I left my uncle's study as if I had been stunned, and as if there was not air enough in all the streets of Hamburg to put me right again. I therefore walked toward the banks of the Elbe, where the steamer connects the city with the Hamburg railway.

Was I convinced of the truth of what I had heard? Had I not bent under Professor Lidenbrock's iron rule? Was I to believe him in earnest in his intention to penetrate to the center of this massive globe? Had I been listening to the mad speculations of a lunatic, or to the scientific conclusions of a great genius? In all this, where did truth stop? Where did error begin?

I was adrift amongst a thousand contradictory assumptions, without being able to grasp any of them firmly.

Yet I remembered that I had been convinced, although now my enthusiasm was beginning to cool down; but I felt a desire to leave at once, and not waste time in calm reflection. Yes, I would have had enough courage enough to pack my suitcase at that moment.

But I must confess that in another hour this unnatural excitement abated, my nerves became unstrung, and from the deep abysses of this earth I ascended to its surface again.

"This is absurd!" I exclaimed, "there's no common sense in it. No sensible young man should entertain such a proposal for a moment. The whole thing is non-existent. I've had a bad night, I've had a nightmare."

But I had followed the banks of the Elbe and passed the town. After going back up to the port, I had reached the Altona road. I was led by a presentiment, a justified presentiment, because soon I saw my little Graüben bravely returning with her light step to Hamburg.

"Graüben!" I called from afar off.

The girl stopped, a little disturbed perhaps to hear her name called after her in the street. With ten steps I had joined her.

"Axel!" she said in surprise. "Ah! you must have come to meet me! That must be it, Sir."

But when she had looked at me, Graüben could not fail to see the uneasiness and distress of my mind.

"What's the matter?" she said, holding out her hand.

"The matter, Graüben!" I exclaimed.

In two seconds and three sentences my pretty Virland girl was fully informed about the situation. She was silent for a few moments. Did her heart palpitate as mine did? I don't know, but her hand did not tremble in mine. We went on a hundred yards without speaking.

"Axel!" she said at last.

"My dear Graüben!"

"It'll be a beautiful journey!"

I leaped up at these words.

"Yes, Axel, a journey worthy of the nephew of a scholar; it's a good thing for a man to be distinguished by some great enterprise."

"What, Graüben, won't you dissuade me from such an expedition?"

"No, dear Axel, and I'd willingly go with you, if a poor girl weren't a burden to you."

"Is that true?"

"Quite true."

Ah! women, girls, how incomprehensible are your feminine hearts! When you are not the most timid, you are the bravest of creatures. Reason has nothing to do with your actions. What! this child encouraged me to take part in the expedition! She wouldn't even have been afraid to join it herself! And she pushed me to do it, the one whom she loved after all!

I was disconcerted and, why not admit it, ashamed.

"Graüben, we'll see whether you say the same thing tomorrow."

"Tomorrow, dear Axel, I'll say what I say today."

Graüben and I, hand in hand, but in silence, continued on our way. The emotions of that day were breaking my heart.

"After all," I thought, "the calends of July are still a long way off, and between now and then, many things can happen that will cure my uncle of his desire to travel underground."

Night had fallen when we arrived at the house in Königstrasse. I expected to find all quiet there, my uncle in bed as was his custom, and Martha giving the dining-room her last touches with the feather brush.

But I had not taken the professor's impatience into account.

I found him shouting and running around among a crowd of porters who were all unloading certain goods in the passage. The old servant was at her wits' end.

"Come, Axel, hurry up, you miserable wretch," my uncle exclaimed from as far off as he could see me. "Your suitcase isn't packed, and my papers aren't in order, and I can't find the key to my overnight bag, and my gaiters haven't arrived!"

I was thunderstruck. My voice failed. Scarcely could my lips formulate the words:

"So we're really going?"

"Of course, you unfortunate boy, walking around instead of being here!"

"We're leaving?" I asked in a weakened voice.

"Yes, the day after tomorrow, early in the morning."

I could listen to no more, and fled to my little room.

There was no more doubt. My uncle had spent his afternoon purchasing some of the items and tools that were necessary for his journey. The passage was packed with rope ladders, knotted cords, torches, flasks, grappling irons, ice picks, iron-tipped walking sticks, pickaxes, enough of a load for at least ten men.

I spent an awful night. Next morning I was called early. I had decided not to open the door. But how to resist the sweet voice that pronounced the words, "My dear Axel"?

I came out of my room. I thought my pale countenance and my red and sleepless eyes would work on Graüben's sympathies and change her mind.

"Ah! my dear Axel," she said to me. "I see you are better, and that the night's rest has calmed you down."

"Calmed me down!" I exclaimed.

I rushed to the mirror. Well, in fact I did look better than I had expected. It was hard to believe.

"Axel," she said, "I've had a long talk with my guardian. He is a bold scholar, a man of immense courage, and you must remember that his blood flows in your veins. He has told me about his plans, his hopes, and why and how he hopes to reach his goal. He will no doubt succeed. My dear Axel, it's a wonderful thing to devote yourself to science like this! What honor will fall on Mr. Lidenbrock, and reflect on his companion! When you return, Axel, you'll be a man, his equal, free to speak and to act independently, and finally free to . . ."

The girl, blushing, did not finish the sentence. Her words revived me. Nevertheless, I still refused to believe we would leave. I drew Graüben toward the professor's study.

"Uncle, is it true, then, that we'll leave?"

"What! You doubt it?"

"No," I said, so as not to irritate him. "Only I'd like to know what need is there to hurry."

"Time, of course! Time, flying with irrecuperable speed!"

"But it is only May 26th, and until the end of June—"

"What, ignorant! do you think you can get to Iceland so easily? If you had not deserted me like a fool, I would have taken you to the Copenhagen office at Liffender & Co., and you would have seen that there's only one trip every month from Copenhagen to Reykjavik, on the 22nd."

"And so?"

"So, if we wait for June 22nd, we'll be too late to see the shadow of Scartaris touch the crater of Snaefells. We must therefore travel to Copenhagen as fast as we can so as to find a means of transportation. Go and pack your suitcase!"

There was not a word I could reply to this. I returned to my room. Graüben followed me. She undertook to pack all things necessary for my voyage. She was no more moved than if I had been starting for a little trip to Lübeck or Helgoland.* Her little hands moved without haste. She talked quietly. She provided me with the most sensible reasons for our expedition. She delighted me, and yet I felt a deep rage against her. Now and then I felt I should break out into a temper, but she took no notice and methodically continued her quiet task.

Finally the last strap was buckled. I went downstairs.

All through the day, the purveyors of instruments, weapons, and electric devices had multiplied. Martha was losing her head.

---

*Lübeck is a city in northern Germany; Helgoland is a German island and vacation resort in the North Sea.

"Is the master mad?" she asked.

I nodded.

"And he's taking you with him?"

I nodded again.

"Where to?" she said.

I pointed to the center of the earth with my finger.

"Into the cellar?" exclaimed the old servant.

"No," I said. "Deeper!"

The evening came. But I was no longer conscious of passing time.

"Tomorrow morning," my uncle said, "we leave at six o'clock."

At ten o'clock I fell on my bed like an inert mass.

During the night, terror gripped me again.

I spent it dreaming of abysses! I was a prey to delirium. I felt myself grasped by the professor's strong hand, dragged along, hurled down, sinking! I dropped down unfathomable precipices with the accelerating speed of bodies falling through space. My life had become nothing but an endless fall.

I awoke at five o'clock, exhausted by fatigue and emotion. I went downstairs to the dining-room. My uncle was at the table. He devoured his breakfast. I looked at him with horror. But Graüben was there. I said nothing. I could eat nothing.

At half-past five there was a rattle of wheels outside. A large carriage was there to take us to the Altona railway station. It was soon loaded up with my uncle's packages.

"Where's your suitcase?" he said.

"It's ready," I replied, with faltering voice.

"Then hurry up to bring it down, or we'll miss the train!"

It was now manifestly impossible to struggle against destiny. I went up again to my room, and rushed after him by letting my suitcase slide down the stairs.

At that moment my uncle was solemnly surrendering "the reins" of the house to Graüben. My pretty Virland girl maintained her usual calm. She kissed her guardian, but could not hold back a tear in brushing my cheek with her sweet lips.

"Graüben!" I exclaimed.

"Go, my dear Axel," she said to me, "you're leaving your fiancée, but you'll find your wife when you return."

I took her into my arms and then seated myself in the carriage. Martha and the girl, standing at the door, waved their last farewell. Then the horses, roused by the driver's whistling, ran off at a gallop on the road to Altona.

VIII

ALTONA, A REAL SUBURB of Hamburg, is the terminus of the Kiel railway, which was supposed to carry us to the Belts. In twenty minutes we were in Holstein.*

At half-past six the carriage stopped at the station; my uncle's numerous packages, his voluminous travel items were unloaded, transported, weighed, labeled, loaded into the luggage car, and at seven we sat facing each other in our compartment. The whistle sounded, the engine started to move. We were off.

Was I resigned? Not yet. Yet the cool morning air and the scenes on the road, rapidly changing due to the speed of the train, distracted me from my great worry.

As for the professor's reflections, they obviously overtook this slow conveyance with his impatience. We were alone in the carriage, but we sat in silence. My uncle examined all his pockets and his traveling bag with the most minute care. I saw that indeed none of the items necessary for the realization of his project were missing.

Among other documents, a carefully folded sheet of paper bore the letterhead of the Danish consulate with the signature of Mr. Christiensen, consul in Hamburg and a friend of the professor's. This should make it easy for us to obtain letters of reference for the Governor of Iceland in Copenhagen.

I also observed the famous document, carefully hidden in the most secret pocket of his portfolio. I cursed it from the bottom of my heart, and then studied the landscape again. It was a vast series of uninteresting, monotonous, loamy and fertile flats; a very favorable landscape for the construction of railways, suitable for the straight lines so beloved by railway companies.

But I had no time to get tired of this monotony; for in three hours we stopped at Kiel, close to the sea.

As our luggage was checked through to Copenhagen, we did not

---

*Kiel is a port city in northern Germany. The Belts are two straits in Denmark that connect the Baltic Sea with the large strait called the Kattegat. Holstein is the region between the Eider and Elbe Rivers, now the southern part of the German state of Schleswig-Holstein.

have to look after it. Nevertheless, the professor kept a cautious eye on it while it was being transported to the steamer. There, it disappeared in the hold.

In his haste, my uncle had so well calculated the connection between the train and the steamer that we had a whole day to kill. The steamer *Ellenora* would not leave until night.

Hence a nine-hour fever during which the irascible traveler sent the steamboat and of railway administrators to the devil, as well as the governments which tolerated such abuses. I was forced to echo him when he approached the captain of the *Ellenora* with this subject. He wanted to force him to heat up the engines without wasting a moment. The captain disposed of him summarily.

In Kiel, as elsewhere, a day eventually passes. What with walking on the verdant shores of the bay at the extreme of which lies the little town, exploring the dense woods which make it look like a nest amongst thick foliage, admiring the villas, each with a little bath house, and moving about and grumbling, at last ten o'clock came.

The heavy coils of smoke from the *Ellenora* rose to the sky; the bridge shook with the shudders of the boiler; we were on board, and owners of two berths, one above the other, in the ship's only cabin.

At a quarter past ten the moorings were loosed and the steamer glided rapidly over the dark waters of the Great Belt.

The night was dark; there was a sharp breeze and rough sea; a few lights appeared on shore through the thick darkness; later on, I cannot tell when, a dazzling light from some lighthouse glittered above the waves; and that is all I can remember of this first passage.

At seven in the morning we landed at Korsör, a small town on the west coast of Zealand. There we transferred from the boat to another train, which took us across just as flat a country as the plain of Holstein.

Three hours' traveling brought us to the capital of Denmark. My uncle had not shut his eyes all night. In his impatience I believe he was trying to accelerate the train with his feet.

At last he discerned a stretch of sea.

"The Sound!" he exclaimed.

At our left was a huge building that looked like a hospital.

"That's a lunatic asylum," said one of our traveling companions.

Very good! I thought, just the place where we should spend the rest of our days! And large though it is, that asylum is not big enough to contain all Professor Lidenbrock's madness!

At ten in the morning, at last, we set foot in Copenhagen; the luggage was loaded on to a carriage and taken to the Hotel Phoenix in Bredgade along with ourselves. This took half an hour, for the station is outside of the town. Then my uncle, after refreshing himself quickly, dragged me along with him. The porter at the hotel could speak German and English; but the professor, as a polyglot, questioned him in good Danish, and it was in the same language that this individual directed him to the Museum of Northern Antiquities.

The director of this curious establishment, in which marvels are piled up from which the ancient history of the country might be reconstructed by means of its stone weapons, its cups and its jewels, was Professor Thomson, a scholar, friend of the Danish consul at Hamburg.

My uncle had a cordial letter of introduction to him. As a general rule one scholar greets another with coolness. But here it was completely different. Mr. Thomson, a helpful man, extended a warm welcome to Professor Lidenbrock and the same to his nephew. It is hardly necessary to mention that the secret was preserved in the presence of the excellent museum director. We simply wanted to visit Iceland as disinterested amateurs.

Mr. Thomson put himself at our disposal, and we visited the quays so as to look for a ship getting ready for departure.

I still hoped that there would be absolutely no means of transportation; but no such luck. A small Danish schooner, the *Valkyrie*, was to set sail for Reykjavik on the 2nd of June. The captain, Mr. Bjarne, was on board. His future passenger, full of joy, shook his hands so hard they almost broke. The good man was a little astonished at this grip. He found it quite simple to go to Iceland, since that was his profession. My uncle considered it sublime. The worthy captain took advantage of this enthusiasm to charge us double for the passage. But we did not trouble ourselves about such trifles.

"Be on board on Tuesday, at seven in the morning," said Captain Bjarne, after having pocketed a considerable number of dollars.

We then thanked Mr. Thomson for his kindness, and returned to the Hotel Phoenix.

"It's going well! It's going very well!" my uncle repeated. "What a fortunate coincidence that we've found this ship that's ready to leave! Now let's have breakfast and go visit the town."

We went first to Kongens Nytorv, an irregular square with a pedestal and two innocent cannons that aim at something but frighten no one. Close by, at No. 5, there was a French "restaurant," kept by a chef called Vincent; we had a sufficient breakfast for the moderate price of four marks each.*

I then took a childish pleasure in exploring the city; my uncle let me take him with me, but he took notice of nothing, neither the insignificant royal palace, nor the pretty seventeenth-century bridge that spans the canal in front of the museum, nor that immense cenotaph of Thorvaldsen's,† decorated with horrible murals, which contains a collection of the sculptor's works, nor the toylike chateau of Rosenberg, nor the beautiful Renaissance building of the Stock Exchange, nor its spire composed of the twisted tails of four bronze dragons, nor the great windmill on the ramparts whose huge arms swelled in the sea breeze like the sails of a ship.

What delicious walks we would have had together, my pretty Virland girl and I, along the harbor where the double-deckers and the frigate slept peaceably under their red roofing, by the green banks of the strait, through the deep shades of the trees amongst which the fort is half concealed, where the cannons thrust their black necks between the branches of alder and willow!

But, alas! she was far away, my poor Graüben, and could I hope ever to see her again?

Meanwhile, whereas my uncle saw none of these delightful places, he was very much struck by the sight of a certain clock tower on the island of Amager, which forms the southwestern part of Copenhagen.

I was ordered to walk in that direction; I embarked on a small steamer which crosses the canals, and in a few minutes it landed at the quay of the dockyard.

---

*Approximately 2 francs and 75 centimes (author's note).
†Bertel Thorvaldsen, Danish neoclassical sculptor (c.1770–1844).

After crossing a few narrow streets where some convicts, in part yellow and part grey trousers, were at work under the orders of the wardens, we arrived at the Vor Frelsers Kirke. There was nothing remarkable about the church. But there was a reason why its tall spire had attracted the professor's attention. Starting from the platform, an external staircase wound around the spire, the spirals circling up into the sky.

"Let's go up," said my uncle.

"But the vertigo?" I replied.

"All the more reason, we must get used to it."

"But—"

"Come, I tell you, let's not waste time."

I had to obey. A guard who lived at the other end of the street handed us the key, and the ascent began.

My uncle went ahead with a lively step. I followed him not without terror, because unfortunately my head turned dizzy very easily. I had neither an eagle's balance nor his steely nerves.

As long as we were enclosed on the interior staircase, everything went well; but after a hundred and fifty steps fresh air hit me in the face, and we were on the platform of the tower. There the aerial staircase began, only guarded by a thin rail, and the narrowing steps seemed to ascend into infinite space.

"I'll never be able to do it!" I exclaimed.

"What kind of a coward are you? Up!" the professor replied mercilessly.

I had to follow, clinging to every step. The keen air made me dizzy; I felt the spire rocking with every gust of wind; my legs began to fail; soon I crawled on my knees, then on my stomach; I closed my eyes; I had space sickness.

At last, my uncle dragging me by the collar, I reached the ball.

"Look down!" he exclaimed. "Look down carefully! We must take *lessons in abysses.*"

I opened my eyes. I saw the houses flattened as if they had been squashed by a fall, in the midst of a fog of smoke. Ragged clouds drifted over my head, and through an optical inversion they seemed stationary, while the steeple, the ball and I were all moving along with fantastic speed. Far away on one side was the green country, on the other the sea sparkled under beams of sunlight. The Sound

Ragged clouds drifted over my head.

stretched away to Elsinore,* dotted with a few white sails, like sea-gulls' wings; and in the misty east and away to the northeast lay out-stretched the faintly-shadowed shores of Sweden. All this immensity of space whirled before my eyes.

Nevertheless I had to get up, stand straight, look. My first lesson in vertigo lasted an hour. When I finally got permission to go down and touch the solid street pavements with my feet, I was aching all over.

"We'll start over again tomorrow," said the professor.

And indeed, for five days, I repeated this vertiginous exercise, and willy-nilly, I made noticeable progress in the art of "lofty contemplations."

---

*English name for the Danish city of Helsingør, the site of Castle Kronberg, the original setting of Shakespeare's tragedy *Hamlet*.

IX

THE DAY OF OUR departure arrived. On the eve, the kind Mr. Thomson had brought us urgent letters of introduction to Count Trampe, the Governor of Iceland, Mr. Pictursson, the bishop's suffragan, and Mr. Finsen, mayor of Reykjavik. By way of thanks, my uncle gave him his warmest handshake.

On the 2nd, at six in the morning, all our precious luggage was put aboard the *Valkyrie*. The captain led us to rather narrow cabins under the deck.

"Do we have favorable winds?" my uncle asked.

"Excellent," replied Captain Bjarne; "wind from the south-east. We'll leave the Sound full speed, with all sails set."

A few moments later the schooner, under her mizzen, brigantine, topsail, and topgallant sails, loosed from her moorings and ran at full sail through the strait. An hour later, the capital of Denmark seemed to sink below the distant waves, and the *Valkyrie* skirted the coast of Elsinore. In my nervous state of mind, I expected to see the ghost of Hamlet wandering on the legendary castle terrace.

"Sublime madman!" I said, "no doubt you would approve of us! Perhaps you'd accompany us to the center of the globe, to find the solution for your eternal doubts!"

But nothing appeared on the ancient walls. The castle is, at any rate, much more recent than the heroic prince of Denmark. It now serves as a sumptuous lodge for the doorkeeper of the Sound's straits, where fifteen thousand ships of all nations pass every year.

Kronberg Castle soon disappeared in the mist, as did the tower of Helsingborg, built on the Swedish coast, and the schooner leaned slightly under the breezes of the Kattegat.*

The *Valkyrie* was a fine sailboat, but you never know just what to expect from a ship under sail. She transported coal, household

---

*Castle Kronberg and the city of Helsingør lie across a sound from Helsingborg. Both these Swedish cities are at the entrance to the Kattegat, a strait between Sweden and Denmark that forms part of the connection between the Baltic Sea and the North Sea.

goods, earthenware, woolen clothing, and a cargo of wheat to Reyk-javik. Five crewmen, all Danes, were enough to navigate her.

"How long will the passage take?" my uncle asked the captain.

"About ten days," the captain replied, "if we don't run into too much north-west wind around the Faroes."

"But so you don't expect to incur any considerable delay?"

"No, Mr. Lidenbrock, don't worry, we'll get there."

Toward evening the schooner sailed around Cape Skagen at the northernmost point of Denmark, crossed the Skagerrak during the night, passed by the tip of Norway at Cape Lindesnes,* and entered the North Sea.

Two days later, we sighted the coast of Scotland near Peterhead, and the *Valkyrie* turned toward the Faroe Islands, passing between the Orkneys and the Shetlands.

Soon the schooner was hit by the waves of the Atlantic; it had to tack against the north wind, and reached the Faroes not without some difficulty. On the 8th, the captain sighted Mykines, the east-ernmost of these islands,† and from that moment he took a straight course toward Cape Portland on the southern coast of Iceland.

Nothing unusual occurred during the passage. I bore the troubles of the sea pretty well; my uncle, to his own intense disgust and his even greater shame, was sick all the way.

He was therefore unable to converse with Captain Bjarne about the Snaefells issue, the connections and means of transportation; he had to put off these explanations until his arrival, and spent all his time lying down in his cabin, whose wooden paneling creaked under the onslaught of the waves. But it must be said that he deserved his fate a little.

On the 11th we reached Cape Portland. The clear weather gave us a good view of Myrdals Jökull, which dominates it. The cape consists of a big hill with steep sides, planted on the beach all by itself.

The *Valkyrie* kept at a reasonable distance from the coast, sailing along it on a westerly course amidst great shoals of whales and

---

*The Skagerrak is an arm of the North Sea that lies between Denmark and Norway; Cape Lindesnes is located at the southernmost tip of Norway.

†Mykines is actually the island farthest to the west.

sharks. Soon an enormous perforated rock appeared, through which the sea dashed furiously. The Westmann islets seemed to rise out of the ocean like a sprinkling of rocks on a liquid plain. From that moment on, the schooner swung out to sea and sailed at a good distance round Cape Reykjanes, which forms the western point of Iceland.

The rough sea prevented my uncle from coming on deck to admire these coasts, shattered and beaten by southwestern winds.

Forty-eight hours later, at the end of a storm that forced the schooner to flee with the sails down, we sighted the beacon of point Skagen* in the east, whose dangerous rocks extend into the sea under the surface. An Icelandic pilot came on board, and in three hours the *Valkyrie* dropped her anchor before Reykjavik, in Faxa Bay.

The professor emerged from his cabin at last, a bit pale, a bit downcast, but still full of enthusiasm, and with a look of satisfaction in his eyes.

The population of the town, intensely interested in the arrival of a vessel from which every one expected something, gathered on the quay.

My uncle was in a hurry to leave his floating prison, or rather hospital. But before stepping off the deck of the schooner he pulled me to the front, and pointed with his finger to the north of the bay at a tall mountain with two peaks, a double cone covered with perpetual snow.

"The Snaefells!" he exclaimed. "The Snaefells!"

Then, after having ordered me with a gesture to keep absolute silence, he climbed down into the boat which was waiting for him. I followed, and soon we set foot on the soil of Iceland.

First of all, a good-looking man in a general's uniform appeared. He was, however, nothing but a magistrate, the governor of the island, Baron Trampe himself. The professor realized whom he was facing. He handed him his letters from Copenhagen, and a short conversation in Danish ensued, to which I remained for good reason completely alien. But the result of this first conversation was

---

*The geographical reference point is unclear.

that Baron Trampe placed himself entirely at the service of Professor Lidenbrock.

My uncle was very cordially received by the mayor, Mr. Finsen, no less military in appearance than the governor, but just as peaceful in temperament and office.

As for the bishop's suffragan, Mr. Pictursson, he was at that moment carrying out an episcopal visit in the northern diocese; for the time being, we had to put off being introduced to him. But Mr. Fridriksson, professor of natural sciences at the school of Reykjavik, was a charming man whose assistance became very valuable to us. This modest scholar spoke only Danish and Latin; he offered his services to me in the language of Horace, and I felt that we were made to understand each other. He was, in fact, the only person with whom I could converse during our stay in Iceland.

This excellent man put at our disposition two out of the three rooms of which his house consisted, and we were soon installed there with our luggage, the quantity of which astonished the inhabitants of Reykjavik a little.

"Well, Axel," my uncle said to me, "we're making progress, and the worst is over."

"What do you mean, the worst!" I exclaimed.

"Of course, now we have nothing left but going down."

"If you mean it like that, you're right; but after all, after we go down, we'll have to go up again, I imagine?"

"Oh, that barely worries me! Come, there's no time to lose! I'm going to the library. Perhaps it has some manuscript of Saknussemm's that I'd like to take a look at."

"Well, in the meantime, I'll go visit the city. Won't you do that also?"

"Oh, that doesn't really interest me. What's remarkable about Icelandic soil is not above but underneath."

I went out, and wandered wherever chance happened to lead me.

It would not be easy to lose your way in Reykjavik. So I had no need to ask for directions, which leads to many mistakes in the language of gestures.

The town extends over low and marshy ground between two hills. An immense bed of lava borders on it on one side, and falls gently towards the sea. On the other side lies the vast bay of Faxa, bounded in the north by the enormous glacier of the Snaefells, where the *Valkyrie* was at the moment the only ship at anchor. Usually the English and French fish-patrols anchor here, but just then they were cruising on the eastern coast of the island.

The longer one of Reykjavik's two streets runs parallel to the beach; here live the merchants and traders, in wooden cabins made of horizontal red boards; the other street, further west, leads to a little lake between the houses of the bishop and other non-commercial people.

I had soon explored these bleak and sad streets. Here and there I caught a glimpse of a bit of faded lawn, looking like an old wool carpet worn out by use, or of some semblance of a kitchen garden whose sparse vegetables, potatoes, cabbages, and lettuce, would have seemed appropriate for a Lilliputian table. A few sickly wallflowers were also trying to look as if they were graced by sunshine.

Toward the middle of the non-commercial street I found the public cemetery, enclosed by a mud wall, where it seemed plenty of room was left. Then, a few steps further, I arrived at the Governor's house, a farmhouse compared to the town hall of Hamburg, a palace in comparison with the cabins of the Icelandic population.

Between the little lake and the town stood the church, built in Protestant style with burnt stones taken from the volcanoes themselves; in strong western winds its red roof tiles would obviously be scattered in the air, endangering the faithful.

From a neighboring hillside I saw the national school where, as I was informed later by our host, Hebrew, English, French, and Danish were taught, four languages of which, to my disgrace, I don't know a single word.* I would have been last among the forty students at this little college, and unworthy of going to bed along with them in one of those closets with two compartments, where the more delicate would die of suffocation the very first night.

In three hours I had visited not only the town but its surroundings. Their aspect was peculiarly melancholy. No trees, no vegetation worth mentioning. Everywhere the bare edges of volcanic rocks. The

---

*Yet in the process of deciphering Saknussemm's manuscript, Axel had in fact identified what he thought were French and Hebrew elements.

Icelanders' huts are made of earth and peat, and the walls lean inward. They resemble roofs placed on the ground. But these roofs are relatively fertile meadows. Due to the heat of the house, the grass grows there almost perfectly, and is carefully mown in the hay season; otherwise domestic animals would come to pasture on top of these green abodes.

During my excursion I met few people. When I returned to the commercial street I saw the greater part of the population busy drying, salting, and loading codfish, their main export item. The men seemed robust but heavy, blond Germans of sorts with pensive eyes, who feel a bit outside the rest of mankind, poor exiles relegated to this land of ice, whom nature should have created as Eskimos, since it had condemned them to live just outside the arctic circle! In vain did I try to detect a smile on their faces; they laughed sometimes with a kind of involuntary contraction of the muscles, but they never smiled.

Their clothes consisted of a coarse jacket of black wool called 'vadmel' in Scandinavian countries, a hat with a very broad brim, trousers with a narrow edge of red, and a piece of leather folded up as a shoe.

The women, with sad and resigned faces of a pleasant but expressionless type, wore a bodice and skirt of dark 'vadmel': unmarried women wore a little knitted brown cap over their braided hair; married women tied a colored handkerchief around their heads, topped with a peak of white linen.

After a good walk I returned to Mr. Fridriksson's house, where I found my uncle already in the company of his host.

X

Dinner was ready; it was eagerly devoured by Professor Lidenbrock, whose compulsory fast on board had converted his stomach into a deep chasm. The meal, more Danish than Icelandic, was unremarkable in and of itself; but our host, more Icelandic than Danish, reminded me of the heroes of ancient hospitality. It seemed obvious that we were more at home than he was himself.

The conversation was carried on in the local language, which my uncle mixed with German and Mr. Fridriksson with Latin for my benefit. It turned on scientific questions, as befits scholars; but Professor Lidenbrock was excessively reserved, and his eyes at every sentence enjoined me to keep the most absolute silence regarding our future plans.

In the first place Mr. Fridriksson asked what success my uncle had had at the library.

"Your library!" exclaimed the latter. "It consists of nothing but a few tattered books on almost empty shelves."

"How so!" replied Mr. Fridriksson. "We possess eight thousand volumes, many of them valuable and rare, works in the ancient Scandinavian language, and we have all the new publications that Copenhagen provides us with every year."

"Where do you keep your eight thousand volumes? For my part—"

"Oh, Mr. Lidenbrock, they're all over the country. In this old island of ice, we are fond of study! There's not a farmer or a fisherman who cannot read and doesn't read. We believe that books, instead of growing moldy behind an iron grating, should be worn out under the eyes of readers. So these volumes pass from one to another, are leafed through, read and reread, and often they find their way back to the shelves only after an absence of a year or two."

"And in the meantime," said my uncle rather spitefully, "foreigners—"

"What can you do! Foreigners have their libraries at home, and the most important thing is that our farmers educate themselves.

I repeat, the love of studying runs in Icelandic blood. So in 1816 we founded a literary society that prospers; foreign scholars are honored to become members of it. It publishes books for the education of our fellow countrymen, and does the country genuine service. If you'll consent to be a corresponding member, Mr. Lidenbrock, you'll give us the greatest pleasure."

My uncle, who was already a member of about a hundred learned societies, accepted with a good grace that touched Mr. Fridriksson.

"Now," he said, "please tell me what books you hoped to find in our library, and I can perhaps advise you on how to consult them."

I looked at my uncle. He hesitated. This question went directly to the heart of his project. But after a moment's reflection, he decided to answer.

"Mr. Fridriksson, I'd like to know whether amongst your ancient books you have those of Arne Saknussemm?"

"Arne Saknussemm!" replied the Reykjavik professor. "You mean that learned sixteenth century scholar, simultaneously a great naturalist, a great alchemist, and a great traveler?"

"Precisely."

"One of the glories of Icelandic literature and science?"

"Just as you say."

"Among the most illustrious men of the world?"

"I grant you that."

"And whose courage was equal to his genius?"

"I see that you know him well."

My uncle was afloat in joy at hearing his hero described in this fashion. He feasted his eyes on Mr. Fridriksson's face.

"Well," he asked, "his works?"

"Ah! His works—we don't have them."

"What—in Iceland?"

"They don't exist either in Iceland or anywhere else."

"But why?"

"Because Arne Saknussemm was persecuted for heresy, and in 1573 his books were burned by the executioner in Copenhagen."

"Very good! Perfect!" exclaimed my uncle, to the great dismay of the science professor.

"What?" he asked.

"Yes! everything's logical, everything follows, everything's clear, and I understand why Saknussemm, after being put on the Index* and compelled to hide his ingenious discoveries, was forced to bury the secret in an unintelligible cryptogram—"

"What secret?" asked Mr. Fridriksson eagerly.

"A secret which—whose—" my uncle stammered.

"Do you have a particular document in your possession?" asked our host.

"No . . . I was making a mere assumption."

"Well," answered Mr. Fridriksson, who was kind enough not to pursue the subject when he noticed the embarrassment of his conversation partner. "I hope," he added, "that you'll not leave our island until you've seen some of its mineralogical wealth."

"Certainly," replied my uncle; "but I'm arriving a little late; haven't other scholars been here before me?"

"Yes, Mr. Lidenbrock; the work of Olafsen and Povelsen, carried out by order of the king, the studies of Troïl, the scientific mission of Gaimard and Robert on the French corvette *La Recherche*,† and lastly the observations of scholars aboard the *Reine Hortense*,[6] have substantially contributed to our knowledge of Iceland. But believe me, there is plenty left."

"Do you think so?" said my uncle with an innocent look, trying to hide the flashing of his eyes.

"Yes. So many mountains, glaciers, and volcanoes to study that are little known! Look, without going any further, look at that mountain on the horizon. That's Snaefells."

"Ah!" said my uncle, "Snaefells."

"Yes, one of the most peculiar volcanoes, whose crater has rarely been visited."

"Extinct?"

"Oh, yes, extinct for more than five hundred years."

"Well," replied my uncle, who was frantically crossing his legs to

---

*The Index Prohibitorius, which specified books forbidden by the Roman Catholic Church.

†*La Recherche* was sent out in 1835 by Admiral Duperré to learn the fate of the lost expedition of Mr. de Blosseville and the Lilloise, which was never heard of again (author's note). See also endnote 6.

keep himself from jumping up, "I'd like to begin my geological studies with that Seffel—Fessel—what do you call it?"

"Snaefells," replied the excellent Mr. Fridriksson.

This part of the conversation had taken place in Latin; I had understood everything, and I could hardly conceal my amusement at seeing my uncle trying to control the satisfaction with which he was brimming over. He tried to put on an air of innocence that looked like the grimace of an old devil.

"Yes," he said, "your words make up my mind for me! We'll try to scale that Snaefells, perhaps even investigate its crater!"

"I deeply regret," replied Mr. Fridriksson, "that my engagements don't allow me to absent myself, or I would have accompanied you with pleasure and profit."

"Oh, no, oh, no!" replied my uncle eagerly, "we wouldn't want to disturb anyone, Mr. Fridriksson; I thank you with all my heart. The company of a scholar such as yourself would have been very useful, but the duties of your profession—"

I like to think that our host, in the innocence of his Icelandic soul, did not understand my uncle's crude malice.

"I very much approve of your beginning with that volcano, Mr. Lidenbrock," he said. "You'll gather an ample harvest of interesting observations. But tell me, how do you plan to get to the Snaefells peninsula?"

"By sea, crossing the bay. That's the fastest route."

"No doubt; but it's impossible."

"Why?"

"Because we don't have a single boat in Reykjavik."

"The devil!"

"You'll have to go overland, following the shore. It'll be longer, but more interesting."

"Well. I'll have to see about a guide."

"I actually have one that I can offer you."

"A reliable, intelligent man?"

"Yes, an inhabitant of the peninsula. He's an eider duck hunter, very skilled, with whom you'll be satisfied. He speaks Danish perfectly."

"And when can I see him?"

"Tomorrow, if you like."

"Why not today?"

"Because he doesn't arrive until tomorrow."

"Tomorrow, then," replied my uncle with a sigh.

This momentous conversation ended a few moments later with warm thanks from the German professor to the Icelandic professor. During this dinner my uncle had learned important facts, among others, Saknussemm's history, the reason for his mysterious document, that his host would not accompany him in his expedition, and that the very next day a guide would be at his service.

XI

In the evening I took a short walk along the Reykjavik shore and returned early to lie down in my bed made of big boards, where I slept deeply.

When I awoke I heard my uncle talking at a great rate in the next room. I immediately got up and hurried to join him.

He was conversing in Danish with a tall man of robust build. This large fellow had to have great strength. His eyes, set in a crude and rather naïve face, seemed intelligent to me. They were of a dreamy blue. Long hair, which would have been considered red even in England, fell on his athletic shoulders. The movements of this native were smooth, but he made little use of his arms in speaking, like a man who knew nothing or cared nothing about the language of gestures. His whole appearance bespoke perfect calm, not indolence but tranquility. One could tell that he would be beholden to nobody, that he worked at his convenience, and that nothing in this world could astonish him or disturb his philosophy.

I became aware of the nuances of this character by the way in which he listened to his interlocutor's impassioned flow of words. He remained with his arms crossed, immobile in the face of my uncle's multiple gesticulations; for a negative his head turned from left to right; it nodded for an affirmative, so slightly that his long hair scarcely moved. It was economy of motion carried to the point of avarice.

Certainly, in looking at this man, I would never have guessed that he was a hunter; he did not look likely to frighten his game, for sure, but how could he reach it?

Everything became clear when Mr. Fridriksson informed me that this calm individual was only a "hunter of the eider duck," whose inner plumage constitutes the greatest wealth of the island. This is in fact what is called eider down, and gathering it requires no great energy of movement.

In the first days of summer the female, a kind of pretty duck, goes to build her nest among the rocks of the fjords that lie all along the coast. After building the nest she feathers it with down plucked from her breast. Immediately the hunter, or rather the trader, comes, robs the nest, and the female starts her work over. This goes on as long as she has any down left. When she has stripped herself bare the male takes his turn to pluck himself. But as the hard and coarse plumage of the male has no commercial value, the hunter does not take the trouble to steal the bedding for his brood; so the nest is completed; the female lays the eggs; the young are hatched, and the following year the down harvest begins again.

Now, since the eider duck does not choose steep cliffs for her nest, but rather the easy and horizontal rocks that slope to the sea, the Icelandic hunter could exercise his calling without any great exertion. He was a farmer who did not have to either sow or reap his harvest, but merely to gather it in.

This grave, phlegmatic, and silent individual was called Hans Bjelke; he came recommended by Mr. Fridriksson. He was our future guide. His manners contrasted strikingly with my uncle's.

Nevertheless, they easily came to terms with each other. Neither one debated the amount of the payment: the one was ready to accept whatever was offered; the other was ready to give whatever was demanded. Never was a bargain struck more easily.

The outcome of the negotiations was that Hans committed himself to lead us to the village of Stapi, on the southern shore of the Snaefells peninsula, at the very foot of the volcano. By land this would be about twenty-two miles,* a journey of about two days, according to my uncle's opinion.

But when he found out that a Danish mile was 24,000 feet long, he was forced to modify his calculations and, given the poor condition of the roads, allow seven or eight days for the march.

Four horses were to be placed at his disposal—two to carry him and me, two for the luggage. Hans would walk, as was his custom. He knew that part of the coast perfectly, and promised to take us the shortest way.

His contract was not to terminate with our arrival at Stapi; he

---

*Just over 100 statute miles.

would continue in my uncle's service for the whole period of his scientific excursions, for the price of three rix-dollars* a week. But it was explicitly agreed that this sum would be paid to the guide every Saturday evening, a *sine qua non* condition of his contract.

The departure was set for June 16. My uncle wanted to pay the hunter a portion in advance, but the latter refused with one word:

"Efter," he said.

"After," said the professor for my edification.

The negotiations concluded, Hans promptly withdrew.

"An excellent man," my uncle exclaimed, "but he doesn't know the marvelous role that the future has in store for him."

"So he goes with us as far as—"

"Yes, Axel, as far as the center of the earth."

Forty-eight hours were left until our departure; to my great regret I had to use them for our preparations; all our intelligence was devoted to pack every item in the most convenient way, instruments on one side, weapons on the other, tools in this package, food supplies in that: four sets of packages in all.

The instruments included:

1. An Eigel centigrade thermometer, graduated up to 150 degrees, which seemed to me either too much or too little. Too much if the surrounding heat was to rise so high, in which case we would be cooked alive. Too little to measure the temperature of springs or any other melted substance;

2. A manometer with compressed air, designed to indicate pressures above that of the atmosphere at sea level. Indeed, an ordinary barometer would not have served the purpose, as the pressure would increase proportionally with our descent below the earth's surface;

3. A chronometer, made by Boissonnas Jun. of Geneva, accurately set to the meridian of Hamburg;

4. Two compasses to measure inclination and declination;

5. A night glass;

---

*16 francs 98 centimes (author's note).

6. Two Ruhmkorff devices, which, by means of an electric current, supplied a highly portable, reliable and unencumbering source of light.*

The weapons consisted of two Purdley More and Co. rifles and two Colt revolvers. Why weapons? We had neither savages nor wild beasts to fear, I suppose. But my uncle seemed to rely on his arsenal as on his instruments, above all on a considerable quantity of gun cotton, which is unaffected by moisture, and whose explosive force far exceeds that of ordinary gunpowder.

The tools included two ice-picks, two pickaxes, a silk rope ladder, three iron-tipped walking sticks, an axe, a hammer, a dozen wedges and iron spikes, and long knotted ropes. Inevitably, this made for a large load, for the ladder was 300 feet long.

Finally there were the food supplies: this parcel was not large, but comforting, for I knew that it contained six months' worth of dried meat and dry biscuits. Gin was the only liquid, and there was no water at all; but we had flasks, and my uncle counted on springs from which to fill them. Whatever objections I had raised as to their quality, their temperature, and even their absence had remained ineffectual.

To complete the exact inventory of all our travel supplies, I should mention a portable medical kit containing blunt scissors, splints for broken limbs, a piece of unbleached linen tape, bandages and compresses, band-aid, a bowl for bleeding, all frightful things; then there was a range of phials containing dextrin, pure alcohol,

---

*A Ruhmkorff device consists of a Bunsen battery operated by means of potassium dichromate, which does not smell; an induction coil puts the electricity generated by the battery in contact with a lantern of a particular design; in this lantern there is a spiral glass tube that contains a vacuum with only a residue of carbon dioxide or nitrogen. When the device is operative, this gas becomes luminous, producing a steady whitish light. The battery and coil are placed into a leather bag that the traveler carries on a shoulder strap. The lantern, carried outside, supplies quite sufficient light even in deep darkness; it allows one to venture into the midst of the most inflammable gases without fear of explosions, and it is not extinguished even in the deepest waters. Mr. Ruhmkorff is a scholar and skilled physicist; his great discovery is the induction coil, which allows one to generate high-tension electricity. In 1864, he won the five-year prize of 50,000 francs reserved by the French government for the most ingenious application of electricity (author's note).

liquid acetate of lead, ether, vinegar, and ammonia, all drugs whose purpose was not reassuring; finally, all the articles necessary for the Ruhmkorff devices.

My uncle took care not to leave out a supply of tobacco, hunting powder, and tinder, nor a leather belt he wore around his waist, where he carried a sufficient quantity of gold, silver, and paper money. Six pairs of good shoes, made waterproof with a layer of tar and rubber, were packed among the tools.

"Clothed, shod, and equipped like this, there's no telling how far we may go," my uncle said to me.

The 14th was entirely spent in arranging all our different items. In the evening we dined at the Baron Trampe's, in the company of the mayor of Reykjavik, and Dr. Hyaltalin, the great doctor of the country. Mr. Fridriksson was not present; I learned afterwards that he and the Governor disagreed on some administrative issue and did not speak to each other. I therefore could not understand a single word of what was said during this semi-official dinner. I only noticed that my uncle talked the whole time.

On the 15th, our preparations were complete. Our host gave the professor very great pleasure by providing him with an immeasurably more perfect map of Iceland than Handerson's: the map of Mr. Olaf Nikolas Olsen, at a scale of 1 to 480,000, and published by the Icelandic Literary Society on the basis of Mr. Frisac Scheel's geodesic works and Bjorn Gumlaugssonn's* topographical survey. It was a precious document for a mineralogist.

Our last evening was spent in intimate conversation with Mr. Fridriksson, with whom I felt the most lively sympathy; the conversation was followed by rather restless sleep, on my part at least.

At five in the morning the neighing of four horses pawing under my window woke me up. I dressed in haste and went down to the street. Hans was finishing the loading of our luggage, as it were without moving a limb. Yet he executed his work with uncommon skill. My uncle generated more noise than effort, and the guide seemed to pay very little attention to his instructions.

---

*Danish mathematician (1788–1876) who traveled to Iceland between 1831 and 1843 to carry out a large-scale topographical survey and design maps on a grant from the Copenhagen Literature Society.

All was ready by six o'clock. Mr. Fridriksson shook hands with us. My uncle thanked him in Icelandic for his kind hospitality, with much heartfelt sentiment. As for me, I sketched a cordial greeting in my best Latin; then we got into the saddle, and with his last farewell Mr. Fridriksson treated me to a line of Virgil that seemed to be made for us, travelers on an uncertain route:

*Et quacumque viam dedent fortuna sequamur.**

---

*And wherever fortune opens up a path, we will follow (Latin; from Virgil's *Aeneid* 11.128).

XII

WE HAD STARTED UNDER an overcast but calm sky. There was no fear of heat, none of disastrous rain. Weather for tourists.

The pleasure of riding on horseback through an unknown country made me easy to please at the start of our venture. I gave myself wholly to the pleasure of the traveler, made up of desires and freedom. I was beginning to take a share in the enterprise.

"Besides," I said to myself, "what's the risk? Traveling in a very interesting country! Scaling very remarkable mountain! At worst, scrambling down into an extinct crater! It's obvious that Saknussemm did nothing more than that. As for a passage leading to the center of the globe, pure fantasy! Perfectly impossible! So let's get all the benefit we can out of this expedition, without haggling."

I had scarcely finished this reasoning when we left Reykjavik behind.

Hans moved on steadily, keeping ahead of us at an even, smooth, and rapid pace. The two pack horses followed him without needing any directions. Then came my uncle and myself, looking not too bad on our small but hardy animals.

Iceland is one of the largest islands in Europe. Its surface is 14,000 square miles, and it has only 60,000 inhabitants. Geographers have divided it into four quarters, and we were traveling almost diagonally across the south-west quarter, called the 'Sudvestr Fjordùngr.'

On leaving Reykjavik Hans took us along the seashore. We crossed lean pastures trying very hard to look green; they succeeded better at yellow. The rugged peaks of the trachytic rocks blurred in the mists on the eastern horizon; at times a few patches of snow, attracting the vague light, glittered on the slopes of the distant mountains; certain peaks, rising up boldly, pierced the grey clouds, and reappeared above the moving mists, like reefs emerging in the sky.

Often these chains of barren rocks reached all the way to the sea, and encroached on the pasture: but there was always enough room to pass. Besides, our horses instinctively chose the proper places without ever slackening their pace. My uncle did not even have the satisfaction of stirring on his beast with voice or whip. He had no reason to be impatient. I could not help smiling to see so tall a man on so small a horse, and as his long legs nearly touched the ground he looked like a six-legged centaur.

"Good animal! good animal!" he kept saying. "You'll see, Axel, that there is no more intelligent animal than the Icelandic horse. Snow, storm, impassable roads, rocks, glaciers, nothing stops it. It's courageous, sober, and reliable. Never a false step, never an adverse reaction. If there is a river or fjord to cross—and we'll encounter them—you'll see it plunge in at once, just as if it were amphibious, and reach the opposite bank. But let's not interfere with it, let's let it have its way, and we'll cover ten miles a day, one carrying the other."

"Undoubtedly we might," I answered, "but how about our guide?"

"Oh, never mind him. People like him walk without even being aware of it. This one moves so little that he'll never get tired. Besides, if necessary, I'll let him have my horse. I'll soon get cramped if I don't move a little. The arms are all right, but I have to think of the legs."

We advanced at a rapid pace. The country was already almost a desert. Here and there an isolated farm, a solitary boër* made of wood, mud, or pieces of lava, appeared like a poor beggar by the wayside. These run-down huts seemed to solicit charity from passersby, and one was almost tempted to give them alms. In this country there were not even roads or paths, and the vegetation, however slow, quickly effaced the rare travelers' footsteps.

Yet this part of the province, at a short distance from the capital, is considered to be among the inhabited and cultivated portions of Iceland. What, then, must other areas look like, more desolate than this desert? In the first half mile we had not yet seen even one farmer standing at his cabin door, nor one shepherd tending a flock less wild than himself, nothing but a few cows and sheep left to themselves. What would the regions look like that were convulsed, turned upside down by eruptive phenomena, sprung from volcanic explosions and subterranean movements?

We would get to know them before long, but when I consulted Olsen's map, I saw that we avoided them by following the sinuous

---

*Icelandic farmer's house (author's note).

edge of the shore. Indeed, the great underground movement is confined to the central portion of the island; there, horizontal layers of superimposed rocks called 'trapps' in Scandinavian, trachytic strips, eruptions of basalt, tuff and all the volcanic mixtures, streams of lava and molten porphyry have created a land of supernatural horror. I had no idea yet of the spectacle which was awaiting us on the Snaefells peninsula, where these residues of a fiery nature create a frightful chaos.

Two hours after leaving Reykjavik we arrived at the town of Gufunes, called 'aoalkirkja,' or principal church. There was nothing remarkable here. Just a few houses. Scarcely enough for a hamlet in Germany.

Hans stopped here for half an hour. He shared our frugal breakfast, answered my uncle's questions about the road with yes and no, and when he was asked where he planned for us to spend the night, he only said, "Gardär."

I consulted the map to see where Gardär was. I saw a small town of that name on the banks of the Hvalfjord, four miles from Reykjavik. I showed it to my uncle.

"Only four miles!" he said. "Four miles out of twenty-two! Now that's a pretty stroll!"

He was about to make an observation to the guide, who without answering resumed his place in front of the horses, and started to walk.

Three hours later, still treading on the discolored grass of the pastures, we had to work around the Kollafjord, an easier and shorter route than crossing it. We soon entered into a 'pingstaœr' or communal gathering place called Ejulberg, from whose steeple twelve o'clock would have struck, if Icelandic churches were rich enough to possess clocks; but they are like the parishioners, who have no watches and do without.

There our horses were fed; then they took a narrow path between a chain of hills and the sea and carried us directly to the aolkirkja of Brantär and one mile farther on, to Saurboër 'Annexia,' a church annex on the south shore of the Hvalfjord.

It was now four o'clock, and we had gone four miles.*

---

*Eight leagues (author's note).

In that place the fjord was at least half a mile wide; the waves broke noisily on the pointed rocks; this bay opened out between walls of rock, a sort of sharp-edged precipice 3,000 feet high, and remarkable for the brown layers which separated beds of reddish tuff. Whatever the intelligence of our horses might be, I hardly cared to put it to the test by crossing a real estuary on the back of quadruped.

If they're intelligent, I thought, they won't try to cross. In any case, I'll be intelligent in their stead."

But my uncle did not want to wait. He spurred his horse on to the shore. His mount sniffed at the waves and stopped. My uncle, who had an instinct of his own, applied more pressure. Renewed refusal by the animal, which shook its head. Then, cussing, and a lashing of the whip; but kicks from the animal, who began to throw off his rider. At last the little horse, bending his knees, crawled out from under the professor's legs, and simply left him standing on two boulders on the shore, like the Colossus of Rhodes.*

"Ah! Damned brute!" exclaimed the horseman suddenly turned pedestrian, as ashamed as a cavalry officer demoted to foot soldier.

"Färja," said the guide, touching his shoulder.

"What! a boat?"

"Der," replied Hans, pointing to a boat.

"Yes," I exclaimed; "there's a boat."

"Why didn't you say so? Let's go!"

"Tidvatten," said the guide.

"What's he saying?"

"He says tide," replied my uncle, translating the Danish word.

"No doubt we must wait for the tide?"

"Förbida?" asked my uncle.

"Ja," replied Hans.

My uncle stamped his foot, while the horses walked toward the boat.

I perfectly understood the necessity to wait for a particular moment of the tide to undertake the crossing of the fjord, when the sea has reached its greatest height and there is no current. Then the ebb

---

*A gigantic statue of the sun god Helios, built between 294 and 282 B.C. in the ancient Greek city of Rhodes.

*The little horse, bending his knees, crawled out from
under the professor's legs.*

and flow have no perceptible effect, and the boat does not risk being carried either to the bottom or out to sea.

That favorable moment arrived only at six o'clock; my uncle, myself, the guide, two ferrymen and the four horses had embarked on a somewhat fragile sort of raft. Accustomed as I was to the steamships on the Elbe, I found the oars of the rowers rather a dismal mechanical device. It took us more than an hour to cross the fjord; but the passage concluded without any mishap.

A half hour later, we reached the aolkirkja of Gardär.

XIII

It SHOULD HAVE BEEN dark, but at the 65th parallel there was nothing surprising about the nocturnal light of the polar regions. In Iceland, during the months of June and July, the sun does not set.

Nevertheless the temperature had gone down. I was cold and above all hungry. Welcome was the "boër" that was hospitably opened to receive us.

It was a peasant's house, but in hospitality it was equal to a king's. On our arrival the master greeted us with outstretched hands, and without ceremony he signaled to us to follow him.

Follow him, indeed, for accompanying him would have been impossible. A long, narrow, dark hallway led into this house made of roughly squared timbers, and gave access to each of the rooms; those were four in number: the kitchen, the weaving room, the 'badstofa' or family bedroom, and the guest bedroom, which was the best of all. My uncle, whose height had not been thought of in building the house, could not avoid hitting his head several times against the beams that projected from the ceilings.

We were led to our bedroom, a large room with an earthen floor, and a window whose panes were made of rather opaque sheep skins. The sleeping accommodation consisted of dry litter, thrown into two wooden frames that were painted red, and decorated with Icelandic proverbs. I did not expect much comfort; but the house was pervaded by a strong smell of dried fish, marinated meat, and sour milk, which caused quite a bit of suffering for my nose.

When we had taken off our traveling clothes, the voice of the host could be heard inviting us to the kitchen, the only room where a fire was lit even in the severest cold.

My uncle hurried to obey the friendly call. I followed him.

The kitchen chimney was of an ancient design: in the middle of the room, a stone for a hearth; in the roof above it, a hole to let the smoke escape. The kitchen also served as dining-room.

When we entered, the host, as if he had not seen us before, greeted us with the word "Sællvertu," which means "be happy," and came and kissed us on the cheek.

After him his wife pronounced the same words, accompanied by the same ritual; then the two placed their hands on their hearts and bowed deeply.

I hasten to mention that this Icelandic woman was the mother of nineteen children, all of them, big and small, swarming in the midst of the dense wreaths of smoke with which the fire on the hearth filled the room. Every moment I noticed a blond and somewhat melancholy face peeping out of this fog. They seemed like a garland of unwashed angels.

My uncle and I treated this 'brood' kindly; and soon we each had three or four of these brats on our shoulders, as many on our laps, and the rest between our knees. Those who could speak kept repeating "Sællvertu," in every conceivable tone. Those who could not speak made up for it with crying.

This concert was brought to a close by the announcement of the meal. At that moment our hunter returned, who had just fed the horses, that is to say, he had economically let them loose in the fields; the poor beasts had to content themselves with grazing on the scanty moss on the rocks and some seaweeds that offered little nourishment, and yet the next day they would not fail to come back by themselves and resume the labors of the previous day.

"Sællvertu," said Hans.

Then calmly, automatically, he kissed the host, the hostess, and their nineteen children, without giving one kiss more emphasis than the next.

This ceremony over, we sat down at the table, twenty-four in number, and therefore one on top of the other, in the most literal sense of the phrase. The luckiest had only two urchins on their knees.

But silence fell in this little world with the arrival of the soup, and the taciturnity that comes naturally even to Icelandic children imposed itself once again. The host served us a lichen soup that was not at all unpleasant, then an enormous serving of dried fish that was floating in butter aged for twenty years, and therefore much preferable to fresh butter, according to Icelandic concepts of gastronomy. Along with this, we had 'skye,' a sort of soured milk, with biscuits, and a liquid prepared from juniper berries; for beverage we had a thin milk mixed with water, called in this country 'blanda.' It is not for me to judge whether this peculiar diet is wholesome or not; I was hungry, and at dessert I swallowed down to the last mouthful of a thick buckwheat broth.

After the meal, the children disappeared; the adults gathered round the hearth which burned peat, briars, cow-dung, and dried fish bones. After this "warm-up," the different groups retired to their respective rooms. Our hostess offered us her assistance in taking off our stockings and pants, according to custom; but as we most gracefully declined, she did not insist, and I was able at last to sink into my bed of hay.

At five the next morning we bade the Icelandic peasant farewell; my uncle had great difficulty persuading him to accept a proper remuneration; and Hans gave the signal for departure.

At a hundred yards from Gardär the soil began to change in appearance; it became swampy and less suitable for walking. On our right, the chain of mountains extended indefinitely like an immense system of natural fortifications, whose counterscarp we followed: often we encountered streams that we had to cross with great care and without getting our luggage too wet.

The desert became more and more desolate; yet from time to time a human shadow seemed to flee in the distance; when a turn in the road unexpectedly brought us close to one of these ghosts, I felt a sudden disgust at the sight of a swollen head with shining and hairless skin, and repulsive sores visible through the rips in the miserable rags.

The unhappy creature did not approach us and offer his misshapen hand; he fled, on the contrary, but not before Hans had greeted him with the customary "Sællvertu."

"Spetelsk," he said.

"A leper!" my uncle repeated.

This word itself had a repulsive effect. The horrible disease of leprosy is fairly common in Iceland; it is not contagious, but hereditary; therefore lepers are forbidden to marry.

These apparitions could not cheer up a landscape that was becoming deeply melancholy. The last tufts of grass had died beneath our feet. Not a tree in sight, unless we except a few tufts of dwarf birch resembling brushwood. Not an animal in sight, except a few horses wandering on the bleak plains, of those whom their master could not feed. Sometimes a hawk glided through the grey clouds, and then darted quickly to the south; I lapsed into the melancholy of this wild nature, and my memories took me back to my home country.

Soon we had to cross several small and insignificant fjords, and at last a genuine bay; the high tide allowed us to cross over without delay, and to reach the hamlet of Alftanes, one mile beyond.

That evening, after having crossed two rivers full of trout and pike, called Alfa and Heta,* we had to spend the night in an abandoned farmhouse worthy of being haunted by all the elves of Scandinavian mythology. The ghost of cold had certainly taken up residence there, and showed us his powers all night long.

No particular event marked the next day. Still the same swampy soil, the same monotony, the same melancholy appearance. By nightfall we had completed half our journey, and we spent the night at the "church annex" of Krösolbt.

On June 19, lava spread beneath our feet for about a mile; this type of soil is called 'hraun' in that country; the wrinkled lava at the surface was shaped like cables, sometimes stretched out, sometimes curled up; an immense stream descended from the nearest mountains, now extinct volcanoes whose past violence was attested by these residues. Yet curls of steam crept along from hot springs here and there.

We had no time to watch these phenomena; we had to proceed on our way. Soon the swampy soil reappeared at the foot of the mountains, intersected by little lakes. Our route now lay westward; we had in fact traveled around the great Bay of Faxa, and the twin peaks of Snaefells rose white into the clouds, less than five miles away.

The horses did their duty well; the difficulties of the soil did not stop them. I myself was getting very tired; my uncle remained as firm and straight as on the first day; I could not help admiring him as much as the hunter, who considered this expedition a simple stroll.

On Saturday, June 20, at six o'clock in the evening, we reached Büdir, a village on the sea shore, and the guide claimed his agreed-upon wages. My uncle settled with him. It was Hans' own family,

---

*The rivers Alfta and Hitard in Iceland.

that is, his uncles and cousins, who offered us hospitality; we were kindly received, and without abusing the kindness of these good folks, I would very much have liked to recover from the exhaustion of the journey at their house. But my uncle, who needed no recovery, would not hear of it, and the next morning we had to mount our brave beasts again.

The soil betrayed the closeness of the mountain, whose granite foundations rose up from the earth like the roots of an ancient oak tree. We traveled around the enormous base of the volcano. The professor hardly took his eyes off it; he gesticulated, he seemed to challenge it and say: "Here's the giant that I'll tame!" Finally, after about four hours' walking, the horses stopped of their own accord at the door of the parsonage at Stapi.

XIV

STAPI IS A VILLAGE consisting of about thirty huts, built right on the lava in the sunlight reflected by the volcano. It extends along the back of a small fjord, enclosed by a basaltic wall of the strangest appearance.

It is known that basalt is a brownish rock of igneous origin. It assumes regular forms, the arrangement of which is often very surprising. Here nature does her work geometrically, with square and compass and plummet. Everywhere else her art consists of huge masses together thrown together without order, its cones barely sketched, its pyramids imperfectly formed, with a bizarre arrangement of lines; but here, as if to exhibit an example of regularity, in advance of the earliest architects, she has created a strict order, never surpassed either by the splendors of Babylon or the wonders of Greece.

I had heard of the Giant's Causeway in Ireland, and Fingal's Cave in Staffa, one of the Hebrides; but I had never yet laid eyes on a basaltic formation.

At Stapi, this phenomenon offered itself in all its beauty.

The wall that enclosed the fjord, like all the coast of the peninsula, consisted of a series of vertical columns, thirty feet high. These straight shafts of pure proportions supported an archivolt of horizontal slabs, the overhanging portion of which formed a half-vault over the sea. At intervals, under this natural shelter, the eye came to rest on vaulted openings of an admirable design, through which the waves came crashing and foaming. A few shafts of basalt, torn off by the fury of the sea, were dispersed on the soil like the remains of an ancient temple, eternally young ruins over which the centuries passed without a trace.

This was the last stage of our journey above ground. Hans had led us here with intelligence, and it gave me comfort to think that he would continue to accompany us.

When we arrived at the door of the rector's house, a simple low cabin, neither more beautiful nor more comfortable than the neighboring ones, I saw a man shoeing a horse, hammer in hand, and with a leather apron on.

"Sællvertu," said the hunter to him.

"God dag," replied the blacksmith in perfect Danish.

"Kyrkoherde," said Hans, turning round to my uncle.

"The rector!" repeated the latter. "It seems, Axel, that this good man is the rector."

In the meantime, our guide informed the 'kyrkoherde' of the situation; the latter, suspending his work, uttered a shout no doubt used among horses and horse dealers, and immediately a tall and ugly hag emerged from the cabin. She must have been almost six feet tall.

I feared that she would come and offer the Icelandic kiss to the travelers; nothing of the sort, nor did she lead us into the house with much grace.

The guest room, narrow, dirty, and foul-smelling seemed to me the worst in the whole house. But we had to resign ourselves to it. The rector seemed not to practice ancient hospitality. Far from it. Before the day was over, I saw that we were dealing with a blacksmith, a fisherman, a hunter, a carpenter, but not at all with a minister of God. To be sure, it was a week-day. Perhaps on Sundays he made amends.

I don't mean to speak ill of these poor priests, who are after all miserably poor; from the Danish Government they receive a ridiculously small pittance, and a fourth of the tithe from their parish, which does not amount to sixty marks* a year. Hence the necessity to work for a living; but when one fishes, hunts, and shoes horses, one ends up adopting the tone and manners of fishermen, hunters, and other somewhat rude folk. That very evening, I found out that temperance was not among the virtues that distinguished our host.

My uncle soon understood what sort of a man he was dealing with; instead of a good and worthy man he found a rude and coarse peasant. He therefore decided to start his great expedition as soon as possible, and to leave this inhospitable parsonage. He cared nothing about his exhaustion and decided to spend some days on the mountain.

The preparations for our departure were therefore carried out the next day after our arrival at Stapi. Hans hired the services of three

---

*In Hamburg currency, about 90 francs (author's note).

Icelanders to replace the horses in the transport of the luggage; but once we arrived at the crater, these natives would turn back and leave us to our own devices. This point was clearly agreed upon.

On this occasion, my uncle had to explain to Hans that it was his intention to pursue the investigation of the volcano to its farthest limits.

Hans merely nodded. There or elsewhere, traveling down into the bowels of his island or on its surface, made no difference to him. For my own part, the incidents of the journey had so far distracted me, and had made me forget the future a little, but now emotion once again got the better of me. What to do? The place to resist Professor Lidenbrock would have been Hamburg, not the foot of Snaefells.

One thought, above all others, tortured me, a frightening idea that might shake firmer nerves than mine.

"Let's see," I said to myself, "we'll climb the Snaefells. Fine. We'll visit the crater. Good. Others have done as much without dying. But that's not all. If there's a way to penetrate into the bowels of the earth, if that unfortunate Saknussemm has told the truth, we'll lose our way among the subterranean passages of the volcano. Now, there's no proof that Snaefells is extinct! Who can prove that an eruption is not brewing at this very moment? Because the monster has slept since 1229,* does it follow that it will never wake up again? And if it wakes up, what becomes of us?"

It was worth thinking about, and I thought about it. I could not sleep without dreaming about eruptions. Now, playing the part of ejected scoria seemed rather brutal to me.

Finally I could not stand it any longer; I decided to lay the case before my uncle as skillfully as possible, in the form of an almost impossible hypothesis.

I went to find him. I conveyed my fears to him, and stepped back to give him room to explode as he liked.

"I thought of that," he replied simply.

What did these words mean? Was he actually going to listen to reason? Was he considering suspending his plans? That was too good to be true.

---

*In chapter VI, Professor Lidenbrock had indicated 1219 as the last eruption date (see p. 31; in fact, it was about A.D. 200.).

After a few moments' silence, during which I dared not question him, he resumed:

"I thought of that. Ever since we arrived at Stapi I've been concerned with the serious question you've just mentioned, for we must not be guilty of carelessness."

"No," I replied forcefully.

"Snaefells hasn't spoken for six hundred years; but he may speak again. Now, eruptions are always preceded by certain well-known phenomena. I have therefore questioned the locals, I have studied the soil, and I can tell you, Axel, that there'll be no eruption."

At this statement I was stunned, and could not answer.

"You doubt my words?" said my uncle. "Well, follow me."

I obeyed mechanically. Leaving the parsonage, the professor took a straight path, which led away from the sea through an opening in the basaltic wall. We were soon in open country, if one can give that name to a vast accumulation of volcanic debris. This land seemed crushed under a rain of enormous rocks, trapp, basalt, granite, and all the pyroxenic rocks.*

Here and there I could see fumaroles curling up into the air; this white steam, called 'reykir' in Icelandic, issued from thermal springs, and they indicated by their force volcanic activity underneath. This seemed to justify my fears. So my spirits sank when my uncle said to me:

"You see all this steam, Axel; well, it proves that we have nothing to fear from the fury of the volcano!"

"How can I believe that?" I exclaimed.

"Remember this," resumed the professor. "At the approach of an eruption these jets increase their activity, but disappear completely during the interval of the eruption. For the gases, which no longer have the necessary pressure, are released by way of the crater instead of escaping through fissures in the soil. Therefore, if this steam remains in its usual condition, if its force does not increase, and if you add to this the observation that the wind and rain are not being replaced by a still and heavy atmosphere, then you can state with certainty that there is no upcoming eruption."

---

*Rocks containing silicates of magnesium, iron, and calcium.

"But . . ."

"Enough. Once science has spoken, one should remain silent."

I returned to the parsonage crestfallen. My uncle had beaten me with scientific arguments. Still I had one hope left, and that was that once we had reached the bottom of the crater, it would prove impossible to descend any further for lack of a passage, in spite of all the Saknussemms of the world.

I spent the following night in constant nightmare in the heart of a volcano, and from the depths of the earth I saw myself tossed up into interplanetary spaces in the form of a volcanic rock.

The next day, June 23, Hans was waiting for us with his companions carrying food, tools, and instruments; two iron–tipped walking sticks, two rifles, and two ammunition belts were set aside for my uncle and myself. Hans, as a cautious man, had added to our luggage a leather bottle full of water that, together with our flasks, would give us a supply for eight days.

It was nine in the morning. The rector and his tall shrew were waiting at the door. They wanted no doubt to bid us the kindest farewell of host to traveler. But this farewell took the unexpected shape of a huge bill, in which we were charged even for the air in the parsonage—foul-smelling air, I might mention. This worthy couple was fleecing us just like a Swiss innkeeper, and estimated their exaggerated hospitality at a high price.

My uncle paid without debate. A man who is setting out for the center of the earth did not care about a few rix-dollars.

This point being settled, Hans gave the signal for departure, and we soon left Stapi behind.

XV

SNAEFELLS IS 5,000 FEET high. Its double cone is the end of a trachytic stratum that stands out from the mountain system of the island. From our point of departure we could see the two peaks boldly projected against the dark grey sky; I noticed an enormous cap of snow drawn down low on the giant's brow.

We walked in single file, headed by the hunter, who ascended on narrow tracks where two could not have gone side by side. Conversation was therefore almost impossible.

After we had passed the basaltic wall of the Stapi fjord we passed first over a grassy, fibrous peat soil, left from the ancient vegetation of this peninsula. The vast quantity of this unused fuel would be sufficient to warm the whole population of Iceland for a century; this vast peat bog was up to seventy feet deep when measured from the bottom of certain ravines, and consisted of layers of carbonized vegetation residues alternating with thinner layers of tufaceous pumice.

As a true nephew of professor Lidenbrock, and in spite of my dismal prospects, I could not help observing with interest the mineralogical curiosities which lay about me as in a vast museum, and I constructed for myself a complete geological account of Iceland.

This most interesting island has evidently been pushed up from the bottom of the sea at a comparatively recent date. Possibly, it is still subject to gradual elevation. If this is so, its origin may well be attributed to subterranean fires. In that case, Sir Humphry Davy's theory, Saknussemm's document, and my uncle's claims would all go up in smoke. This hypothesis led me to examine the appearance of the surface with more attention, and I soon arrived at a conclusion as to the nature of the forces which presided at its creation.

Iceland, which is entirely devoid of alluvial soil, is wholly composed of volcanic tuff, that is to say, an agglomeration of porous rocks and stones. Before the volcanoes erupted, it consisted of trapp rocks slowly raised to sea level by the action of central forces. The interior fires had not yet forced their way through.

But at a later period a wide chasm opened up diagonally from the south-west to the north-east of the island, through which the trachytic mass was gradually squeezed out. No violence accompanied this change; the quantity of ejected matter was vast, and the molten substances oozing out from the bowels of the earth slowly spread over extensive plains or in hillocky masses. In this period feldspar, syenites, and porphyries appeared.

But with the help of this outflow the thickness of the crust of the island increased materially, and therefore also its powers of resistance. It may easily be conceived what vast quantities of elastic gases, what masses of molten matter accumulated beneath its solid surface while no exit was practicable after the cooling of the trachytic crust. Therefore a moment came when the mechanical force of these gases was such that it lifted up the heavy crust and forced their way out through tall chimneys. Hence the volcano created by pushing up the crust, then the crater suddenly formed at the summit of the volcano.

Eruptive phenomena were succeeded by volcanic phenomena. Through the newly created outlets, basalt residues were first ejected, of which the plain we were crossing offered the most wonderful specimens. We walked over heavy rocks of a dark grey color, which the cool-down had shaped into hexagonal prisms. In the distance we could see a large number of flattened cones that were once fire-spitting mouths.

Then, after the basalt eruption had exhausted itself, the volcano, whose power increased through the extinction of the lesser craters, provided a passage for lava and tuff of ashes and scoriae, whose scattered streams I noticed on the mountain sides like abundant hair.

This was the succession of phenomena that produced Iceland, all deriving from the action of interior fire. To suppose that the mass within was not still in a state of liquid incandescence was madness. Madness above all trying to reach the earth's center.

So I felt a little comforted as we advanced to the assault of Snaefells.

The path grew more and more arduous, the ascent steeper and steeper; loose fragments of rock trembled beneath us, and utmost care was needed to avoid dangerous falls.

Hans continued on as calmly as if he were on level ground; sometimes he disappeared behind huge blocks, and we momentarily lost sight of him; then a shrill whistle from his lips would indicate the direction we should follow. Often he would stop, pick up a few bits of stone, stack them up into a recognizable shape, and thereby create

We could see the two peaks boldly projected
against the dark grey sky.

landmarks to guide us on our way back. A wise precaution in itself, but as things turned out, quite useless.

Three exhausting hours of walking had only brought us to the base of the mountain. There Hans signaled to us to stop, and a hasty breakfast was divided up among us. My uncle swallowed two mouthfuls at a time to get on faster. But whether he liked it or not, this was a rest as well as a breakfast hour, and he had to wait until it pleased our guide to move on, he gave the signal for departure after an hour. The three Icelanders, just as taciturn as their comrade the hunter, did not say a single word and ate soberly.

We were now beginning to scale the steep sides of Snaefells. Through an optical illusion that occurs frequently in the mountains, its snowy summit appeared very close; and yet, how many long hours it took to reach! And above all, what exhaustion! The rocks, not tied together by any connection of soil or plants, rolled away from under our feet and lost themselves in the plain with the speed of an avalanche.

In some places the flanks of the mountain formed an angle of at least 36 degrees with the horizon; it was impossible to climb them, and we had to walk around these stony slopes, not without difficulty. We helped each other with our sticks.

I must admit that my uncle kept as close to me as he could; he never lost sight of me, and on many occasions his arm provided me with powerful support. He himself seemed to possess an innate sense of balance, for he never stumbled. The Icelanders, though they were burdened, climbed with the agility of mountaineers.

Judging by the distant appearance of the summit of Snaefells, it seemed impossible to me to reach it from on our side, if the angle of the slopes did not diminish. Fortunately, after an hour of exhaustion and exertions, a kind of staircase appeared unexpectedly in the midst of the vast snow cover on the back of the volcano, which greatly facilitated our ascent. It originated from one of those torrents of stones thrown up by eruptions that are called 'stinâ' by the Icelanders. If this torrent had not been checked in its fall by the shape of the mountain sides, it would have fallen into the sea and formed new islands.

Such as it was, it served us well. The steepness increased, but these stone steps allowed us to climb up easily, and even so quickly that, having rested for a moment while my companions continued their ascent, I perceived them already reduced to microscopic dimensions by the distance.

At seven in the evening, we had ascended the two thousand steps of this grand staircase, and we had attained a bulge in the mountain, a kind of bed on which the cone proper of the crater rested.

Three thousand two hundred feet below us stretched the sea. We had passed the limit of eternal snow, which is not very high up in Iceland because of the constant humidity of the climate. It was savagely cold. The wind blew powerfully. I was exhausted. The professor saw that my legs completely refused to do their duty, and in spite of his impatience he decided to stop. He therefore spoke to the hunter, who shook his head saying:

"Ofvanför."

"It seems we must go higher," said my uncle.

Then he asked Hans for his reason.

"Mistour," replied the guide.

"Ja Mistour," said one of the Icelanders in a tone of alarm.

"What does that word mean?" I asked uneasily.

"Look!" said my uncle.

I looked down on the plain. An immense column of pulverized pumice, sand and dust was rising up with a whirling circular motion like a waterspout; the wind was lashing it on to that side of Snaefells where we were holding on; this dense veil, hung across the sun, threw a deep shadow over the mountain. If this tornado leaned over, it would sweep us up into its whirlwinds. This phenomenon, which is not infrequent when the wind blows from the glaciers, is called in Icelandic 'mistour.'

"Hastigt! hastigt!" exclaimed our guide.

Without knowing Danish I understood at once that we must follow Hans at top speed. He began to circle round the cone of the crater, but in a diagonal direction so as to facilitate our progress. Presently the dust storm fell on the mountain, which quivered under the shock; the loose stones, caught in the blasts of wind, flew about in a hail as in an eruption. Fortunately we were on the opposite side, and sheltered from all harm. Without the guide's precaution, our torn-up bodies, shattered to smithereens, would have fallen down in the distance like the residue of an unknown meteor.

Yet Hans did not think it prudent to spend the night on the sides of the cone. We continued our zigzag climb. The fifteen hundred remaining feet took us five hours to clear; the circuitous route, the diagonal and the counter marches, must have measured at least three leagues. I could not go on; I succumbed to hunger and cold. The slightly thinner air was not enough for my lungs.

At last, at eleven o'clock, we reached the summit of Snaefells in darkness, and before going into the crater for shelter, I had time to observe the midnight sun, at its lowest point, casting its pale beams on the island sleeping at my feet.

XVI

DINNER WAS RAPIDLY CONSUMED, and the little company housed itself as best it could. The bed was hard, the shelter insubstantial, and our situation uncomfortable at five thousand feet above sea level. Yet I slept particularly well; it was one of the best nights I had ever had, and I did not even dream.

Next morning we awoke half frozen by the sharp keen air, but in the light of a splendid sun. I rose from my granite bed and went out to enjoy the magnificent spectacle that spread out before my eyes.

I stood on the summit of the southernmost of Snaefells' peaks. From there, my view extended over the greatest part of the island. By an optical law which obtains at all great heights, the shores seemed raised and the center depressed. It seemed as if one of Helbesmer's relief maps lay at my feet. I could see deep valleys intersecting each other in every direction, precipices like wells, lakes reduced to ponds, rivers shortened to creeks. On my right innumerable glaciers and multiple peaks succeeded each other, some plumed with feathery clouds of smoke. The undulations of these endless mountains, whose layers of snow made them look foamy, reminded me of the surface of a stormy sea. When I turned westward, the ocean lay spread out majestically, like a continuation of these sheep-like summits. The eye could hardly tell where the earth ended and the waves began.

I plunged into the famous ecstasy that high summits create in the mind, and this time without vertigo, for I was finally getting used to these sublime contemplations. My dazzled eyes were bathed in the bright flood of the solar rays. I was forgetting who I was, where I was, and lived instead the life of elves and sylphs, imaginary inhabitants of Scandinavian mythology. I felt intoxicated by the pleasure of the heights without thinking of the abysses into which fate would soon plunge me. But I was brought back to reality by the arrival of Hans and the professor, who joined me on the summit.

My uncle, turning west, pointed out to me a light steam, a mist, a semblance of land that dominated the horizon line.

"Greenland," he said.

"Greenland?" I exclaimed.

"Yes; we're only thirty-five leagues from it; and during thaws the polar bears come all the way to Iceland, carried atop icebergs. But that doesn't matter. Here we are at the top of Snaefells, and there are two peaks, one north and one south. Hans will tell us the name of the one on which we're standing."

The question being put, Hans replied:

"Scartaris."

My uncle shot a triumphant glance at me.

"To the crater!" he exclaimed.

The crater of Snaefells resembled an inverted cone, whose opening might have been half a league in diameter. Its depth appeared to be about two thousand feet. Imagine the aspect of such a container when it filled with thunder and flames. The bottom of the funnel was about 250 feet in circumference, so that its rather gentle slopes allowed its lower brim to be reached without difficulty. Involuntarily I compared the whole crater to an enormous hollow grenade launcher, and the comparison frightened me.

"What madness," I thought, "to go down into a grenade launcher when it's perhaps loaded and can go off at the slightest impact!"

But there was no way out. Hans resumed the lead with an air of indifference. I followed him without a word.

In order to make the descent easier, Hans wound his way down the cone on a spiral path. We had to walk amidst eruptive rocks, some of which, shaken out of their sockets, fell bouncing down into the abyss. Their fall gave rise to surprisingly loud echoes.

In certain parts of the cone there were glaciers. Here Hans advanced only with extreme caution, sounding his way with his iron-tipped walking stick, to discover any crevasses in it. At particularly dubious passages it was necessary to tie ourselves to each other with a long cord, so that anyone who unexpectedly lost his foothold could be held up by his companions. This solidarity was prudent, but did not eliminate all danger.

Yet, notwithstanding the difficulties of the descent, on slopes unknown to the guide, the journey was accomplished without accidents, except the loss of a coil of rope, which escaped from the hands of an Icelander, and took the shortest way to the bottom of the abyss.

At mid-day we had arrived. I raised my head and saw straight above me the upper aperture of the cone, framing a bit of sky of very small circumference, but almost perfectly round. Just on the edge appeared the snowy peak of Scartaris reaching into infinity.

At the bottom of the crater three chimneys opened up, through which Snaefells, during its eruptions, had evacuated lava and steam from its central furnace. Each of these chimneys was about a hundred feet in diameter. They gaped before us right in our path. I did not have the courage to look down into them. But Professor Lidenbrock had quickly examined all three; he was panting, running from one to the other, gesticulating, and uttering unintelligible words. Hans and his comrades, seated on pieces of lava, looked on; they clearly thought he was mad.

Suddenly my uncle uttered a cry. I thought his foot must have slipped and that he had fallen down one of the holes. But no. I saw him, arms outstretched, legs apart, standing in front of a granite rock that was placed in the center of the crater like a pedestal ready to receive a statue of Pluto.* He stood with the posture of a stunned man, but one whose amazement was rapidly giving way to irrational joy.

"Axel, Axel," he exclaimed. "Come, come!"

I ran. Hans and the Icelanders never stirred.

"Look!" said the professor.

And, sharing his astonishment, though not his joy, I read on the western face of the block, in Runic characters half eaten away by time, this thousand times accursed name:

"Arne Saknussemm!" replied my uncle. "Do you yet doubt?"

I made no answer; and I returned to my lava seat in consternation. The evidence crushed me.

How long I remained plunged into my reflections I cannot tell. All I know is that when I raised my head again, I saw only my uncle and Hans at the bottom of the crater. The Icelanders had been dismissed, and they were now descending the outer slopes of Snaefells to return to Stapi.

---

*God of the underworld in Greek mythology.

Hans slept peaceably at the foot of a rock, in a lava bed, where he had made an improvised bed for himself; but my uncle was pacing around the bottom of the crater like a wild beast in a trapper's pit. I had neither the wish nor the strength to rise, and following the guide's example I went off into a painful slumber, thinking I could hear noises or feel tremors in the sides of the mountain.

Thus the first night at the bottom of the crater passed.

The next morning, a grey, heavy, cloudy sky hung over the summit of the cone. I did not realize this so much because of the darkness in the chasm as because of the rage that seized my uncle.

I understood the reason, and a glimmer of hope came back to my heart. Here is why.

Of the three routes open to us, only one had been taken by Saknussemm. According to the Icelandic scholar, one had to identify it by the detail mentioned in the cryptogram, that the shadow of Scartaris would touch its edges during the last days of the month of June.

That sharp peak might hence be considered the hand of a vast sun dial, whose shadow on a given day would indicate the path to the center of the earth.

But if there were to be no sun, no shadow. Consequently, no indicator. It was June 25. If the sky remained overcast for six days, we would have to postpone the observation to another year.

I decline to describe Professor Lidenbrock's impotent rage. The day passed, and no shadow came to stretch along the bottom of the crater. Hans did not move from his spot; yet he must be asking himself what we were waiting for, if he asked himself anything at all. My uncle did not address a single word to me. His gaze, invariably turned to the sky, lost itself in its gray and misty hue.

On the 26th, nothing yet. Rain mingled with snow fell all day long. Hans built a hut with pieces of lava. I took a certain pleasure in watching the thousands of improvised waterfalls on the sides of the cone, where every stone increased the deafening murmur.

My uncle could no longer control himself. It was indeed enough to irritate a more patient man than him, because this was really shipwreck before leaving the port.

But Heaven always mixes great grief with great joy, and for Professor Lidenbrock there was satisfaction equal to his desperate troubles in store.

It softly brushed the edge of the middle chimney.

The next day the sky was again overcast; but on the 29th of June, the next-to-last day of the month, a change of weather came with the change of the moon. The sun poured a flood of light down the crater. Every hill, every stone, every roughness got its share of the luminous flow and instantly threw its shadow on the ground. Among them all, that of Scartaris was outlined with a sharp edge and began to move slowly in the opposite direction from that of the radiant star.

My uncle turned with it.

At noon, when it was shortest, it softly brushed the edge of the middle chimney.

"There it is! there it is!" shouted the professor. "To the center of the globe!" he added in Danish.

I looked at Hans.

"Forüt!" he said quietly.

"Forward!" replied my uncle.

It was thirteen minutes past one.

XVII

THE REAL JOURNEY BEGAN. So far our effort had overcome all difficulties, now difficulties would really spring up at every step.

I had not yet ventured to look down at the bottomless pit into which I was about to plunge. The moment had come. I could still either take my part in the venture or refuse to undertake it. But I was ashamed to withdraw in front of the hunter. Hans accepted the adventure so calmly, with such indifference and such perfect disregard for any danger that I blushed at the idea of being less brave than he. If I had been alone I might have once more tried a series of long arguments; but in the presence of the guide I held my peace; my memory flew back to my pretty Virland girl, and I approached the central chimney.

I have already mentioned that it was a hundred feet in diameter, and three hundred feet in circumference. I bent over a projecting rock and gazed down. My hair stood on end with terror. The feeling of emptiness overcame me. I felt the center of gravity shifting in me, and vertigo rising up to my brain like drunkenness. There is nothing more treacherous than this attraction toward the abyss. I was about to fall. A hand held me back. Hans'. I suppose I had not taken as many lessons in abysses as I should have at the Frelsers Kirke in Copenhagen.

But however briefly I had looked down this well, I had become aware of its structure. Its almost perpendicular walls were bristling with innumerable projections which would facilitate the descent. But if there was no lack of steps, there was still no rail. A rope fastened to the edge of the aperture would have been enough to support us. But how would we unfasten it when we arrived at the lower end?

My uncle used a very simple method to overcome this difficulty. He uncoiled a cord as thick as a finger and four hundred feet long; first he dropped half of it down, then he passed it round a lava block that projected conveniently, and threw the other half down the chimney. Each of us could then descend by holding both halves of the rope with his hand, which would not be able to unroll itself from its hold; when we were two hundred feet down, it would be easy to retrieve the entire rope by letting one end go and pulling down by the other. Then we would start this exercise over again *ad infinitum*.

"Now," said my uncle, after having completed these preparations, "let's see about our loads. I'll divide them into three lots; each of us will strap one on his back. I mean only fragile articles."

The audacious professor obviously did not include us in this last category.

"Hans," he said, "will take charge of the tools and a part of the food supplies; you, Axel, will take another third of the food supplies, and the weapons; and I will take the rest of the food supplies and the delicate instruments."

"But," I said, "the clothes, and that mass of ladders and ropes, who'll take them down?"

"They'll go down by themselves."

"How so?" I asked.

"You'll see."

My uncle liked to use extreme means, without hesitation. At his order, Hans put all the unbreakable items into one package, and this packet, firmly tied up, was simply thrown down into the chasm.

I heard the loud roar of the displaced layers of air. My uncle, leaning over the abyss, followed the descent of the luggage with a satisfied look, and only rose up again when he had lost sight of it.

"Well," he said. "Now it's our turn."

I ask any sensible man if it was possible to hear those words without a shudder!

The professor tied the package of instruments to his back; Hans took the tools, myself the weapons. The descent started in the following order: Hans, my uncle, and myself. It was carried out in profound silence, broken only by the fall of loose stones into the abyss.

I let myself fall, so to speak, frantically clutching the double cord with one hand and buttressing myself from the wall with the other with my stick. One single idea obsessed me: I feared that the rock from which I was hanging might give way. This cord seemed very fragile for supporting the weight of three people. I used it as little as possible, performing miracles of equilibrium on the lava projections which my foot tried to seize like a hand.

When one of these slippery steps shook under Hans' steps, he said in his quiet voice:

"Gif akt!"

"Attention!" repeated my uncle.

In half an hour we were standing on the surface of a rock wedged in across the chimney from one side to the other.

Hans pulled the rope by one of its ends, the other rose in the air; after passing the higher rock it came down again, bringing with it a rather dangerous shower of bits of stone and lava.

Leaning over the edge of our narrow platform, I noticed that the bottom of the hole was still invisible.

The same maneuver was repeated with the cord, and half an hour later we had descended another two hundred feet.

I do not suppose even the most obsessed geologist would have studied the nature of the rocks that we were passing under such circumstances. As for me, I hardly troubled myself about them. Pliocene, Miocene, Eocene, Cretaceous, Jurassic, Triassic, Permian, Carboniferous, Devonian, Silurian, or Primitive was all one to me. But the professor, no doubt, was pursuing his observations or taking notes, for during one of our stops he said to me:

"The farther I go the more confident I am. The order of these volcanic formations absolutely confirms Davy's theories. We're now in the midst of primordial soil in which the chemical reaction of metals catching flame through the contact of water and air occurred. I absolutely reject the theory of heat at the center of the earth. We'll see, in any case."

Always the same conclusion. Of course, I was not inclined to argue. My silence was taken for consent, and the descent continued.

After three hours, and I still did not see bottom of the chimney. When I raised my head I noticed how the opening was getting smaller. Its walls, due to their gentle slope, were drawing closer to each other, and it was beginning to grow darker.

Still we kept descending. It seemed to me that the stones breaking loose from the walls fell with a duller echo, and that they must be reaching the bottom of the chasm promptly.

As I had taken care to keep an exact account of our maneuvers with the rope, I could tell exactly what depth we had reached and how much time had passed.

We had by that time repeated this maneuver fourteen times, each one taking half an hour. So it had been seven hours, plus fourteen quarter of an hour or a total of three hours to rest. Altogether, ten hours and a half. We had started at one, it must now be eleven o'clock.

As for the depth we had reached, these fourteen rope maneuvers of 200 feet each added up to 2,800 feet.

At that moment I heard Hans' voice.

"Stop!" he said.

I stopped short just as I was going to hit my uncle's head with my feet.

"We've arrived," said the latter.

"Where?" I said, sliding down next to him.

"At the bottom of the vertical chimney," he answered.

"Is there any way out?"

"Yes, a kind of tunnel that I can see and which veers off to the right. We'll see about that tomorrow. Let's have dinner first, and afterwards we'll sleep."

The darkness was not yet complete. We opened the bag with the supplies, ate, and each of us lay down as well as he could on a bed of stones and lava fragments.

When I lay on my back, I opened my eyes and saw a sparkling point of light at the extremity of this 3,000-foot long tube, which had now become a vast telescope.

It was a star without any glitter, which by my calculation should be ß of *Ursa minor*.

Then I fell into a deep sleep.

XVIII

At eight in the morning a ray of daylight came to wake us up. The thousand facets of lava on the walls received it on its passage, and scattered it like a shower of sparks.

There was light enough to distinguish surrounding objects.

"Well, Axel, what do you say?" exclaimed my uncle, rubbing his hands. "Did you ever spend a quieter night in our little house in the Königstrasse? No noise of carts, no cries of merchants, no boatmen vociferating!"

"No doubt it's very quiet at the bottom of this well, but there's something alarming in the quietness itself."

"Now come!" my uncle exclaimed; "if you're frightened already, what will you be later on? We've not gone a single inch yet into the bowels of the earth."

"What do you mean?"

"I mean that we've only reached the ground level of the island. This long vertical tube, which terminates at the mouth of the crater, has its lower end at about sea level."

"Are you sure of that?"

"Quite sure. Check the barometer."

In fact, the mercury, which had gradually risen in the instrument as we descended, had stopped at twenty-nine inches.

"You see," said the professor, "we only have a pressure of one atmosphere, and can't wait for the manometer to take the place of the barometer."

And indeed, this instrument would become useless as soon as the weight of the atmosphere exceeded the pressure at sea level.

"But," I said, "isn't there reason to fear that this steadily increasing pressure will become very painful?"

"No; we'll descend at a slow pace, and our lungs will become used to breathing a denser atmosphere. Aeronauts lack air as they rise to high elevations, and we'll perhaps have too much. But I prefer that. Let's not waste a moment. Where's the packet we sent down before us?"

I then remembered that we had searched for it in vain the evening before. My uncle questioned Hans who, after having looked around attentively with his hunter's eyes, replied:

"Der huppe!"

"Up there."

And so it was. The bundle had been caught by a projection a hundred feet above us. Immediately the agile Icelander climbed up like a cat, and in a few minutes the package was in our possession.

"Now," said my uncle, "let's have breakfast, but let's have it like people who may have a long route in front of them."

The biscuit and extract of meat were washed down with a draught of water mingled with a little gin.

Breakfast over, my uncle drew from his pocket a small notebook, intended for scientific observations. He consulted his instruments, and recorded:

Monday, July 1

Chronometer: 8.17 a.m.
Barometer: 29 7/12".
Thermometer: 6°C.
Direction: E.S.E.

This last observation applied to the dark tunnel, and was indicated by the compass.

"Now, Axel," exclaimed the professor with enthusiasm, "we're really going into the bowels of the globe. At this precise moment the journey begins."

That said, my uncle took the Ruhmkorff device that was hanging from his neck with one hand; and with the other he connected the electric current with the coil in the lantern, and a rather bright light dispersed the darkness of the passage.

Hans carried the other device, which was also turned on. This ingenious electrical appliance would enable us to go on for a long time by creating an artificial light even in the midst of the most inflammable gases.

"Let's go!" exclaimed my uncle.

Each of us took his package. Hans pushed the load of cords and clothes before; and, myself going last, we entered the tunnel.

At the moment of penetrating into this dark tunnel, I raised my head, and saw for the last time through the length of that vast tube the sky of Iceland, "which I was never to behold again."

The lava, in the last eruption of 1229, had forced a passage through this tunnel. It still lined the walls with a thick and glistening coat. The electric light was here intensified a hundredfold by reflection.

The only difficulty in advancing lay in not sliding too fast down an incline of about forty-five degrees; fortunately certain abrasions and a few blisters here and there formed steps, and we descended, letting our baggage slip before us from the end of a long rope.

But what made steps under our feet had turned into stalactites overhead. The lava, porous in some places, had taken the shape of small round blisters; opaque quartz crystals, decorated with limpid drops of glass and suspended like chandeliers from the vaulted roof, seemed to light up at our passage. It seemed as if the spirits of the abyss were illuminating their palace to receive their earthly guests.

"It's magnificent!" I exclaimed spontaneously. "My uncle, what a sight! Don't you admire these hues of lava, which blend from reddish brown to bright yellow by imperceptible gradations? And these crystals that seem to us like globes of light?"

"Ah! you're coming around, Axel!" replied my uncle. "So you find this splendid, my boy! Well, you'll see many others yet, I hope. Let's go! Let's go!"

He had better have said "slide," for we did nothing but drop down the steep slopes. It was the *facilis descensus Averni* of Virgil.* The compass, which I consulted frequently, gave our direction as southeast with inflexible steadiness. This lava stream deviated neither to the right nor to the left.

Yet there was no sensible increase in temperature. This justified Davy's theory, and more than once I consulted the thermometer with surprise. Two hours after our departure it only showed 10°, an increase of only 4°. This was reason to believe that our descent was more horizontal than vertical. As for the exact depth we had reached,

---

*The descent to Hell is easy (Latin; from Virgil's *Aeneid* 6.126); the literal meaning of the phrase—"the descent to Avernus is easy"—refers to Lake Avernus, near what is now Naples, Italy; the lake was once believed to be an entrance to the underworld.

it was very easy to ascertain that; the professor measured the angles of deviation and inclination accurately on the road, but he kept the results of his observations to himself.

At about eight in the evening he signaled to stop. Hans sat down at once. The lamps were hung on a projection in the lava; we were in a sort of cavern where there was no lack of air. On the contrary. Certain breezes reached us. What caused them? That was a question I did not try to answer at the moment. Hunger and exhaustion made me incapable of reasoning. A descent of seven consecutive hours is not accomplished without considerable expenditure of strength. I was exhausted. The word 'stop' therefore gave me pleasure. Hans spread some provisions out on a block of lava, and we ate with a good appetite. But one thing troubled me; our supply of water was half consumed. My uncle counted on a fresh supply from underground sources, but so there had been none. I could not help drawing his attention to this issue.

"Are you surprised at this lack of springs?" he said.

"More than that, I'm anxious about it; we have only water enough for five days."

"Don't worry, Axel, I guarantee you that we'll find water, and more than we'll want."

"When?"

"When we have left this layer of lava behind us. How can springs break through such walls as these?"

"But perhaps this passage runs to a very great depth. It seems to me that we've not yet made much progress vertically."

"Why do you suppose that?"

"Because if we had advanced far into the crust of earth, it would be hotter."

"According to your theory," said my uncle. "What does the thermometer say?"

"Hardly 15°C, which means an increase of only 9° since our departure."

"So, draw your conclusion."

"This is my conclusion. According to exact observations, the temperature in the interior of the globe increases at the rate of 1° Celsius for every hundred feet. But certain local conditions may modify this rate. For example, at Yakutsk in Siberia it's been observed that the increase of 1° takes place every 36 feet. This difference clearly depends on the heat-conducting power of the rocks. Moreover, in the neighborhood of an extinct volcano, through gneiss, it's been observed that the increase of 1° is only attained every 125 feet. Let's therefore assume this last hypothesis as the most appropriate for our situation, and calculate."

"Do calculate, my boy."

"Nothing's easier," I said, putting down figures in my notebook. "Nine times a hundred and twenty-five feet adds up to a depth of eleven hundred and twenty-five feet."

"Very accurate indeed."

"Well?"

"By my observation we are 10,000 feet below sea level."

"Is that possible?"

"Yes, or numbers aren't numbers anymore!"

The professor's calculations were accurate. We had already reached a depth of six thousand feet beyond that so far reached by the foot of man, such as the mines of Kitzbühl in Tyrol, and those of Wuttemberg in Bohemia.

The temperature, which should have been 81°C in this place, was scarcely 15°. This was serious cause for reflection.

XIX

THE NEXT DAY, TUESDAY, June 30, at six in the morning, the descent began again.

We continued to follow the tunnel of lava, really a natural, gently sloping ramp like those inclined planes which are still found in old houses instead of staircases. And so we continued on until seventeen minutes past noon, the precise moment when we rejoined Hans, who had just stopped.

"Ah! here we are," exclaimed my uncle, "at the very end of the chimney."

I looked around me. We were standing at the intersection of two roads, both dark and narrow. Which one should we take? This was a difficulty.

But my uncle did not want to seem hesitant, either before me or the guide; he pointed to the Eastern tunnel, and all three of us were soon deep inside it.

In any case, any hesitation about this double path would have prolonged itself indefinitely, as there was no indicator to guide our choice of one or the other; we had to leave it absolutely to chance.

The slope of this tunnel was scarcely perceptible, and its sections very unequal. Sometimes we passed a series of arches succeeding each other like the majestic arcades of a gothic cathedral. Medieval artists could have studied all the forms of sacred architecture here that derive from the ogival arch. A mile farther we had to bow our heads under low arches in the Roman style, and massive pillars growing from the rock bent under the burden of the vaults. In certain places, this magnificence gave way to low structures which looked like beaver dams, and we had to crawl through narrow tubes.

The temperature remained bearable. Involuntarily I thought of the heat when the lava ejected from Snaefells was boiling and working through this now silent passage. I imagined the torrents of fire breaking at every turn in the tunnel, and the accumulation of overheated steam in this close environment!

"I only hope," I thought, "that this old volcano doesn't come up with any belated fantasies!"

I did not convey these fears to Professor Lidenbrock; he would not have understood them. His only idea was to move on. He walked, he slid, he even fell with a conviction that one could only admire.

By six in the evening, after an undemanding walk, we had gone two leagues south, but scarcely a quarter of a mile down.

My uncle gave the signal to rest. We ate without talking, and went to sleep without reflection.

Our arrangements for the night were very simple; a travel blanket into which we rolled ourselves was our only bedding. We had neither cold nor intrusive visits to fear. Travelers who penetrate into the wilds of central Africa, and into the pathless forests of the New World, are obliged to watch over each other by night. But here, absolute safety and utter seclusion. Savages or wild beasts, we did not need to fear any of these wicked species.

We awoke the next morning refreshed and in good spirits. We resumed the road. As on the previous day, we followed a lava path. Impossible to identify the nature of the rock it passed through. The tunnel, instead of leading down into the bowels of the globe, gradually became absolutely horizontal. I even thought I noticed that it rose again toward the surface of the earth. This tendency became so obvious at about ten in the morning, and therefore so tiring, that I was forced to slow down our pace.

"Well, Axel?" said the professor impatiently.

"Well, I can't stand it any longer," I replied.

"What! after three hours' walk over such easy ground."

"It may be easy, but it's tiring all the same."

"What, when we have nothing to do but keep going down!"

"Going up, if you please."

"Going up!" said my uncle, with a shrug.

"No doubt. For the last half-hour the slopes have gone the other way, and at this rate we'll go back to the surface of Iceland."

The professor shook his head like a man who refuses to be convinced. I tried to resume the conversation. He answered not a word, and gave the signal for departure. I saw that his silence was nothing but concentrated bad humor.

Still I courageously shouldered my burden again, and rapidly followed Hans, whom my uncle preceded. I was anxious not to be left behind. My greatest care was not to lose sight of my companions. I shuddered at the thought of losing my way in the depths of this labyrinth.

Besides, if the ascending road became harder, I comforted myself by thinking that it was taking us closer to the surface. There was hope in this. Every step confirmed me in it, and I rejoiced at the thought of meeting my little Graüben again.

At noon there was a change in the appearance of the tunnel walls. I noticed it through a decrease in the amount of light that was reflected from the sides. Solid rock was replacing the lava coating. The mass was made up of slanted and sometimes vertical strata. We were passing through rocks of the Transition or Silurian system.*

"It's obvious," I exclaimed, "marine deposits in the Secondary period have formed these shales, limestones, and sandstones! We're turning away from the primary granite! We're like people from Hamburg who go to Lübeck by way of Hanover!"†

I should have kept my observations to myself. But my geological instinct was stronger than my prudence, and Uncle Lidenbrock heard my exclamation.

"What's the matter?" he asked.

"Look," I said, pointing to the varied succession of sandstones and limestones, and the first indication of slate.

"And?"

"We're now in the period when the first plants and animals appeared."

"Do you think so?"

"Well, look, examine it, study it!"

I forced the professor to move his lamp over the walls of the tunnel. I expected some outcry on his part. But he didn't say a word, and continued on his way.

Had he understood me or not? Did he refuse to admit, out of self-love as an uncle and a scholar, that he had made a mistake when he chose the eastern tunnel, or was he determined to explore this passage

---

*So called because the soils of this period are wide-spread in England, in the regions once inhabited by the celtic tribe of the Silurians (author's note). The Silurian period occurred 438 to 410 million years ago.

†That is, who take a long detour to reach a place nearby.

to the end? It was obvious that we had left the lava path, and that this route could not possibly lead to the fiery core of the Snaefells.

Yet I wondered if I was not attributing too much importance to this change in the rock. Was I not myself mistaken? Were we really crossing layers of rock above the granite foundation?

"If I'm right," I thought, "I should find some residue of primitive plants, and then we'll have to acknowledge the evidence. Let's look."

I had not gone a hundred paces before incontestable proofs presented themselves. It could not be otherwise, for in the Silurian age the seas contained at least fifteen hundred vegetable and animal species. My feet, which had become accustomed to the hard lava ground, suddenly touched dust composed of plant and shell residue. In the walls were distinct impressions of fucus and lycopods.* Professor Lidenbrock must have noticed; but he closed his eyes, I imagine, and pushed on with a steady step.

This was stubbornness pushed beyond all bounds. I could not hold out any longer. I picked up a perfectly formed shell, which had belonged to an animal not unlike the woodlouse; then, joining my uncle, I said:

"Look!"

"Very well," he replied quietly, "it's the shell of a crustacean, of an extinct species called a trilobite. Nothing more."

"But don't you conclude from this . . . ?"

"What you yourself conclude? Yes. I do, perfectly. We've left the granite and the lava. It's possible that I made a mistake. But I can't be sure of that until I've reached the end of this tunnel."

"You're right in doing this, Uncle, and I'd approve if there were not a more and more threatening danger."

"Which one?"

"The lack of water."

"Well, Axel, we'll put ourselves on rations."

---

*Fucus is a type of brown algae; lycopods are club mosses, spore-bearing evergreen plants with leaves that resemble needles.

In the walls were distinct impressions of fucus
and lycopods.

XX

INDEED, WE DID HAVE to ration ourselves. Our supply of water could not last more than three days. I found that out for certain when dinnertime came. Dismal prospect, we had little hope of finding a source in those rocks of the Transition period.

The whole next day the tunnel opened its endless arcades before us. We moved on almost without a word. Hans' silence spread to us.

The road was not ascending now, at least not perceptibly. Sometimes, it even seemed to slope downward. But this tendency, which was at any rate very slight, did not reassure the professor; for there was no change in the nature of the strata, and the Transition period became more and more manifest.

The electric light made the schist, the limestone, and old red sandstone of the walls glitter splendidly. One might have thought that we were passing through an open trench in Devonshire, the region whose name has been given to this kind of soil.* Magnificent marble specimens covered the walls, some of a grayish agate with veins fancifully outlined in white, others in a crimson color, or yellow dotted with spots of red; farther on, samples of dark cherry-red marbles in which limestone showed up in bright hues.

The greater part of this marble bore impressions of primitive organisms. Creation had made obvious progress since the previous day. Instead of rudimentary trilobites, I noticed remains of a more perfect order of beings, amongst others ganoid fishes† and some of those saurians in which paleontologists have discovered the earliest reptile forms. The Devonian seas were inhabited by animals of these species, and deposited them by thousands in the newly formed rocks.

It was obvious that we were ascending the scale of animal life in which man holds the highest place. But Professor Lidenbrock seemed not to care.

He was waiting for one of two events: either that a vertical well would be opening under his feet and allow him to resume his de-

---

*That is, soils of the Devonian period (410–360 million years ago).
†Primitive fishes that have thick, bony scales with a shiny surface.

scent, or that an obstacle would prevent him from continuing on this route. But evening came, and this hope was not fulfilled.

On Friday, after a night during which I began to feel the pangs of thirst, our little troop again plunged into the winding passages of the tunnel.

After ten hours' walking I noticed that the reflection of our lamps on the walls diminished strangely. The marble, the schist, the limestone, and the sandstone were giving way to a dark and lusterless lining. At one moment where the tunnel became very narrow, I leaned against the left wall.

When I pulled my hand back, it was black. I looked more closely. We were in a coal formation.

"A coal mine!" I exclaimed.

"A mine without miners," my uncle replied.

"Ah! Who knows?" I asked.

"I know," the professor pronounced decidedly, "I'm certain that this tunnel piercing through layers of coal was never created by the hand of man. But whether it's the work of nature or not doesn't matter. Dinnertime has come; let's have dinner."

Hans prepared some food. I scarcely ate, and I swallowed the few drops of water rationed out to me. One half-full flask was all we had left to quench the thirst of three men.

After their meal my two companions laid down on their blankets, and found in sleep a remedy for their exhaustion. But I could not sleep, and I counted the hours until morning.

On Saturday, at six, we started afresh. In twenty minutes we reached a vast open space; I then knew that the hand of man could not have hollowed out this coal mine; the vaults would have been shored up, and really they seemed to be held up only by a miracle of equilibrium.

This cavern was about a hundred feet wide and a hundred and fifty high. The ground had been pushed aside by a subterranean motion. The massive rock, impacted by a powerful thrust, had been displaced, leaving this large empty space that inhabitants of the earth entered for the first time.

The whole history of the Carboniferous period* was written on

---

*360–286 million years ago.

these dark walls, and a geologist might with ease trace all its diverse phases. The beds of coal were separated by strata of sandstone or compact clays, and appeared crushed by the strata above.

At the age of the world which preceded the Secondary period, the earth was covered with immense vegetable forms, produced by the double influence of tropical heat and constant moisture; a vaporous atmosphere enveloped the earth, depriving it again of the direct rays of the sun.

Hence the conclusion that the high temperature was due to some other source than the heat of the sun. Perhaps the day star was not ready to play its brilliant role. There were no 'climates' as yet, and a torrid heat, equal from pole to equator, spread over the whole surface of the globe. Where did it come from? Was it from the interior of the earth?

Notwithstanding Professor Lidenbrock's theories, a violent heat did at that time smolder in the bowels of the spheroid. Its effect was felt up to the last layers of the terrestrial crust; the plants, deprived of the beneficent influence of the sun, produced neither flowers nor scent, but their roots drew vigorous life from the burning soil of the first days.

There were only a few trees, only herbaceous plants, enormous meadows, ferns, lycopods, sigillarias, asterophyllites,* rare families whose species numbered in the thousands then.

Coal owes its existence to this period of profuse vegetation. The still flexible crust of the earth followed the movements of the liquid masses it covered. Hence numerous fissures and depressions. The plants, pushed under water, gradually accumulated in considerable quantities.

Then the reactions of natural chemistry intervened; at the bottom of the oceans, the vegetable accumulations first became peat; then, due to the influence of gases and the heat of fermentation, they underwent a process of complete mineralization.

In this way those immense coalfields were formed, which excessive exploitation will nonetheless exhaust in less than three centuries, unless industrialized countries prevent it.

---

*Sigillaria is a tree-size lycopod that is found as a fossil in ancient coal formations, where the asterophyllite, a fossil plant, also occurs.

These reflections came to my mind while I was contemplating the mineral wealth stored up in this portion of the globe. Undoubtedly, I thought, these will never be discovered; the exploitation of such deep mines would require too large a sacrifice, and what would be the use as long as coal is spread far and wide close to the surface? Therefore, such as I see these intact layers, such they will be when this world comes to an end.

But still we marched on, and I alone forgot the length of the way by losing myself in the midst of geological contemplations. The temperature remained what it had been during our passage through the lava and schist. Only my sense of smell was affected by an odor of hydrocarbon. I immediately recognized in this tunnel the presence of a considerable quantity of the dangerous gas called firedamp by miners, whose explosion has often caused dreadful catastrophes.

Luckily, our light came from Ruhmkorff's ingenious device. If by misfortune we had carelessly explored this tunnel with torches, a terrible explosion would have put an end to traveling by eliminating the travelers.

This excursion through the coal formation lasted until night. My uncle could scarcely restrain his impatience at the horizontal road. The darkness, always twenty steps ahead of us, prevented us from estimating the length of the tunnel; and I was beginning to think it must be endless, when suddenly at six o'clock a wall very unexpectedly arose before us. Right or left, top or bottom, there was no passage; we were at the end of a blind alley.

"Well, all the better!" exclaimed my uncle, "I know what the facts are. We're not on Saknussemm's route, and all we have to do is go back. Let's take a night's rest, and in three days we'll get back to the point where the two tunnels branch off."

"Yes," I said, "if we have any strength left!"

"And why not?"

"Because tomorrow we'll have no water left at all."

"Or courage either?" asked my uncle, looking at me severely.

I dared make no answer.

XXI

THE NEXT DAY WE started very early. We had to hurry. We were a five days' walk away from the crossroads.

I will not insist on the suffering we endured during our return. My uncle bore them with the rage of a man who does not feel his strongest; Hans with the resignation of his passive nature; I, I confess, with complaints and expressions of despair. I had no spirit to oppose this misfortune.

As I had foreseen, we ran completely out of water by the end of the first day's march. Our liquid food was now nothing but gin, but this infernal fluid burned my throat, and I could not even endure the sight of it. I found the temperature stifling. Exhaustion paralyzed me. More than once I almost fell and lay motionless. Then we stopped; and my uncle and the Icelander comforted me as best they could. But I saw already that the former was struggling painfully against excessive fatigue and the tortures of thirst.

At last, on Tuesday, July 7, we arrived half dead at the junction of the two tunnels by dragging ourselves on our knees, on our hands. There I dropped down like an inert mass, stretched out on the lava soil. It was ten in the morning.

Hans and my uncle, clinging to the wall, tried to nibble a few bits of biscuit. Long moans escaped from my swollen lips.

After some time my uncle approached me and raised me up in his arms.

"Poor boy!" he said, in a genuine tone of compassion.

I was touched by these words, not being used to tenderness in the fierce professor. I seized his trembling hands with mine. He let me hold them and looked at me. His eyes were moist.

Then I saw him take the flask that was hanging at his side. To my amazement, he placed it at my lips.

"Drink!" he said.

Had I heard him right? Was my uncle beside himself? I stared at him stupidly, as if I could not understand him.

"Drink!" he said again.

And raising his flask he emptied every drop between my lips.

Oh! infinite pleasure! A sip of water came to moisten my burning mouth, just one, but it was enough to call back my ebbing life.

I thanked my uncle with clasped hands.

"Yes," he said, "a draught of water! The last one! Do you hear me? The last one! I had carefully kept it at the bottom of my flask. Twenty times, a hundred times, I've had to resist a frightening desire to drink it! But no, Axel, I kept it for you."

"Uncle!" I murmured, while big tears came to my eyes.

"Yes, poor child, I knew that as soon as you arrived at this crossroads you would drop half dead, and I kept my last drops of water to reanimate you."

"Thank you, thank you!" I exclaimed.

Although my thirst was only partially quenched, I had nonetheless regained some strength. My throat muscles, until then contracted, relaxed again, and the inflammation of my lips abated somewhat. I was able to speak.

"Let's see," I said, "now we have only one choice. We're out of water; we must go back."

As I said this, my uncle avoided looking at me; he lowered his head; his eyes avoided mine.

"We must return!" I exclaimed, "and go back on the way to the Snaefells. May God give us strength to climb up the crater again!"

"Return!" said my uncle, as if he was answering himself rather than me.

"Yes, return, without losing a minute."

A long silence followed.

"So then, Axel," replied the professor in a strange voice, "these few drops of water have given you no courage and energy?"

"Courage?"

"I see you just as discouraged as you were before, and still expressing only despair!"

What kind man was I dealing with, and what plans was his daring mind hatching yet?

"What! you don't want to . . . ?"

"Give up this expedition just when all the signs are that it can succeed! Never!"

"Then must we resign ourselves to dying?"

"No, Axel, no! Go back. I don't want your death! Let Hans accompany you. Leave me to myself!"

"Leave you here!"

"Leave me, I tell you! I've started this journey; I'll continue to the end, or I won't return. Go, Axel, go!"

My uncle spoke in extreme overexcitement. His voice, tender for a moment, had once again become hard, threatening. He struggled against the impossible with a sinister energy! I did not want to leave at the bottom of this chasm, yet on the other hand the instinct of self-preservation prompted me to flee.

The guide watched this scene with his usual indifference. Yet he understood what was going on between his two companions. The gestures themselves were sufficient to indicate the different paths on which each of us was trying to lead the other; but Hans seemed to take little interest in the question on which his life depended, ready to start if the signal for departure were given, or to stay according to his master's least wish.

How I wished at that moment that I could make him understand me! My words, my moans, my tone would have overcome that cold nature. These dangers which our guide did not seem to anticipate, I would have made him understand and confront them. Together we might perhaps have convinced the obstinate professor. If necessary, we would have forced him to climb back up to the heights of the Snaefells!

I approached Hans. I put my hand on his. He did not move. I showed him the route to the crater. He remained immobile. My panting face revealed all my suffering. The Icelander gently shook his head, and calmly pointing to my uncle, he said:

"Master."

"Master!" I shouted; "you madman! no, he isn't the master of your life! We must flee, we must take him along with us! Do you hear me? Do you understand me?"

I had seized Hans by the arm. I wanted to force him to get up. I struggled with him. My uncle intervened.

"Calm down, Axel," he said. "You'll achieve nothing with that impassive servant. So listen to what I want to propose to you."

I crossed my arms and looked my uncle straight in the face.

"The lack of water," he said, "is the only obstacle for the realization of my plans. In this eastern tunnel, made up of lava, schist, and coal, we have not found a single particle of moisture. It's possible that we'll be more fortunate if we follow the western tunnel."

I shook my head with an air of profound skepticism.

"Hear me out," the professor continued with a firm voice. "While you were lying here motionlessly, I went to explore the structure of that tunnel. It goes directly into the bowels of the globe, and in a few hours it'll take us to the granite formation. There we should find abundant springs. The nature of the rock implies this, and instinct agrees with logic to support my conviction. Now, this is what I propose to you. When Columbus asked his ships' crew for three more days to discover new land, his crew, frightened and sick as they were, recognized the legitimacy of his claim, and he discovered the new world. I am the Columbus of this nether world, and I only ask for one more day. If after that day I haven't found the water that we're missing, I swear to you we'll return to the surface of the earth."

In spite of my irritation I was moved by these words and by the violence my uncle was doing to himself by speaking in this manner.

"Well then!" I exclaimed, "let's do what you wish, and may God reward your superhuman energy. You now have only a few hours left to tempt fortune. Let's go!"

XXII

THE DESCENT STARTED OVER again, this time by way of the other tunnel. Hans walked first, as was his custom. We had not walked a hundred paces when the professor, moving his lantern along the walls, exclaimed:

"Here are primitive rocks. Now we're on the right way. Let's go! Let's go!"

When the earth was slowly cooling in its early stages, its contraction produced displacements, ruptures, retrenchments, and cracks in its crust. Our current tunnel was such a fissure, through which eruptive granite flowed at one time. Its thousand turns formed an inextricable labyrinth in the primeval soil.

As we descended, the succession of layers that made up the primitive foundation manifested itself more distinctly. Geological science considers this primitive matter the base of the mineral crust, and has discovered that it is made up of three different strata, schists, gneisses, and mica schists resting on that unshakable rock called granite.

Never had mineralogists found themselves in such wonderful circumstances to study nature in situ. What the drill, an unintelligent and brutal machine, could not relay to the surface about the inner texture of the globe, we were able to examine with our own eyes and touch with our own hands.

Through the beds of schist, colored in beautiful shades of green, meandered metallic threads of copper and manganese with traces of platinum and gold. I thought about these riches buried in the bowels of the globe that greedy humanity will never enjoy! These treasures have been buried at such depths by the upheavals of primeval days that neither ice-pick nor pickaxe will ever be able to tear them from their grave.

The schists were succeeded by stratified gneisses, remarkable for the parallelism and regularity of its laminae, then mica schists arranged in large sheets that were outlined to the eye by the sparkling of white mica.

The light from our devices, reflected from the small facets in the mass of rock, shot sparkling rays at every angle, and I imagined I was traveling through a hollow diamond, on whose inside the light beams shattered in a thousand coruscations.

At about six o'clock this feast of light diminished appreciably, then almost ceased; the walls took on a crystalline but dark appearance; mica mingled more intimately with feldspar and quartz to form the essential rock, the hardest stone of all, the one that supports the four layered terrains of the globe. We were immured in an immense prison of granite.

It was eight in the evening. There was still no water. I was suffering horribly. My uncle walked at the front. He refused to stop. He listened anxiously for the murmur of some spring. But nothing!

But my legs refused to carry me any further. I resisted my torture so as not to force my uncle to stop. It would have been a stroke of desperate misfortune for him, because the day was coming to an end, the last one that belonged to him.

Finally my strength left me. I uttered a cry and fell.

"Come to me! I'm dying!"

My uncle retraced his steps. He looked at me with his arms crossed; then these muttered words passed his lips:

"It's all over!"

The last thing I saw was a frightening gesture of rage, and I closed my eyes.

When I reopened them I saw my two companions motionless and rolled up in their blankets. Were they asleep? As for me, I could not get one moment's sleep. I was suffering too much, especially from the thought that there was no remedy. My uncle's last words echoed in my ear: "It's all over!" For in such a state of weakness it was impossible to think of going back to the surface of the globe.

We had a league and a half of terrestrial crust on top of us! It seemed to me that the weight of this mass bore down on my shoulders with all its power. I felt crushed, and exhausted myself with violent exertions to turn round on my granite couch.

A few hours passed. Deep silence reigned around us, the silence of the grave. Nothing reached us through these walls, the thinnest of which was five miles thick.

Yet in the midst of my slumber I believed I heard a sound. It was dark in the tunnel. I looked more carefully, and I seemed to see the Icelander vanishing with the lamp in his hand.

Why this departure? Was Hans going to abandon us? My uncle was fast asleep. I wanted to shout. My voice could not find a passage through my parched lips. The darkness became deeper, and the last sounds died away.

"Hans is abandoning us," I shouted. "Hans! Hans!"

But these words were only uttered within me. They did not go any further. Yet after the first moment of terror I felt ashamed of my suspicions against a man whose conduct had had nothing suspect so far. His departure could not be an escape. Instead of ascending the tunnel, he was descending. Evil intentions would have taken him up, not down. This reasoning calmed me down a little, and I returned to another set of thoughts. Only a serious motive could have torn so peaceful a man from his sleep. Was he going on discovery? Had he heard a murmur in the silent night that had not reached me?

XXIII

FOR A WHOLE HOUR I tried to work out in my delirious brain the reasons which this quiet huntsman might have. The most absurd ideas were entangled in my mind. I thought I was going mad!

But at last a noise of footsteps sounded in the depths of the abyss. Hans was returning. The dim light began to glimmer on the walls, then showed up at the opening of the tunnel. Hans appeared.

He approached my uncle, put his hand on his shoulder, and gently woke him. My uncle rose up.

"What's the matter?" he asked.

"Vatten!" replied the hunter.

It seems that under the impact of violent pain, everybody becomes polyglot. I did not know a word of Danish, and yet instinctively I understood our guide's word.

"Water! water!" I exclaimed, clapping my hands and gesticulating like a madman.

"Water!" repeated my uncle. "Hvar?" he asked, in Icelandic.

"Nedat," replied Hans.

Where? Down below! I understood it all. I seized the hunter's hands, and pressed them while he looked at me calmly.

The preparations for our departure were not long in making, and we were soon on our way along a passage sloping down at a rate of two feet per fathom.

In an hour we had gone a thousand fathoms, and descended two thousand feet.

At that moment, I began to hear distinctly an unusual sound of something running inside the granite wall, a kind of dull rumbling like distant thunder. During the first half-hour of our walk, when we did not find the promised spring, I felt my anguish returning; but then my uncle told me the cause of these noises.

"Hans was not mistaken," he said. "What you hear is the rushing of a torrent."

"A torrent?" I exclaimed.

"There can be no doubt. A subterranean river is flowing around us."

We hurried forward, overexcited because of our hope. I no longer sensed my fatigue. This sound of murmuring water was refreshing me already. It increased perceptibly. The torrent, after having for some time flowed over our heads, was now running within the left wall, roaring and bouncing. I often brushed with my hand over the rock, hoping to feel some seeping or moisture. But in vain.

Yet another half-hour passed. We put another half league behind us.

Then it became clear that the hunter had not been able to extend his investigation further during his absence. Guided by an instinct peculiar to mountaineers, to water-dowsers, he 'felt' this torrent through the rock, but he had certainly not seen the precious liquid; he had drunk nothing himself.

Soon it became obvious that if we continued on our walk, we would move away from the stream, whose noise was growing more faint.

We returned. Hans stopped at the precise point where the torrent seemed closest.

I sat near the wall, while the waters were rushing past me at a distance of two feet with extreme violence. But there was a thick granite wall still separating us from it.

Without reflection, without wondering if there was not some means of accessing this water, I gave way to a first moment of despair.

Hans looked at me, and I thought I saw a smile on his lips.

He rose and took the lamp. I followed him. He moved towards the wall. I looked on. He pressed his ear against the dry stone, and moved it slowly to and fro, listening intently. I understood at once that he was looking for the exact point where the torrent could be heard the loudest. He found that point on the left side of the tunnel, three feet from the ground.

How stirred up I was! I hardly dared guess what the hunter was about to do! But I had to understand and cheer him on when I saw him lay hold of the pickaxe to attack the rock.

"Saved!" I exclaimed.

"Yes," exclaimed my uncle frantically. "Hans is right. Ah! Brave hunter! We wouldn't have thought of this!"

Absolutely true! Such an expedient, however simple, would never have entered into our minds. Nothing more dangerous than to strike a blow of the pickaxe in this part of the earth's structure. What if there were a collapse that would crush us all! What if the torrent, bursting through, would drown us in a sudden flood! There was nothing chimerical about these dangers; but still no fears of landslides of floods could stop us now, and our thirst was so intense that, to satisfy it, we would have dug into the very bottom of the ocean.

Hans set about the task which neither my uncle nor I could have accomplished. With impatience guiding our hands, we would have shattered the rock into a thousand fragments. The guide, by contrast, calm and moderate, gradually wore down the rock with a succession of light strokes, creating a six-inch opening. I could hear the noise of the torrent grow louder, and I thought I could already feel the healing water touch my lips.

The pickaxe had soon penetrated two feet into the granite partition. The work had lasted more than an hour. I writhed with impatience! My uncle wanted to use more forceful measures. I had some difficulty stopping him and he had already taken a pickaxe in his hand, when a sudden hissing was heard. A jet of water spurted out of the rock and hit the opposite wall.

Hans, almost thrown off his feet by the shock, could not hold back a cry of pain. I understood it when, just as I had plunged my own hands into the liquid jet, I shouted out loudly in my turn. The water was scalding hot.

"The water is a hundred degrees!" I exclaimed.

"Well, it'll cool down," my uncle replied.

The tunnel filled with steam, while a stream formed which lost itself in subterranean meanderings; soon we had the satisfaction of swallowing our first draught.

Ah! What enjoyment! What incomparable pleasure! What was this water? Where did it come from? No matter. It was water, and though it was still warm, it brought back to one's heart the life that had been on the point of vanishing. I drank without stopping or even tasting.

It was only after a minute of enjoyment that I exclaimed, "Why, this water contains iron!"

"Excellent for the stomach," replied my uncle, "and full of minerals! This journey will be as good for us as going to Spa or Töplitz!"*

"Well, it's delicious!"

---

*Spa is a famous site of therapeutic hot springs in Belgium. Töplitz is the German name for Teplice, a town in what is today the north of the Czech Republic; it was a famous spa in the eighteenth and nineteenth centuries.

"Of course it is, water found two leagues underground should be. It has an inky flavor, which is not at all unpleasant. What an excellent resource Hans has found for us here! We'll give his name to this wholesome creek."

"Great!" I exclaimed.

And Hansbach* it was from that moment.

Hans was none the prouder. After a moderate draught, he went to rest in a corner with his usual calm.

"Now," I said, "we mustn't lose this water."

"What for?" my uncle replied. "I imagine that the source is inexhaustible."

"Never mind! Let's fill the leather bottle and our flasks, and then we can try to stop up the opening."

My advice was followed. Hans tried to stop the cut in the wall with pieces of granite and tow. It was not an easy task. One scalded one's hands without succeeding; the pressure was too strong, and our efforts remained fruitless.

"It's obvious," I said, "that the upper reaches of this course of water are very high up, judging by the force of the jet."

"No doubt," answered my uncle. "If this column of water is 32,000 feet high, it has a thousand atmospheres of pressure. But I've got an idea."

"What idea?"

"Why should we trouble ourselves to close up this opening?"

"Because . . ."

I could not come up with a reason.

"When our flasks are empty, are we sure we'll be able to fill them again?"

"No, obviously."

"Well, then let's allow the water to run on. It'll flow down, and will both guide and refresh us on the way."

"That's well planned!" I exclaimed. "With this stream as our guide, there's no reason why we should not succeed in our undertaking."

"Ah! You're coming around to my way of thinking, my boy," said the professor laughing.

Bach is the German word for creek.

A jet of water spurted out of the rock and hit the opposite wall.

"I'm not coming around to it, I'm with it."

"Just a moment! Let's start by resting for a few hours."

I had really forgotten that it was night. The chronometer soon informed me of that fact; and soon all of us, sufficiently restored and refreshed, fell into a deep sleep.

XXIV

THE NEXT MORNING, WE had already forgotten all our sufferings. At first, I was amazed that I was no longer thirsty, and wondered about the reason. The creek murmuring at my feet provided the answer.

We had breakfast, and drank of this excellent ferrous water. I felt completely restored, and quite resolved to push on. Why would not so firmly convinced a man as my uncle succeed, with so industrious a guide as Hans and so 'determined' a nephew as myself? Such were the beautiful ideas that floated into my brain! If it had been proposed to me to return to the summit of Snaefells, I would have indignantly declined.

But fortunately, all we had to do was descend.

"Let's take off!" I exclaimed, awakening the ancient echoes of the globe with my enthusiastic tone.

We resumed our walk on Thursday at eight in the morning. The granite tunnel meandered in sinuous contortions and confronted us with unexpected turns in what appeared to be the intricacies of a labyrinth; but, on the whole, its main direction was always southeast. My uncle constantly checked his compass to keep track of the ground we had covered.

The tunnel stretched almost horizontally, with at most two inches of slope per fathom. The stream ran gently murmuring at our feet. I compared it to a friendly spirit guiding us underground, and with my hand I caressed the tepid naiad whose songs accompanied our steps. My good mood spontaneously led me to this mythological train of thought.

As for my uncle, a man of the vertical, he raged against the horizontal route. His path prolonged itself indefinitely, and instead of sliding down along the earth's radius, in his words, it followed the hypotenuse. But we did not have any choice, and as long as we were making progress toward the center, however slowly, we could not complain.

From time to time, at any rate, the slopes became steeper; the naiad began to rush down with a roar, and we descended with her to a greater depth.

On the whole, that day and the next we made considerable headway horizontally, very little vertically.

On Friday evening, July 10, according to our calculations, we were thirty leagues south-east of Reykjavik, and at a depth of two and a half leagues.

At our feet a rather frightening well then opened up. My uncle could not keep from clapping his hands when he calculated the steepness of its slopes.

"This'll take us a long way," he exclaimed, "and easily, because the projections in the rock make for a real staircase!"

The ropes were tied by Hans in such a way as to prevent any accident. The descent began. I can hardly call it dangerous, because I was already familiar with this kind of exercise.

This well was a narrow cleft cut into the rock, of the kind that's called a 'fault.' The contraction of the earth's frame in its cooling period had obviously produced it. If it had at one time been a passage for eruptive matter thrown up by Snaefells, I could not understand why this material had left no trace. We kept going down a kind of spiral staircase which seemed almost to have been made by the hand of man.

Every quarter of an hour we were forced to stop, to get the necessary rest and restore the flexibility of our knees. We then sat down on some projecting rock, let our legs hang down, and chatted while we ate and drank from the stream.

Needless to say, in this fault the Hansbach had turned into a waterfall and lost some of its volume; but there was enough, more than enough, to quench our thirst. Besides, on less steep inclines, it would of course resume its peaceable course. At this moment it reminded me of my worthy uncle, in his frequent fits of impatience and anger, whereas on gentle slopes it ran with the calmness of the Icelandic hunter.

On July 11 and 12, we kept following the spiral curves of this singular well, penetrating two more leagues into the earth's crust, which added up to a depth of five leagues below sea level. But on the 13th, about noon, the fault fell in a much gentler slope of about forty-five degrees towards the south-east.

The path then became easy and perfectly monotonous. It could hardly be otherwise. The journey could not vary by changes in the landscape.

Finally on Wednesday, the 15th, we were seven leagues underground and about fifty leagues away from Snaefells. Although we were a little tired, our health was still reassuringly good, and the medicine kit had not yet been opened.

My uncle noted every hour the indications of the compass, the chronometer, the manometer, and the thermometer just as he has published them in his scientific report of his journey. He could therefore easily identify our location. When he told me that we had gone fifty leagues horizontally, I could not repress an exclamation.

"What's the matter?" he exclaimed.

"Nothing, I was just thinking."

"Thinking what?"

"That if your calculations are correct we're no longer underneath Iceland."

"Do you think so?"

"It's easy enough to find out."

I made my compass measurements on the map.

"I'm not mistaken," I said. "We have left Cape Portland behind, and those fifty leagues place us right under the sea."

"Right under the sea," my uncle repeated, rubbing his hands.

"So the ocean is right above our heads!" I exclaimed.

"Bah! Axel, what would be more natural? Aren't there coal mines at Newcastle that extend far under the sea?"

It was all very well for the professor to call this so simple, but the idea that I was walking around under masses of water kept worrying me. And yet it really mattered very little whether it was the plains and mountains of Iceland that were suspended over our heads or the waves of the Atlantic, as long as the granite structure was solid. At any rate, I quickly got used to this idea, for the tunnel, sometimes straight, sometimes winding, as unpredictable in its slopes as in its turns, but always going south-east and penetrating ever deeper, led us rapidly to great depths.

Four days later, on Saturday, July 18, in the evening, we arrived at a kind of rather large grotto; my uncle paid Hans his three weekly rix-dollars, and it was settled that the next day, Sunday, should be a day of rest.

XXV

I THEREFORE WOKE UP on Sunday morning without the usual pre-occupations of an immediate departure. And even though we were in the deepest abyss, that was still pleasant. In any case, we had gotten used to this troglodyte life. I hardly thought of sun, stars, moon, trees, houses, and towns anymore, or of any of those earthly super-fluities which sublunary beings have turned into necessities. Being fossils, we did not care about such useless wonders.

The grotto was an immense hall. Along its granite floor our faithful stream ran gently. At this distance from its spring, the water had the same temperature as its surroundings and could be drunk without difficulty.

After breakfast the professor wanted to devote a few hours to putting his daily notes in order.

"First," he said, "I'll calculate our exact position. I hope, after our return, to draw a map of our journey, a kind of vertical section of the globe which will retrace the itinerary of our expedition."

"That'll be very interesting, Uncle; but are your observations sufficiently accurate?"

"Yes; I've carefully noted the angles and the slopes. I'm sure there's no mistake. Let's see where we are now. Take your compass, and note the direction."

I looked at the instrument and replied after careful study:

"East-a-quarter-south-east."

"Good," answered the professor, writing down the observation and calculating quickly. "I infer that we've gone eighty-five leagues from our point of departure."

"So we're under the mid-Atlantic?"

"Exactly."

"And perhaps at this very moment there's a storm unleashed above, and ships over our heads are being tossed by the waves and the hurricane?"

"Possible."

"And whales are lashing the roof of our prison with their tails?"

"Don't worry, Axel, they won't manage to break it. But let's go back to our calculation. We're eighty-five leagues south-east of the foot of Snaefells, and I estimate that we're at a depth of sixteen leagues."

"Sixteen leagues!" I exclaimed.

"No doubt."

"But that's the upper limit that science has calculated for the thickness of the earth's crust."

"I don't deny it."

"And here, according to the law of increasing temperature, there should be a heat of 1,500°C!"

" 'Should,' my boy."

"And all this solid granite could not remain solid and would be completely molten."

"You see that it's not so, and that, as so often happens, facts contradict theories."

"I'm forced to agree, but it does amaze me."

"What does the thermometer say?"

"27 and 6/10°C."

"Therefore the scholars are wrong by 1,474 and 4/10°. So the proportional increase in temperature is a mistake. So Humphry Davy was right. So I am not wrong in following him. What do you say now?"

"Nothing."

In truth, I had a great deal to say. In no way did I accept Davy's theory. I still believed in core heat, although I did not feel its effects. I preferred to believe, really, that this chimney of an extinct volcano was covered with a refractive lava coating that did not allow the heat to pass through its walls.

But without bothering to find new arguments, I simply accepted the situation such as it was.

"Uncle," I resumed, "I believe all your calculations are accurate, but allow me to draw one rigorous conclusion from them."

"Go ahead, my boy."

"At the latitude of Iceland, where we now are, the radius of the earth is about 1,583 leagues?"

"1,583 leagues and 1/3."

"Let's say 1,600 leagues in round numbers. Out of 1,600 leagues we have covered twelve?"

"Just as you say."

*"Perhaps at this very moment there's a storm
unleashed above."*

"And these twelve by going 85 leagues diagonally?"

"Exactly."

"In about twenty days?"

"In twenty days."

"Now, sixteen leagues are the hundredth part of the earth's radius. At this rate we'll take two thousand days, or nearly five years and a half, to get to the center."

The professor gave no answer.

"Without mentioning that if a vertical depth of sixteen leagues can be reached only by a diagonal descent of eighty-four, we have to go eight thousand miles to the south-east, and we'll emerge from some point in the earth's circumference long before we get to the center!"

"To Hell with your calculations!" replied my uncle in a fit of rage. "To Hell with your hypotheses! What's the basis of them all? How do you know that this passage doesn't run straight to our goal? Besides, we have a precedent. What I'm doing, another man has done before me, and where he's succeeded, I'll succeed in my turn."

"I hope so; but, still, I may be permitted—"

"You're permitted to hold your tongue, Axel, if you're going to talk in that irrational way."

I could see the awful professor threatening to reappear under the surface of the uncle, and I took the hint.

"Now look at your manometer. What does it indicate?"

"Considerable pressure."

"Good; so you see that by going down gradually, and by getting accustomed to the density of the atmosphere, we don't suffer at all."

"Not at all, except a little pain in the ears."

"That's nothing, and you can get rid of that discomfort by putting the outside air in rapid contact with the air in your lungs."

"Exactly," I said, determined not to say a word that might contradict my uncle. "There's even genuine pleasure in being immersed in this denser atmosphere. Have you noticed how far the sound carries down here?"

"Undoubtedly. A deaf man would end up hearing perfectly."

"But won't this density increase?"

"Yes, according to a rather ill-defined law. It's well known that gravity decreases as we descend. You know that it's at the surface of the earth that weight is most acutely felt, and that at the center objects have no weight."

"I'm aware of that; but tell me, won't the air at last become as dense as water?"

"No doubt, under a pressure of seven hundred and ten atmospheres."

"And lower down?"

"Lower down the density will increase even more."

"So how will we go down then?"

"Well, we'll fill our pockets with stones."

"Really, Uncle, you're never at a loss for an answer."

I dared venture no farther into the region of hypotheses, for I might once again stumble over an impossibility that would make the professor jump with rage.

Still, it was obvious that the air, under a pressure that might reach thousands of atmospheres, would at last turn solid, and then, even if our bodies could resist, we would have to stop, in spite of all reasoning in the world.

But I did not insist on this argument. My uncle would have held against it his inevitable Saknussemm, a precedent without value, for even if the journey of the Icelandic scholar had really taken place, there was one very simple question to answer:

In the sixteenth century neither barometer or manometer had been invented; so how could Saknussemm have determined whether he had arrived at the center of the globe?

But I kept this objection to myself and let events take their course.

The rest of the day was spent in calculations and conversations. I always agreed with Professor Lidenbrock's opinions, and I envied Hans his complete indifference; without looking so hard for effects and causes, he went blindly wherever his destiny guided him.

XXVI

It was true that so far things had gone well, and it would have been ungraceful of me to complain. If the 'average' number of difficulties did not increase, we could not fail to reach our goal. And then, what glory! I had come around to reasoning in this way, quite like a Lidenbrock. Seriously. Was this due to the strange environment in which I was living? Perhaps.

For several days steeper slopes, some even frighteningly vertical, took us deep into the interior rock. Some days we got a league and a half or two leagues closer to the center. Dangerous descents, during which Hans' skill and marvelous calm were very useful to us. That impassive Icelander devoted himself with incomprehensible unconcern to his tasks; and thanks to him, we overcame more than one dangerous spot that we would never have cleared alone.

But his silence increased day by day. I believe it even infected us. External forces have real effects on the brain. Whoever shuts himself up between four walls soon loses the power to bring words and ideas together. How many prisoners in solitary confinement become idiots, if not mad, for lack of exercise for their thinking faculty!

During the two weeks following our last conversation, no incident worthy of reporting occurred. I only find in my memory a single, very important event, for good reason. It would have been difficult for me to forget even its slightest detail.

By August 7, our successive descents had taken us to a depth of thirty leagues, which means that there were thirty leagues of rock, ocean, continents, and towns over our heads. We must have been two hundred leagues from Iceland then.

On that day the tunnel went down a gentle slope.

I was ahead of the others. My uncle was carrying one of the Ruhmkorff devices and myself the other. I was examining layers of granite.

Suddenly, when I turned around, I found that I was alone.

"Well," I thought, "I've gone too fast, or Hans and my uncle have stopped on the way. Let's go, I must join them again. Fortunately the path doesn't go up appreciably."

I retraced my steps. I walked for a quarter of an hour. I looked. Nobody. I called. No response. My voice was lost in the midst of the cavernous echoes it suddenly called forth.

I began to feel uneasy. A shudder ran all over my body.

"A bit of calm!" I said aloud to myself, "I'm sure I'll find my companions again. There's only one path. Now, I was ahead, so let's go further back!"

For half an hour I climbed back up. I listened for a call, and in that dense atmosphere, it could come from far away. An extraordinary silence reigned in the immense tunnel.

I stopped. I could not believe my isolation. I had only strayed from the path, not lost my way completely. After having strayed, one finds one's path again.

"Let's see," I repeated, "since there's only one path, and since they're on it, I must run into them. I just have to go further up. Unless, when they didn't see me, they forgot that I was ahead, and retraced their steps also. Well! Even in that case, if I hurry up, I'll find them again. It's obvious!"

I repeated these last words like a man who is not convinced. In addition, even coming up with these simple ideas and bringing them together in coherent reasoning took me a very long time.

A doubt then assailed me. Was I really ahead? Yes, Hans followed me, preceding my uncle. He had even stopped for a few moments to strap his baggage more tightly to his shoulder. This detail came back to me. It was at that very moment that I must have continued on my way.

"Besides," I thought, "I have a reliable means of not getting lost, a thread that cannot break to guide me in this labyrinth, my faithful stream. All I have to do is to follow its course in reverse, and I'll inevitably find the traces of my companions."

This reasoning revived me, and I decided to go on my way again without losing a moment.

How I blessed my uncle's foresight then in keeping the hunter from stopping up the hole in the granite wall! This beneficent spring, which had quenched our thirst on the route, would now guide me through the meanderings of the earth's crust.

Before starting out, I thought a wash would do me good.

I bent down to bathe my forehead in the Hansbach.

Who can imagine my dismay!

I touched dry, rough granite! The stream no longer ran at my feet!

XXVII

I CANNOT DESCRIBE MY despair. No human words could express my feelings. I was buried alive, with the prospect of dying from the tortures of hunger and thirst.

Mechanically I swept the ground with my burning hands. How dry the rock seemed to me!

But how had I left the course of the stream? For it was definitely no longer there! Then I understood the reason for that strange silence when I listened for the last time for any call from my companions that might reach my ears. But at the moment when I took my first step on the wrong path, I had not noticed this absence of the stream. It is obvious that at that moment a fork in the tunnel had opened up before me, while the Hansbach, following the whim of another slope, had gone away with my companions toward unknown depths.

How to get back? There were no traces. My foot left no mark on this granite. I racked my brain for a solution of this unsolvable problem. My situation could be summed up in a single word: Lost!

Yes! Lost at a depth that seemed immeasurable to me! Those thirty leagues of terrestrial crust weighed on my shoulders with a dreadful weight. I felt crushed.

I tried to take my mind back to the things of the earth. I could hardly manage it. Hamburg, the house in the Königstrasse, my poor Graüben, all that world underneath which I had lost my way passed rapidly before my terrified memory. In a vivid hallucination, I relived all the incidents of the journey, the passage, Iceland, Mr. Fridriksson, the Snaefells. I told myself that if I still hung on to some glimmer of hope in my position, it would be a sign of madness, and that it would be better to give in to despair.

Indeed, what human power could take me back to the surface of the globe and break apart the enormous vaults of rock that buttressed each other above my head? Who could put me back on the right path and take me back to my companions?

"Oh, Uncle!" I cried in a tone of despair.

It was the only word of reproach that passed my lips, for I knew how much that unfortunate man must suffer in his turn in searching for me.

When I saw myself like this, beyond all human help, unable to do anything for my own well-being, I thought of heavenly help. Memories of my childhood, especially of my mother whom I had only known in my tender early years, came back to me. I resorted to prayer, in spite of the few rights I had of being heard by a God to whom I directed myself so late, and I fervently implored him.

This return to Providence calmed me a little, and I was able to concentrate all the power of my intelligence on my situation.

I had three days' worth of food supplies with me and my flask was full. However, I could not remain alone much longer. Should I go up or down?

Up, of course; always up!

I had to get back to the point where I had left the stream, that deadly fork in the road. There, with the stream at my feet, I might be able to return to the summit of Snaefells.

Why had I not thought of that sooner! This was obviously a possibility for rescue. The most pressing task, therefore, was to find the course of the Hansbach again.

I rose, and leaning on my iron-tipped stick I walked back up the tunnel. The slope was rather steep. I walked on without hope and without indecision, like a man who has no choice as to what course he might take.

For half an hour I met with no obstacle. I tried to recognize my path by the shape of the tunnel, by the projections of certain rocks, by the arrangement of the crevices. But no particular detail struck me, and I soon realized that this tunnel could not take me back to the fork. It came to a dead end. I struck against an impenetrable wall, and fell down on the rock.

The fear, the despair that then seized me cannot be described. I lay overwhelmed. My last hope was shattered by this granite wall.

Lost in this labyrinth, whose meandering paths intersected in all directions, I could no longer attempt an impossible escape. I had to die the most dreadful of deaths! And, strange to say, the thought crossed my mind that if my fossilized body were to be found one day, its discovery thirty leagues deep in the bowels of the earth would raise serious scientific questions!

I wanted to speak aloud, but only hoarse sounds came from my parched lips. I panted.

In the midst of these fears, a new terror laid hold of me. My lamp had been damaged when it fell. I had no means of repairing it. Its light was fading and would soon disappear!

I watched the luminous current diminish in the wire coil of the appliance. A procession of moving shadows unfolded on the darkening walls. I no longer dared to shut my eyes, for fear of missing the smallest atom of this elusive light! Every moment it seemed to me that it was about to vanish and that blackness would engulf me.

Finally a last glimmer trembled in the lamp. I followed it, I drank it in with my gaze, I concentrated all the power of my eyes on it as the very last sensation of light they would ever perceive, and then I was plunged into immense darkness.

What horrible cry burst from me! On earth, even in the midst of the darkest nights, light never vanishes altogether. It is diffuse, it is subtle, but however little there may be, the eye's retina manages to perceive it. Here, nothing. The total darkness blinded me in the word's most literal significance.

Then I began to lose my head. I rose up with my arms stretched out before me, attempting to feel my way in the most painful manner. I began to run, rushing haphazardly through this inextricable maze, always going down, running through the earth's crust like an inhabitant of subterranean faults, calling, crying, shouting, soon bruised by the projections of the rocks, falling and getting up again bloody, trying to drink the blood that covered my face, and always expecting that some wall would present the obstacle on which I would fracture my skull.

Where did this mad career take me? I will never know. After several hours, no doubt at the end of my strength, I fell down like a lifeless mass at the foot of the wall, and lost all awareness of my existence!

XXVIII

WHEN I RETURNED TO life my face was wet, but wet with tears. How long that state of unconsciousness had lasted I cannot say. I no longer had any means of telling time. Never had there been a solitude like mine, never had an abandonment been so complete!

After my fall I had lost a great deal of blood. I felt it flowing over me! Ah! how I regretted that I was not yet dead, "and that it remained to be done"! I did not want to think any longer. I drove away every idea, and overcome by pain, I rolled close to the opposite wall.

I was already beginning to lose consciousness again and plunging into supreme annihilation, when a loud noise struck my ear. It resembled the continuous rumble of thunder, and I heard the sound waves gradually fading in the distant recesses of the abyss.

Where did this noise come from? No doubt from some phenomenon that was occurring right inside the mass of the earth. A gas explosion, or the fall of some mighty foundation of the globe!

I continued to listen. I wanted to know if the noise would repeat itself. A quarter of an hour passed. Silence reigned in the tunnel. I could not even hear the beating of my heart anymore.

Suddenly my ear, resting haphazardly against the wall, seemed to catch vague, ungraspable, distant words. I trembled.

"This is a hallucination!" I thought.

But no. Listening more attentively, I really heard a murmur of voices. But my weakness did not allow me to understand what was being said. Yet it was language. That I was sure of.

For a moment I feared these words might be my own, brought back by an echo. Perhaps I had cried out without knowing it. I closed my lips firmly, and pressed my ear against the wall again.

"Yes, truly, someone is speaking! Someone is speaking!"

By moving several feet further along the wall, I could hear distinctly. I succeeded in catching uncertain, bizarre, unintelligible words. They came to me as if they had been pronounced at a low volume, murmured, so to speak. The word 'forlorād' was repeated several times, in a tone of pain.

What did it mean? Who was pronouncing it? My uncle or Hans, obviously. But if I heard them, they could hear me.

"Help!" I shouted with all my force. "Help!"

I listened, I watched in the shadows for an answer, a cry, a sigh. Nothing came. Several minutes passed. A whole world of ideas had opened up in my mind. I thought that my weakened voice could never reach my companions.

"For it is they," I repeated. "What other men would be thirty leagues underground?"

I listened again. Moving my ear over the wall from one place to another, I found a mathematical point where the voices seemed to attain maximum volume. The word 'forlorad' again reached my ear; then that rolling of thunder which had roused me from my torpor.

"No," I said, "no. These voices cannot be heard through solid rock. The wall is made of granite, and it would not allow even the loudest detonation to penetrate! This noise comes from the tunnel itself. There must be some very special acoustic effect here!"

I listened again, and this time, yes! this time! I distinctly heard my name flung across space!

It was my uncle who pronounced it! He was talking to the guide, and the word 'forlorad' was a Danish word!

Then I understood it all. To make myself heard, I precisely had to speak along this wall which would conduct the sound of my voice just as wire conducts electricity.

But there was no time to lose. If my companions moved only a few steps away, the acoustic phenomenon would cease. I therefore approached the wall, and I pronounced these words as clearly as possible:

"Uncle Lidenbrock!"

I waited with the most acute anxiety. Sound does not travel at great speed. Even increased density of air does not affect its velocity; it merely increases its intensity. Seconds, centuries passed, and at last these words reached my ears:

"Axel! Axel! is it you?"

. . . .

"Yes! yes!" I replied.

. . . .

"My child, where are you?"

. . . .

"Lost, in the deepest darkness."

. . . .

"But your lamp?"

. . . .

"Extinguished."

. . . .

"And the stream?"

. . . .

"Disappeared."

. . . .

"Axel, my poor Axel, take courage!"

. . . .

"Wait a little, I'm exhausted! I don't have the strength to answer. But speak to me!"

. . . .

"Courage," resumed my uncle. "Don't speak, listen to me. We've looked for you up and down the tunnel. Couldn't find you. Ah! I wept much for you, my child! At last, assuming that you were still on the path of the Hansbach, we went back down and fired a few shots from our rifles. Now, if our voices are audible to each other, it's purely an acoustic effect! Our hands cannot touch! But don't despair, Axel! It's already something that we can hear each other!"

. . . .

During this time I had been thinking. A certain hope, still vague, was returning to my heart. Above all, there was one thing that it was important to me to find out. I placed my lips close to the wall and said:

"Uncle?"

. . . .

"My boy?" came the reply after a few moments.

. . . .

"We must first find out how far we are apart."

. . . .

"That's easy."

. . . .

"You have your chronometer?"

. . .

"Yes."

. . . .

"Well, take it. Pronounce my name, noting exactly the second when you speak. I'll repeat it as soon as it reaches me, and you'll also note the exact moment when you get my answer."

. . . .

"Yes, and half the time between my call and your answer will indicate exactly the time my voice takes to reach you."

. . . .

"That's it, Uncle."

. . . .

"Are you ready?"

. . . .

"Yes."

. . . . . .

"Now, attention. I'm going to pronounce your name."

. . . .

I put my ear to the wall, and as soon as the name 'Axel' reached me, I immediately replied "Axel," then waited.

. . . .

"Forty seconds," said my uncle. "Forty seconds have passed between the two words; so the sound takes twenty seconds. Now, at a rate of 1,020 feet per second, that adds up to 22,400 feet, or a league and a half, and one-eighth."

. . . .

"A league and a half!" I murmured.

. . . .

"Eh! That can be overcome, Axel."

. . . .

"But must I go up or down?"

. . . .

"Down—for this reason: We've arrived in a vast space where a large number of tunnels end. Yours must lead into it, for it seems as if all the clefts and crevices of the globe radiate out from this immense cavern where we are. So get up, and start walking. Walk on, drag yourself along, if necessary slide down the steep slopes, and you'll find us with our arms open to receive you at the end of the path. Go ahead, my child, get going!"

. . . .

These words cheered me up.

"Good-bye, Uncle!" I exclaimed. "I'm leaving. Our voices won't be able to communicate anymore once I leave this place. So good-bye!"

. . . .

"Good-bye, Axel, I'll see you soon!"

. . . .

These were the last words I heard.

This surprising conversation, carried on across the mass of the earth, with a distance of a league and a half between us, concluded with these words of hope. I prayed a prayer of gratitude to God, for he had guided me through these immense dark spaces to perhaps the only point where the voices of my companions could reach me.

This amazing acoustic effect is easily explained just in terms of the laws of physics. It came from the concave shape of the tunnel and the conducting power of the rock. There are many examples of this propagation of sounds which remain imperceptible in the intermediate spaces. I remember that this phenomenon has been observed in many places, among others on the inner gallery of the dome of St. Paul's in London, and especially in the midst of those curious caverns in Sicily, those quarries near Syracuse, the most wonderful of which is known by the name of Ear of Dionysus.

These memories came back to my mind, and I realized clearly that since my uncle's voice did reach me, there was no obstacle between us. Following the direction of the sound, I would logically reach him, if my strength did not fail me.

I therefore rose. I dragged myself rather than walked. The slope was steep. I let myself slide.

Soon the speed of my descent increased in a frightening way, and threatened to turn into a fall. I no longer had the strength to stop myself.

Suddenly the ground failed under my feet. I felt myself revolving in the air, striking against the craggy projections of a vertical tunnel, a real well; my head struck a sharp rock, and I lost consciousness.

XXIX

When I regained consciousness, I found myself in half-darkness, lying on thick blankets. My uncle was watching over me, to discover the least sign of life on my face. At my first sigh he took my hand; when I opened my eyes he uttered a cry of joy.

"He's alive! He's alive!" he exclaimed.

"Yes," I answered feebly.

"My child," said my uncle, hugging me to his breast, "you're saved."

I was deeply touched by his tone as he uttered these words, and even more by the care that accompanied them. But it took trials such as this to trigger this kind of outpouring from the professor.

At this moment Hans came. He saw my hand in my uncle's, and I dare say that his eyes expressed a deep satisfaction.

"God dag," he said.

"Hello, Hans, hello," I murmured. "And now, Uncle, tell me where we are at present?"

"Tomorrow, Axel, tomorrow. Now you're still too weak. I've bandaged your head with compresses which must not be disturbed. Sleep now, and tomorrow I'll tell you all."

"But at least," I insisted, "tell me what time it is, and what day?"

"Eleven o'clock at night, it's Sunday today, August 9, and I won't allow you to ask any more questions until the 10th."

In truth I was very weak, and my eyes closed involuntarily. I needed a good night's rest; and I therefore let myself doze off with the thought that my isolation had lasted four long days.

Next morning, on awakening, I looked around me. My bed, made up of all our traveling blankets, had been made in a charming grotto, adorned with splendid stalagmites, and whose ground was covered with fine sand. It was half-dark. There was no torch, no lamp, yet an explicable lightness from outside seeped in through a narrow opening in the grotto. I also heard a vague and indistinct noise, something like the murmuring of waves breaking on a pebbled shore, and at times the whistling of wind.

I wondered whether I was really awake, whether I was still dreaming, whether my brain, injured by the fall, was not perceiving purely imaginary noises. Yet neither eyes nor ears could be so utterly deceived.

"It's a ray of daylight," I thought, "seeping in through this cleft in the rock! That really is the murmuring of waves! That's the whistling of wind! Am I quite mistaken, or have we returned to the surface of the earth? Has my uncle given up the expedition, or might it have happily concluded?"

I was asking myself these unanswerable questions when the professor entered.

"Good morning, Axel!" he said joyfully. "I bet that you're doing well."

"Yes, indeed," I said, sitting up on the blankets.

"You should be, because you've slept quietly. Hans and I watched you by turns, and we noticed that your recovery was making good progress."

"Indeed, I do feel a great deal better, and I'll give you proof of that presently if you'll let me have my breakfast."

"You'll eat, my lad. The fever has left you. Hans rubbed your wounds with some ointment or other of which the Icelanders keep the secret, and they've healed marvelously. Our hunter is a splendid fellow!"

While he talked, my uncle prepared a few provisions, which I devoured eagerly, in spite of his instructions. All the while I overwhelmed him with questions which he answered promptly.

I then learned that my providential fall had brought me exactly to the extremity of an almost vertical shaft; and as I had landed in the midst of an accompanying torrent of stones, the least of which would have been enough to crush me, the conclusion was that a part of the rock mass had come down with me. This frightening vehicle had transported me in this way to the arms of my uncle, where I fell bleeding, unconscious.

"Really," he said to me, "it's amazing that you've not been killed a hundred times over. But, by God, let's not separate again, or we risk never seeing each other again."

"Not separate!" The journey was not over, then? I opened my eyes wide in astonishment, which immediately triggered the question:

"What's the matter, Axel?"

"I have a question to ask you. You say that I'm safe and sound?"

"Undoubtedly."

"And all my limbs unbroken?"

"Certainly."

"And my head?"

"Your head, except for a few bruises, is perfectly fine and on your shoulders, where it ought to be."

"Well then, I'm afraid my brain is troubled."

"Troubled!"

"Yes. We haven't returned to the surface of the globe?"

"No, certainly not!"

"Then I must be crazy, because I see daylight, I hear the wind blowing, and the sea breaking on the shore!"

"Ah! is that all?"

"Will you explain . . . ?"

"I won't explain anything because it's inexplicable; but you'll soon see and understand that the science of geology has not spoken its last word yet."

"Then let's go," I exclaimed, rising up quickly.

"No, Axel, no! The open air might be bad for you."

"Open air?"

"Yes, the wind is rather strong. I don't want you to expose yourself like that."

"But I assure you that I'm perfectly well."

"A little patience, my boy. A relapse would get us into trouble, and we have no time to lose, because the passage may be long."

"The passage?"

"Yes, rest today, and tomorrow we'll set sail."

"Set sail!"

This last word made me jump up.

What! Set sail! Did we then have a river, a lake, a sea at our disposal? Was there a ship anchored in some underground harbor?

My curiosity was aroused to the maximum. My uncle tried in vain to restrain me. When he saw that my impatience would do me more harm than satisfying my desire, he gave in.

I dressed in haste. As a precaution, I wrapped myself in one of the blankets, and stepped out of the grotto.

XXX

AT FIRST I SAW nothing. My eyes, unaccustomed to the light, closed quickly. When I was able to reopen them, I stood more stunned even than amazed.

"The sea!" I exclaimed.

"Yes," my uncle replied, "the Lidenbrock Sea, and I like to believe that no other navigator will ever dispute me the honor of discovery and the right to name it after myself!"

A vast surface of water, the beginnings of a lake or an ocean, spread far away beyond the range of the eye. The deeply indented shore met the lapping of the waves with a fine, golden sand, strewn with those small shells that were once inhabited by the first beings of creation. The waves broke on this shore with the resonant murmur that is typical of vast enclosed spaces. A light foam was blown away by the breeze of a moderate wind, and some spray fell on my face. On this gently sloping shore, about a hundred fathoms from the edge of the waves, rested the foot of enormous cliffs that rose up widening to an immeasurable height. Some of them, dividing the beach with their sharp ridge, formed capes and promontories eaten away by the erosive force of the surf. Farther on, the eye discerned their sharply outlined mass against the hazy background of the horizon.

It was a real ocean, with the irregular outline of earthly shores, but deserted and frighteningly wild.

If my eyes were able to range widely over this great sea, it was because a special "light" illuminated its most minor details. It was not the light of the sun, with its shafts of brightness and the splendid radiation of its beams, nor was it the pale and uncertain gleam of the night star, which is only a reflection without heat. No. The illuminating power of this light, its trembling diffusiveness, its clear, dry whiteness, its low temperature and its brightness which surpassed that of the moon showed that it must obviously be of electric origin. It was like an aurora borealis, a constant cosmic phenomenon that filled a cavern large enough to contain an ocean.

The vault suspended above my head, the sky, so to speak, seemed made up of vast clouds, shifting and moving steam, which through condensation had to turn into torrential rain on certain days. I would have thought that under such high atmospheric pressure, there could be no evaporation; and yet, for a physical reason that eluded me, large clouds of steam extended in the air. But at that time 'the weather was good.' The electric layers produced astonishing effects of light on the highest clouds. Deep shadows were sketched on their lower wreaths, and often, between two separate layers, a beam pierced through to us with remarkable intensity. But overall it was not the sun because its light had no heat. Its effect was sad, supremely melancholy. Instead of a firmament glittering with stars, I sensed a granite vault above these clouds that crushed me with all its weight, and all this space, enormous it was, would not have been enough for the movement of the humblest satellite.

Then I remembered the theory of an English captain, who likened the earth to a vast hollow sphere,* inside of which the air remained luminous because of the immense pressure, while its two stars, Pluto and Proserpine,† followed their mysterious orbits there. Could he have been right?

We were in reality imprisoned inside an immense cavity. Its width was impossible to judge, since the shore ran as far as the eye could reach, and so was its length, for the eye soon came to a halt at a somewhat indistinct horizon. As for its height, it must have exceeded several leagues. Where this vault rested on its granite base no eye could tell; but there was a cloud suspended in the atmosphere whose height we estimated at two thousand fathoms, a greater height than that of any terrestrial steam, due no doubt to the considerable density of the air.

The word "cavern" obviously does not convey any idea of this immense space; but the words of the human language are inadequate for one who ventures into the abyss of earth.

I did not know, at any rate, what geological fact would explain the existence of such a cavity. Had the cooling of the globe been able to produce it? I knew of certain famous caverns from the descriptions of travelers, but had never heard of any with such dimensions.

---

*John Cleves Symmes (1780–1829), a former American army officer and an ardent advocate of a theory that the Earth is hollow and has entrances thousands of miles wide at the poles.
†Goddess of the underworld in Roman mythology.

Even if the grotto of Guachara in Colombia, visited by Humboldt,* had not yielded the secret of its depth to the scholar who explored 2,500 feet of it, it probably did not extend much farther. The immense mammoth cave in Kentucky is of gigantic proportions, since its vaulted roof rises five hundred feet above an unfathomable lake, and travelers have explored more than ten leagues without finding the end. But what were these cavities compared to the one which I was now admiring, with its sky of steam, its electric radiation, and its vast enclosed ocean? My imagination felt powerless before such immensity.

I gazed on all these wonders in silence. Words failed me to express my feelings. I felt as if I were witnessing phenomena on some distant planet, Uranus or Neptune, of which my "terrestrial" nature had no knowledge. For such novel sensations, new words were needed, and my imagination failed to supply them. I gazed, I thought, I admired with amazement mingled with a certain amount of fear.

The unforeseen nature of this spectacle brought healthy color back to my cheeks. I treated myself with astonishment, and was effecting a cure with this new therapy; besides, the keenness of the very dense air reinvigorated me, supplying more oxygen to my lungs.

It will be easy to understand that after an imprisonment of forty-seven days in a narrow tunnel, it was an infinite pleasure to breathe this air full of moisture and salt.

So I had no reason to regret that I had left my dark grotto. My uncle, already used to these wonders, was no longer astonished.

"You feel strong enough to walk a little?" he asked me.

"Yes, certainly," I answered, "and nothing could be more pleasant."

"Well, take my arm, Axel, and let's follow the meanderings of the shore."

I eagerly accepted, and we began to walk along the edge of this new ocean. On the left steep cliffs, piled on top of one another, formed a titanic heap with a prodigious appearance. Down their sides flowed innumerable waterfalls, which turned into limpid, resounding streams. A few bits of steam, leaping from rock to rock,

---

*Verne is confused. German explorer Alexander von Humboldt visited the Cuevas del Guácharo in Venezuela in 1799 and wrote about them in 1816. Von Humboldt never visited Guácharo Cave in Colombia.

marked the location of hot springs, and streams flowed gently toward the shared basin, taking the slopes as an opportunity to murmur even more pleasantly.

Among these streams I recognized our faithful traveling companion, the Hansbach, which came to lose itself quietly in the ocean, just as if it had done nothing else since the beginning of the world.

"We'll miss it," I said, with a sigh.

"Bah!" replied the professor, "this one or another one, what does it matter?"

I found this remark rather ungrateful.

But at that moment my attention was attracted to an unexpected spectacle. At a distance of five hundred feet, at the turn of a high promontory, a high, tufted, dense forest appeared before our eyes. It consisted of moderately tall trees shaped like normal parasols, with precise geometrical outlines. The currents of wind seemed to have no impact on their leaves, and in the midst of the breezes they stood unswerving like a clump of petrified cedars.

I hastened forward. I could not give a name to these peculiar specimens. Did they not form part of the two hundred thousand plant species known to date, and was it necessary to give them a place of their own among the water plants? No. When we arrived in their shade my surprise turned into admiration.

In fact, I was facing products of the earth, but grown to gigantic stature. My uncle immediately called them by their name.

"It's just a forest of mushrooms," he said.

And he was right. Imagine the development of these plants, which prefer a warm, moist climate. I knew that according to Bulliard,* the *Lycoperdon giganteum* reaches a circumference of eight or nine feet; but these were white mushrooms thirty to forty feet tall, with a cap of the same diameter. There they stood by the thousands. No light could penetrate into their shade, and complete darkness reigned beneath these juxtaposed domes that resembled the round, thatched roofs of an African town.

Yet I wanted to go further. A deadly cold descended from these

---

*Jean-Baptiste-François Bulliard (1752–1793), French botanist who researched and published extensively on plants and fungi.

fleshy vaults. For half an hour we wandered in the humid darkness, and it was with a genuine feeling of well-being that I returned to the seashore.

But the vegetation of this subterranean region was not limited to mushrooms. Farther on there were clusters of tall trees with faded foliage. They were easy to identify; these were the lowly shrubs of earth in prodigious sizes, lycopods a hundred feet tall, giant sigillarias, tree ferns as tall as pines in northern latitudes, lepidodendra with cylindrical forked stems ending in long leaves and bristling with coarse hairs like monstrous fat plants.

"Amazing, magnificent, splendid!" exclaimed my uncle. "Here is the entire flora of the Secondary period of the world, the Transition period. Look at these humble garden plants that were trees in the early ages of the globe! Look, Axel, and admire them! Never has a botanist been at a celebration such as this!"

"You're right, Uncle. In this immense greenhouse, Providence seems to have wanted to preserve the prehistoric plants which the wisdom of scholars has so successfully reconstructed."

"You put it well, my boy, it is a greenhouse; but you'd put it even better if you added that it's perhaps a zoo."

"A zoo."

"Yes, no doubt. Look at this dust under our feet, these bones scattered on the ground."

"Bones!" I exclaimed. "Yes, bones of prehistoric animals!"

I rushed toward these centuries-old remains made of an indestructible mineral substance.* Without hesitation I could name these gigantic bones that resembled dried-up trunks of trees.

"Here is the lower jaw of a mastodon," I said. "These are the molar teeth of the deinotherium; this femur must have belonged to the greatest of those beasts, the megatherium.† It certainly is a zoo, for these remains were not brought here by a cataclysm. The animals to whom they belonged lived on the shores of this subterranean sea, under the shade of those tree-sized plants. Look, I see entire skeletons. And yet . . ."

---

*Calcium phosphate (author's note).

†The mastodon and the deinotherium were elephant-like species of fossil mammals; the megatherium was a type of ground-dwelling sloth that is now extinct.

"And yet?" said my uncle.

"I don't understand the presence of such quadrupeds in this granite cavern."

"Why?"

"Because animal life existed on the earth only in the Secondary period, when a sedimentary soil had been created through alluvial deposits and had taken the place of the white-hot rocks of the Primitive period."

"Well, Axel, there's a very simple answer to your objection, and that is that this soil is alluvial."

"What! at such a depth below the surface of the earth?"

"No doubt; and there's a geological explanation for this fact. At a certain period the earth consisted only of a flexible crust, subject to alternating movements from above or below, by virtue of the laws of gravity. Probably there were landslides, and some alluvial soil was precipitated to the bottom of these chasms that had suddenly opened up."

"That must be it. But if prehistoric animals have lived in these underground regions, who says that one of these monsters is not still roaming in these gloomy forests or behind these steep crags?"

At this thought, I surveyed the various directions not without fear; but no living creature appeared on the barren strand.

I felt rather tired, and went to sit down at the end of a promontory, at whose foot the waves broke noisily. From here my view included this entire bay formed by an indentation of the coast. In the background, a little harbor lay between pyramidal cliffs. Its still water rested untouched by the wind. A brig and two or three schooners could easily have cast anchor in it. I almost expected to see some ship leave it with sails set and take to the open sea under the southern breeze.

But this illusion vanished quickly. We were the only living creatures in this subterranean world. When there was a lull in the wind, a silence deeper than that of the desert fell on the arid rocks and weighed down on the surface of the ocean. I then tried to pierce the distant haze and to tear the curtain that hung across the mysterious horizon. What questions lay at the tip of my tongue? Where did that ocean end? Where did it lead to? Could we ever explore its opposite shores?

These were white mushrooms thirty to forty feet tall.

My uncle had no doubt about it. I both desired and feared it at the same time.

After spending an hour in the contemplation of this marvelous spectacle, we walked back on the pebbles to the grotto, and I fell into a deep sleep in the midst of the strangest thoughts.

XXXI

THE NEXT MORNING I woke up feeling perfectly well. I thought a bath would do me good, and I went to dive into the waters of this Mediterranean sea for a few minutes. Certainly it deserved this name more than any other ocean.*

I came back to breakfast with a good appetite. Hans knew how to cook our little meal; he had water and fire at his disposal, so that he could change our ordinary fare a bit. For dessert he served us a few cups of coffee, and this delicious beverage never seemed more pleasant to my sense of taste.

"Now," said my uncle, "this is the time of the high tide, and we mustn't miss the opportunity to study this phenomenon."

"What, the tide!" I exclaimed.

"No doubt."

"Can the influence of the sun and moon be felt even here?"

"Why not? Aren't all bodies subject to universal gravity in their entirety? So this mass of water can't escape the general law. And in spite of the heavy atmospheric pressure on the surface, you'll see it rise like the Atlantic itself."

At that moment we walked on the sand of the shore, and the waves were gradually encroaching on the pebbles.

"Here's the beginning of high tide," I exclaimed.

"Yes, Axel, and judging from these tidemarks of foam, you can see that the ocean rises about ten feet."

"That's wonderful!"

"No, it's natural."

"It's easy for you to say, Uncle, but all of this seems extraordinary to me, and I can hardly believe my eyes. Who would ever have imagined an ocean under this terrestrial crust, with ebbing and flowing tides, with winds and storms!"

"Why not? Is there any physical reason against it?"

"I don't see any, so long as we abandon the theory of core heat."

"So this far Davy's theory has been confirmed?"

---

*Literally, this term means "in the middle of the Earth."

"Obviously, and therefore nothing contradicts the existence of oceans and continents in the interior of the earth."

"No doubt, but uninhabited."

"Well! Why wouldn't this water be the sanctuary of fishes of an unknown species?"

"At any rate, we haven't seen a single one so far."

"Well, let's make some lines, and see if the bait draws as much here as it does in surface oceans."

"We'll try, Axel, because we must penetrate all the secrets of these new regions."

"But where are we, Uncle? For I haven't asked you that question yet, which your instruments must be able to answer."

"Horizontally, three hundred and fifty leagues from Iceland."

"As much as that?"

"I'm sure that I'm not off even by five hundred fathoms."

"And does the compass still show south-east?"

"Yes, with a westerly deviation of 19° 45', just as above ground. As for its dip, something curious is occurring that I've observed with the greatest care."

"What is that?"

"It's that the needle, instead of dipping toward the pole as in the northern hemisphere, on the contrary points upward."

"Must we then conclude that the magnetic pole is somewhere between the surface of the globe and the point where we are?"

"Exactly, and it's likely that if we were to reach the polar regions at about the seventieth degree, where Sir James Ross* discovered the magnetic pole, we would see the needle point straight up. Therefore that mysterious center of attraction does not lie at a great depth."

"Indeed, and that's a fact which science had not anticipated."

"Science, my boy, is built on errors, but errors which it's good to commit because they gradually lead to the truth."

"What depth have we reached now?"

"Thirty-five leagues below the surface."

"So," I said, examining the map, "the Highlands of Scotland are

---

*Scottish explorer (1800–1862) who investigated magnetic phenomena in the Arctic and Antarctic and discovered the magnetic north pole in 1831.

over our heads, and the snow-covered peaks of the Grampian Mountains rise up to prodigious heights."

"Yes," answered the professor laughing. "It's a bit of a heavy load to bear, but the vault is solid. The great architect of the universe has built it of the best materials, and man could never have given it such a reach! What are the arches of bridges and the naves of cathedrals compared to this vault with a three-league radius, beneath which an ocean and its storms can unfold at their ease?"

"Oh, I'm not afraid that it'll fall down on my head. But now, Uncle, what are your plans? Aren't you thinking of returning to the surface now?"

"Return! No, indeed! We'll continue our journey, since everything has gone well so far."

"But I don't see how we can go down beneath this liquid surface."

"Oh! I'm not going to dive in head foremost. But if all oceans are properly speaking only lakes, since they are surrounded by land, of course this interior sea is also encircled by a granite coast."

"That's beyond question."

"Well then, on the opposite shores we'll find new passages opening up."

"How wide do you estimate this ocean to be?"

"Thirty or forty leagues."

"Ah!" I remarked, thinking that this estimate might well be inaccurate.

"So we have no time to lose, and we'll set sail tomorrow."

Involuntarily I looked about for the ship that was supposed to transport us.

"Ah!" I said, "set sail, will we? Fine! But aboard what ship will we travel?"

"It'll not be aboard a ship at all, my boy, but on a good, solid raft."

"A raft!" I exclaimed. "A raft is just as impossible to build as a ship, and I don't see . . ."

"You don't see, Axel, but if you listened, you might hear."

"Hear?"

"Yes, certain strikes of the hammer that would tell you that Hans is already at work on it."

"He's building a raft?"

"Yes."

"What! He's already felled trees with his axe?"

"Oh, the trees were already down. Come, and you'll see him at work."

After a walk of a quarter of an hour, on the other side of the promontory which formed the little natural harbor, I saw Hans at work. A few more steps, and I was at his side. To my great surprise, a half-finished raft was already lying on the sand; it was made out of beams of a peculiar wood, and a great number of planks, hinges and frames were strewn about the ground. It was enough material for an entire fleet.

"Uncle," I exclaimed, "what wood is this?"

"It is pine, fir, birch, all kinds of northern conifers, mineralized by the seawater."

"Is that possible?"

"It's called 'surturbrand' or fossil wood."

"But then, like lignite, it must be as hard as stone, and cannot float?"

"Sometimes that happens; some of these woods have become true anthracites; but others, like these, have only gone through the beginnings of fossil transformation. Just look," added my uncle, throwing one of those precious remains into the sea.

The piece of wood, after disappearing, returned to the surface of the waves and swung back and forth with their movements.

"Are you convinced?" said my uncle.

"Convinced, although it's incredible!"

The next evening, thanks to our guide's skill, the raft was completed; it was ten feet by five feet; the beams of surturbrand, tied together with strong rope, offered an even surface, and when it was launched, this improvised vessel floated calmly on the waves of the Lidenbrock Sea.

XXXII

On August 13 we awoke early. We planned to inaugurate a new mode of fast and easy transportation.

The rigging of the raft consisted of a mast made from two poles tied together, a yard made of a third, a sail from our blankets. There was no lack of rope. The whole thing was solid.

At six o'clock, the professor gave the signal to embark. The food supplies, the baggage, the instruments, the guns, and a good quantity of fresh water gathered from the rocks were all put in their place.

Hans had installed a rudder so as to be able to steer his floating vessel. He took the tiller. I detached the rope that moored us to the shore. The sail was set, and we rapidly left the land behind.

At the moment of leaving the little harbor, my uncle, who insisted on his geographical nomenclature, wanted to give it a name, proposing mine among others.

"Really," I said, "I have another proposal."

"Which one?"

"Graüben. Port Graüben, that'll look very good on the map."

"Let it be Port Graüben then."

In this way, the memory of my beloved Virland girl connected with our adventurous expedition.

The wind blew from the north-west. We sailed at great speed with the wind from behind. The very dense layers of the atmosphere had considerable force and acted on the sail like a powerful fan.

After an hour, my uncle was able to estimate our speed with a good deal of precision.

"At this rate," he said, "we'll travel at least thirty leagues in twenty-four hours, and we'll soon come in sight of the opposite shore."

I made no answer, but went and sat at the front of the raft. The northern shore was already beginning to dip under the horizon. The eastern and western strands spread wide as if to make our departure easier. An immense ocean stretched out before my eyes. The grayish shadows of great clouds glided over its surface, which seemed to weigh down this somber water. The silvery rays of the electric light, here and there reflected by the spray, shot out little points of light from our wake. Soon we lost sight of land entirely, all points

159

of orientation disappeared, and without the foamy wake of the raft, I might have thought that it was perfectly motionless.

Toward noon, immense algae could be seen floating at the surface of the water. I was aware of the vital power of these plants, which grow at a depth of over twelve thousand feet under the sea, reproduce under a pressure of four hundred atmospheres, and sometimes form barriers strong enough to impede the course of a ship; but there were never, I think, more gigantic algae than those in the Lidenbrock Sea.

Our raft passed along fucus that were three or four thousand feet long, immense serpents that continued beyond the reach of sight; I entertained myself in tracing these endless ribbons, always thinking that I had reached the end, and for hours my patience competed with my surprise.

What natural force could produce such plants, and what must the earth have looked like in the first centuries of its formation, when under the impact of heat and humidity, the vegetable kingdom alone developed on its surface!

Evening came and, as I had noted on the previous day, the luminosity of the air did not diminish. It was a constant phenomenon whose permanence could be relied on.

After dinner I lay down at the foot of the mast, and immediately fell asleep in the midst of carefree reveries.

Hans, motionless at the helm, let the raft run, which at any rate did not even need steering, with the wind blowing from behind.

Since our departure from Port Graüben, Professor Lidenbrock had charged me with keeping the "ship log," writing down even the smallest observation, recording interesting phenomena, the direction of the wind, the speed, the route we had taken—in a word, all the details of our strange sea voyage.

I will therefore limit myself here to reproducing these daily notes, written, so to speak, as events directed, so as to provide a more exact account of our passage.

Friday, August 14. —Steady breeze from the northwest. The raft makes rapid progress in a straight line. The coast is thirty leagues behind us in the direction of the wind. Nothing on the horizon.

Intensity of light remains the same. Good weather, that is, the clouds are high up, not very dense, and bathed in a white atmosphere that looks like molten silver. Thermometer: +32°C.

At noon Hans fastens a hook to the end of a line. He baits it with a small piece of meat and throws it into the sea. For two hours he catches nothing. Are these waters uninhabited, then? No. A pull on the line. Hans draws it in and lifts up a fish that struggles vigorously.

"A fish!" exclaims my uncle.

"That's a sturgeon!" I exclaimed in turn. "A small sturgeon!"

The professor looks carefully at the animal and does not share my opinion. The fish has a flat, round head, and the front of its body is covered with bony plates; its mouth has no teeth; large, well-developed pectoral fins are attached to a body without tail. This animal does belong to the same order where naturalists place the sturgeon, but it differs from it in many essential aspects.

My uncle makes no mistake about this, and after a rather brief examination, he says:

"This fish belongs to a family that has been extinct for centuries, of which only fossil traces are found in the Devonian formations."

"How could we have taken one of those inhabitants of the primitive oceans alive?"

"Yes," replies the professor as he continues his examination, "and you can see that these fossil fishes are not at all identical with the contemporary species. So having one of these creatures alive in one's hand is a real joy for a naturalist."

"But to what family does it belong?"

"Order ganoids, family cephalaspidae, species . . ."

"Well?"

"Species pterichthys, I'd swear! But this one has a peculiarity which is apparently found in fish that inhabit subterranean waters."

"Which one?"

"It's blind!"

"Blind!"

"Not just blind, but it has no organ of sight at all."

I look. It's true. But this could be a special case. So the fish line is baited once again, and thrown again into the ocean. This ocean is most certainly full of fish, for in two hours, we catch a large quantity of pterichthys, as well as fish belonging to another extinct family, the dipterides,* whose species my uncle is unable to identify. None of them have any organ of sight. This unexpected catch nicely restocks our food supplies.

So it seems certain that this ocean contains only fossil species, among which the fish as well as the reptiles are the more perfect the more ancient they are in their creation.

Perhaps we will find some of those saurians that science has reconstructed out of a bit of bone or cartilage?

I take up the telescope and scan the ocean. It is deserted. Undoubtedly we are still too close to the shores.

I gaze upward in the air. Why should not some of the birds restored by the immortal Cuvier[†] again flap their wings in these heavy atmospheric layers? The fish would provide them with sufficient food. I survey the whole space, but the air is as uninhabited as the shore.

Still my imagination carries me away into those wonderful speculations of paleontology. Wide awake, I dream. I think I see enormous chelonians on the surface of the water, antediluvian turtles that resemble floating islands. Across the dimly lit beach walk the huge mammals of the first ages of the world, the leptotherium found in the caverns of Brazil, the mericotherium[7] from the icy regions of Siberia. Farther on, the pachydermatous lophiodon, a giant tapir, hides behind the rocks, ready to fight for its prey with the anoplotherium, a strange animal that resembles the rhinoceros, the horse, the hippopotamus and the camel, as if the Creator, in too much of a hurry in the first hours of the world, had combined several animals into one. The giant mastodon curls his trunk, and smashes rocks on the shore with his tusks, while the megatherium, resting on its enormous paws, digs through the soil, its roars echoing sonorously off the granite rocks. Higher up, the protopithecus—the first monkey that appeared on the globe—climbs up the steep summits. Higher yet, the pterodactyl with its winged hand glides on

---

*Genus of fish with two fins.

†Georges Cuvier (1769–1832), French statesman and zoologist who did groundbreaking work on comparative anatomy and paleontology and extensively studied fossil animals.

the dense air like a large bat. In the uppermost layers, finally, immense birds, more powerful than the cassowary and larger than the ostrich, spread their vast wings and are about to strike their heads against the granite vault.

All this fossil world is born again in my imagination. I travel back to the biblical age of the world, long before the advent of man, when the unfinished world was as yet insufficient to sustain him. My dream then goes back farther to the ages before the advent of living beings. The mammals disappear, then the birds, then the reptiles of the Secondary period, and finally the fish, the crustaceans, mollusks, and articulated beings. The zoophytes of the Transition period also return to nothingness. All the world's life is concentrated in me, and my heart is the only one that beats in this depopulated world. There are no more seasons; climates are no more; the heat of the globe continually increases and neutralizes that of the radiant star. Vegetation grows excessively. I glide like a shade amongst arborescent ferns, treading with unsteady feet the iridescent clay and the multicolored sand; I lean against the trunks of immense conifers; I lie in the shade of sphenophylla, asterophylla, and lycopods, a hundred feet tall.

Centuries pass by like days! I move back through the series of terrestrial transformations. Plants disappear; granite rocks lose their purity; solids give way to liquids under the impact of increasing heat; water covers the surface of the globe; it boils, evaporates; steam envelops the earth, which gradually dissolves into a gaseous mass, white-hot, as large and radiant as the sun!

In the midst of this nebula, fourteen hundred thousand times more voluminous than this globe that it will one day become, I am carried into planetary spaces! My body subtilizes, sublimates itself in its turn and, like an imponderable atom, mingles with these immense vapors that follow their flaming orbits through infinite space.

What a dream! Where is it carrying me? My feverish hand sketches the strange details out on paper! I have forgotten everything, the professor, the guide, and the raft! A hallucination possesses my spirit . . .

"What's the matter?" my uncle says.

My eyes, wide open, gaze at him without seeing him.

"Take care, Axel, or you'll fall overboard!"

At the same moment, I feel the vigorous grip of Hans' hand.

Without him, I would have thrown myself into the sea under the influence of my dream.

"Is he going crazy?" exclaims the professor.

"What's going on?" I finally say, returning to myself.

"Are you sick?"

"No, I had a momentary hallucination, but it's over now. Is everything alright?"

"Yes! Nice wind and beautiful sea! We're making good progress, and if I'm not wrong in my calculation, we'll soon land."

At these words I rise up, I look at the horizon; but the water line still blurs into the line of clouds.

XXXIII

SATURDAY, AUGUST 15. —THE sea remains monotonously uniform. No land is in sight. The horizon seems excessively far removed.

My head is still weighted down by the vividness of my dream.

My uncle has had no dreams, but he is in a bad mood. He examines all directions with his telescope and folds his arms with a vexed look.

I notice that Professor Lidenbrock is becoming the impatient man of the past again and note this fact in my log. It took my danger and suffering to strike a spark of human feeling in him; but now that I am cured, his nature has once again gained the upper hand. And yet, why lose one's temper? Is not the journey progressing under the most favorable circumstances? Is not the raft gliding along with marvelous speed?

"You seem anxious, Uncle," I say, seeing him lift the telescope frequently to his eye.

"Anxious? No."

"Impatient, then?"

"There's reason to be!"

"Yet we're going very fast . . ."

"What does that matter? It's not the speed that's too slow, it's the ocean that's too large!"

I then remember that the professor, before our departure, had estimated the width of this underground ocean at thirty leagues. Now we have already covered three times this distance, and still the southern coast has not emerged.

"We're not going down!" the professor resumes. "All this is a waste of time, and after all, I've not come this far to take a little boat trip on a pond!"

He calls this passage a little boat trip, and this ocean a pond!

"But," I say, "since we've followed the route that Saknussemm indicated . . ."

"That's exactly the question. Have we followed that route? Did Saknussemm find this expanse of water? Did he cross it? Hasn't this stream that we took as our guide led us completely astray?"

"At any rate, we can't regret having come this far. This spectacle is magnificent, and . . ."

"This isn't about seeing spectacles. I had set myself an objective, and I want to attain it! So don't talk to me about admiring spectacles!"

I take the point and let the professor gnaw his lips with impatience. At six in the evening, Hans asks for his wages, and his three rix-dollars are counted out to him.

Sunday, August 16. —Nothing new. Weather unchanged. The wind is becoming a little colder. When I wake up, my first concern is to determine the intensity of the light. I always fear that the electric phenomenon might grow dim, then disappear altogether. Nothing of the sort. The shadow of the raft is clearly outlined on the surface of the waves.

Really this ocean is unending! It must be as large as the Mediterranean or even the Atlantic. Why not?

My uncle probes the depth several times. He ties the heaviest of our pickaxes to a long rope which he lets run down to two hundred fathoms. No bottom. We have a lot of difficulty in bringing our probe back up.

But when the pickaxe is back on board, Hans points out to me two deep imprints on its surface. It looks as if this piece of iron had been vigorously gripped between two hard objects.

I look at the hunter.

"Tänder," he says.

I do not understand. I turn to my uncle, who is completely absorbed in his reflections. I do not bother to disturb him. I return to the Icelander. Opening and closing his mouth several times, he makes me understand his idea.

"Teeth!" I say with amazement, examining the iron bar more attentively.

Yes! These are indeed teeth marks imprinted on the metal! The jaws that are equipped with these must have prodigious strength! Is it a monster of some long-lost species that moves about in the depths of the water, more voracious than the shark, more formidable than the whale? I cannot take my eyes off this half-gnawed bar! Will my dream of last night turn into reality?

These thoughts trouble me all day, and my imagination hardly calms down during a few hours' sleep.

Monday, August 17. —I try to recall the particular instincts of those prehistoric animals in the Secondary period that succeeded mollusks, crustaceans and fishes and preceded the appearance of mammals on the earth. The world then belonged to reptiles. Those monsters ruled as masters over the Jurassic oceans.* Nature had bestowed on them a perfect structure. What a gigantic framework! What prodigious strength! The saurians of our day, alligators and crocodiles, are only weaker, smaller reproductions of their forefathers in the primitive ages!

I shudder as I imagine those monsters. No human eye has ever seen them alive. They appeared on this earth a thousand ages before man, but their fossil remains, found in the argillaceous limestone called lias by the English,† have made it possible to reconstruct their anatomy and to discover their colossal frames.

At the Hamburg Museum, I saw the skeleton of one of these saurians that measured thirty feet in length. Am I then destined— me, an inhabitant of earth—to find myself face to face with these representatives of a prehistoric family? No! It's impossible. Yet the mark of powerful teeth is engraved on the iron bar, and by their imprint, I realize that they are cone-shaped like the crocodile's.

My eyes stare at the sea with dread. I fear seeing one of those inhabitants of submarine caverns rushing out.

I assume that Professor Lidenbrock shares my thoughts, if not my fears, for after having examined the pickaxe, his eyes roam across the ocean.

"To Hell with that idea of sounding the depth!" I say to myself. "He's probably disturbed some animal in its shelter, and if we're not attacked on our route . . . !"

I glance at our weapons and make sure that they are in good shape. My uncle notices it and approves with a gesture.

Already big commotions at the surface of the water point to some upheaval in the deeper layers. Danger is near. We must be vigilant.

---

*Oceans of the Secondary period that generated the soil which the Jura Mountains consist of (author's note). Jurassic period: 208–144 million years ago.

†Blue argillaceous limestone that occurs in southwestern England; it also forms part of Jurassic layers that typically contain many fossils.

Tuesday, August 18. —Evening comes, or rather the time when sleep weighs down our eyelids, for this ocean knows no night, and the relentless light tires our eyes continually, as if we were sailing under an arctic sun. Hans is at the helm. During his watch I fall asleep.

Two hours later a terrible jolt wakes me up. The raft has been lifted up outside the water with indescribable force and thrown back again twenty fathoms away.

"What's the matter?" shouts my uncle. "Have we struck land?"

Hans points with his finger at a blackish mass two hundred fathoms away, which rises and falls again and again. I look and exclaim:

"It's an enormous porpoise!"

"Yes," replies my uncle, "and now there's a sea lizard of extraordinary size."

"And farther on a monstrous crocodile! Look at its huge jaw and the rows of teeth it's equipped with! Ah! It's disappearing!"

"A whale! A whale!" then exclaims the professor. "I can see its enormous fins! Look at the air and the water it blows out through its blow-holes!"

Indeed, two water columns rise up to a considerable height above the sea. We stand surprised, thunderstruck, frightened in the presence of this herd of marine monsters. They are of supernatural size, and the smallest among them could break our raft with one snap of its teeth. Hans wants to tack before the wind to get away from this dangerous neighborhood; but he discovers no less fearsome enemies on the other side: a forty-foot turtle and a thirty-foot snake that shoots its enormous head above the flood.

Impossible to get away. The reptiles approach; they wheel around our little raft at a speed that express trains could not match; they swim concentric circles around it. I've gripped my rifle. But what can a bullet do against the scales that cover the bodies of these animals?

We are speechless with fear. They come closer! On one side the crocodile, on the other the snake. The rest of the marine herd has disappeared. I prepare to fire. Hans stops me with a gesture. The two monsters pass within fifty fathoms of the raft, and hurl themselves at each other with a fury that prevents them from seeing us.

The battle is fought a hundred fathoms from the raft. We can clearly see the two monsters in mortal combat.

But now it seems to me as if the other animals were participating in the battle—the porpoise, the whale, the lizard, the turtle. Every instant I catch sight of one of them. I point them out to the Icelander. He shakes his head in negation.

"Tva," says he.

"What! Two? He claims only two animals . . ."

"He's right," exclaims my uncle, whose telescope has never left his eye.

"It can't be!"

"Yes! One of these monsters has the snout of a porpoise, the head of a lizard, the teeth of a crocodile, that's what deceived us. It's the most formidable of the prehistoric reptiles, the ichthyosaurus!"*

"And the other one?"

"The other one's a snake hidden in the shell of a turtle, a plesiosaurus,† the terrible enemy of the first one!"

Hans has spoken the truth. Only two monsters disrupt the surface of the ocean, and I have two reptiles of the primitive oceans before my eyes. I can distinguish the bloody eye of the ichthyosaurus, large as a man's head. Nature has endowed it with an extremely powerful optical device that can withstand the water pressure at the depths it inhabits. It has rightly been called a saurian whale, because it has both the latter's speed and its size. This one is no less than a hundred feet long, and I can judge its size when it raises the vertical fins on its tail above the water. Its jaw is enormous, and according to the naturalists it has no less than one hundred and eighty-two teeth.

The plesiosaurus, a snake with a cylindrical body and a short tail, has four paws shaped like oars. Its body is entirely covered by a shell, and its neck, as flexible as a swan's, rises thirty feet above the waves.

These animals attack each other with indescribable rage. They heave up liquid mountains that roll back to our raft. Twenty times we are about to capsize. Prodigiously loud hisses can be heard. The two beasts are locked together. I cannot distinguish one from the other. We must fear the fury of the winner.

One hour, two hours pass. The struggle continues with the same

---

*Extinct marine animal with the body of a fish, a head like a dolphin's, and flippers.
†Extinct marine reptile with a long neck, typically found in fossils from about 200 million years ago.

Two monsters disrupt the surface of the ocean.

ferocity. The combatants alternately move toward and away from our raft. We remain motionless, ready to fire.

Suddenly the ichthyosaurus and the plesiosaurus disappear, creating a genuine maelstrom in the water. Several minutes pass. Will the battle end in the depths of the ocean?

Suddenly an enormous head shoots up, the head of the plesiosaurus. The monster is fatally injured. I no longer see his enormous shell. Only his long neck shoots up, drops, rises up again, droops, lashes the waters like a gigantic whip, and writhes like a worm cut in two. The water splashes to a considerable distance. It blinds us. But soon the reptile's agony draws to an end, its movements diminish, its contortions decrease, and the long serpentine shape extends like a lifeless mass on the calm waters.

As for the ichthyosaurus, has he returned to his submarine cavern, or will he reappear at the surface of the ocean?

XXXIV

WEDNESDAY, AUGUST 19. —FORTUNATELY the wind blows power-fully, and has allowed us to flee quickly from the scene of the battle. Hans keeps his post at the helm. My uncle, drawn out of his absorb-ing reflections by the incidents of the combat, falls back into his im-patient contemplations of the ocean.

The voyage resumes its monotonous uniformity, which I would not like to break with a repetition of yesterday's dangers.

Thursday, August 20. —Unsteady wind N.N.E. Temperature high. We sail at a rate of three and a half leagues per hour.

At about noon, a very distant noise can be heard. I note the fact here without being able to provide an explanation. It is a continuous roar.

"In the distance," says the professor, "there is a rock or islet against which the sea breaks."

Hans climbs up on the mast, but sees no breakers. The ocean is smooth all the way to the horizon.

Three hours pass. The roar seems to come from a distant waterfall.

I point this out to my uncle, who shakes his head. But I am con-vinced that I am right. Are we then speeding toward some waterfall that will precipitate us into an abyss? This method of descent might possibly please the professor, because it is almost vertical, but as for me . . .

In any case, there must be some noisy phenomenon several leagues windward, for now the roar resounds with great intensity. Does it come from the sky or the ocean?

I look up at the steam suspended in the atmosphere and try to probe its depth. The sky is calm. The clouds, having floated to the top of the vault, seem motionless and fade in the intense glare of the light. The cause of this phenomenon must therefore lie else-where.

Then I examine the clear horizon with no trace of mist. Its ap-pearance has not changed. But if this noise comes from a waterfall, if this entire ocean crashes into a lower basin, if this roar is produced by a mass of falling water, the current should accelerate, and its increasing speed will give me the measure of the peril that threatens us. I check the current. There is none. An empty bottle that I throw into the ocean stays in the direction of the wind.

At about four Hans rises, grips the mast, climbs to its top. From there his gaze sweeps the partial circle of the ocean in front of the raft and stops at one point. His face expresses no surprise, but his eye remains at that point.

"He's seen something," says my uncle.

"I believe so."

Hans comes back down, then points with his arm to the south and says:

"Dere nere!"

"Down there?" replies my uncle.

Then, seizing his telescope, he gazes attentively for a minute, which seems to me a century.

"Yes, yes!" he exclaims.

"What do you see?"

"I see an immense fountain rising from the water."

"Another sea animal?"

"Perhaps."

"Then let's steer farther westward, because we know about the danger of running into prehistoric monsters!"

"Let's go straight," replies my uncle.

I turn to Hans. He maintains the helm with inflexible rigor.

Yet if at our current distance from the animal, which is at least twelve leagues, we can see the fountain of water from its blow-hole, it must be of a supernatural size. Taking flight would be nothing more than following the rules of the most elementary caution. But we did not come here to be cautious.

So we press on. The closer we draw, the taller the water fountain becomes. What monster can possibly fill itself with such a quantity of water, and spurt it up so continuously?

At eight in the evening, we are less than two leagues away. Its blackish, enormous, mountainous body rests on the sea like an island. Is it imagination, is it fear? Its length seems to exceed a thousand fathoms! What can be this cetacean that neither Cuvier nor

Blumenbach* anticipated? It lies motionless, as if asleep; the sea seems unable to lift it, and the waves play on its sides. The fountain of water propelled to a height of five hundred feet falls back down in a rain with deafening noise. And here we speed like madmen toward this powerful mass that a hundred whales would not nourish even for a day!

Terror grips hold of me. I don't want to go any further! I will cut the halyard if necessary! I am in open mutiny against the professor, who does not reply.

Suddenly Hans rises and points with his finger at the threatening object:

"Holme!" he says.

"An island!" cries my uncle.

"An island!" I say in turn, shrugging my shoulders.

"Obviously," replies the professor, breaking out into a loud laugh.

"But that fountain of water?"

"Geyser," utters Hans.

"Ah! Undoubtedly, a geyser!" my uncle replies, "a geyser like those in Iceland."†

At first I refuse to admit that I have been so crudely mistaken. Taking an island for a sea monster! But the evidence is against me, and I finally have to acknowledge my error. It is nothing more than a natural phenomenon.

As we draw nearer, the dimensions of the water column become magnificent. The islet deceptively resembles an enormous cetacean whose head rests above the waves at a height of six fathoms. The geyser, a word that the Icelanders pronounce 'geysir' and which means 'fury,' rises majestically to its full height. Dull explosions take place from time to time, and the enormous jet, gripped by a more furious rage, shakes its plume of steam and leaps up to the first layer of clouds. It stands alone. Neither steam vents nor hot springs

---

*Johann Friedrich Blumenbach (1752–1840), German physiologist and founder of physical anthropology, proposed one of the first classifications of humans into different races.

†Very famous spring at the foot of Mount Hekla (author's note). Mount Hekla is in southern Iceland.

surround it, and all the volcanic power gathers in it. Rays of electric light mingle with the dazzling fountain, every drop of which refracts all the prismatic colors.

"Let's land," says the professor.

But we must carefully avoid this waterspout, which would sink our raft in a moment. Hans, steering skillfully, takes us to the other end of the islet.

I jump onto the rock; my uncle follows me nimbly, while the hunter remains at his post, like a man beyond amazement.

We walk on granite mixed with siliceous tuff. The ground trembles under our feet, like the sides of an overheated boiler filled with steam struggling to get loose; it is scalding hot. We come in sight of a small lake at the center, from which the geyser springs. I dip an overflow thermometer into the boiling water, and it indicates a temperature of 163°C.

So this water comes out of a burning furnace. This markedly contradicts Professor Lidenbrock's theories. I cannot help but point it out.

"Well," he replies, "what does this prove against my doctrine?"

"Nothing," I say dryly, realizing that I am up against inflexible obstinacy.

Nevertheless I am forced to admit that we have so far enjoyed extraordinarily favorable circumstances, and that for some reason that eludes me, our journey takes place under special temperature conditions. But it seems obvious to me that one day we will reach the areas where the core heat reaches its highest limits and exceeds all the gradations of our thermometers.

We shall see. That is what the professor says who, after naming this volcanic islet after his nephew, gives the signal to embark.

I continue to contemplate the geyser for a few minutes. I notice that its jet is variable in strength: sometimes its intensity decreases, then it returns with renewed vigor, which I attribute to the variable pressure of the steam that has gathered in its reservoir.

At last we leave by steering around the very pointed rocks in the south. Hans has taken advantage of the stop-over to fix up the raft.

But before going any further, I make a few observations to calculate the distance we have covered, and note them in my journal. We have crossed two hundred and seventy leagues of ocean since leaving Port Graüben, and we are six hundred and twenty leagues away from Iceland, underneath England.

XXXV

Friday, August 21. —The next day, the magnificent geyser has disappeared. The wind has become colder, and has rapidly carried us away from Axel Island. The roar has gradually faded.

The weather, if it is appropriate to call it that, will change before long. The atmosphere fills up with steam clouds that carry with them electricity generated by the evaporation of the salt water. The clouds sink perceptibly lower, and take on a uniform olive-colored hue. The electric rays can scarcely penetrate through this opaque curtain, drawn on the theater in which the drama of a thunderstorm is about to be staged.

I feel particularly affected, as do all creatures on earth just before a cataclysm. The piled-up cumulus clouds* in the south look sinister; they have that 'merciless' look that I have often noticed at the beginning of a thunderstorm. The air is heavy, the sea is calm.

In the distance the clouds resemble big bales of cotton, piled up in picturesque disorder; by degrees they dilate, and lose in number what they gain in size. Their weight is such that they cannot lift from the horizon; but in the breeze of air currents high up, they dissolve little by little, grow darker and soon turn into a single, formidable-looking layer. From time to time a ball of steam, still lit up, bounces off this grayish carpet and soon loses itself in the opaque mass.

The atmosphere is obviously saturated with liquid; I am impregnated with it; my hair bristles on my head as it would close to an electrical appliance. It seems to me that if my companions touched me at that moment, they would receive a powerful shock.

At ten in the morning the symptoms of a storm become more pronounced; it seems as if the wind lets up only to catch its breath; the cloud bank resembles a huge goatskin in which hurricanes are building up.

I am reluctant to believe in the threatening signs from the sky, and yet I cannot keep from saying:

"Here's some bad weather coming on."

---

*Clouds in round shapes (author's note).

The professor gives no answer. He is in a murderous mood as he sees the ocean stretching out indefinitely before him. He shrugs his shoulders at my words.

"We'll have a thunderstorm," I exclaim, pointing at the horizon. "Those clouds are coming down on the sea as if they were going to crush it!"

General silence. The wind stops. Nature looks as if it is dead and breathes no more. On the mast, where I already see a small St. Elmo's fire sprouting, the tensionless sail hangs in heavy folds. The raft lies motionless in the middle of a sluggish sea without waves. But if we no longer move, why leave that sail on the mast, which could wreck us at the first onslaught of the tempest?

"Let's reef the sail and take the mast down!" I say. "That's safer."

"No, by the Devil!" shouts my uncle. "A hundred times no! Let the wind seize us! Let the thunderstorm take us away! But let me finally see the rocks of a shore, even if our raft were to be smashed to smithereens!"

The words are hardly out of his mouth when a sudden change takes place on the southern horizon. The built-up steam condenses into water, and the air, violently attracted to the voids produced by the condensation, turns into a hurricane. It rushes in from the farthest recesses of the cavern. The darkness deepens. I can scarcely jot down a few incomplete notes.

The raft rises up, takes a leap. My uncle falls. I crawl to him. He has firmly gripped the end of a thick rope and seems to watch this spectacle of unbridled elements with pleasure.

Hans does not move. His long hair, blown by the hurricane and falling over his immobile face, gives him a strange physiognomy, because each of its ends is tipped with little luminous feathers. His frightening mask is that of a prehistoric man, a contemporary of the ichthyosaurus and the megatherium.

The mast holds firm yet. The sail stretches tight like a bubble ready to burst. The raft flies at a speed I cannot guess, but not as fast as the drops of water it pushes aside below itself in straight, clear lines of speed.

"The sail! the sail!" I say, motioning to lower it.

"No!" replies my uncle.

"Nej!" repeats Hans, gently shaking his head.

But now the rain is like a roaring waterfall in front of that horizon toward which we speed like madmen. But before it reaches us, the veil of clouds breaks apart, the sea begins to boil, and the electricity produced by a powerful chemical reaction in the upper layers comes into play. Glittering flashes of lightning mix with crashes of thunder; innumerable flashes interlace in the midst of detonations; the mass of steam glows white-hot; hailstones light up as they hit the metal of our tools and of our weapons; the heaving waves resemble fire-breathing hills, each belching forth its own interior flames, and every crest is plumed with dancing fire. My eyes are blinded by the dazzling light, my ears are stunned by the roar of thunder. I have to hold on to the mast, which bends like a reed under the violence of the hurricane!!!

....

[Here my notes became quite incomplete. I have only been able to find a few quick observations, jotted down mechanically, so to speak. But their brevity and their obscurity are saturated with the emotion that gripped me, and they convey the gist of the situation better than my memory.]

Sunday, August 23. —Where are we? Driven on at incalculable speed.

The night has been horrible. The thunderstorm does not abate. We live in the midst of noise, a constant explosion. Our ears are bleeding. We cannot exchange a word.

The lightning flashes never stop. I see reverse zigzags that after flashing momentarily rebound back up and strike against the granite vault. What if it crumbled! Other lightning flashes bifurcate or take the shape of fiery spheres that explode like bombshells. But the general noise does not seem to increase when they do; it has exceeded the volume that the human ear can perceive, and even if all the powder kegs of the world exploded at once, we would not hear it anymore.

There is continuous light emission at the surface of the clouds; the electric substance is constantly discharged from their molecules; obviously the gaseous principles in the air have changed; innumerable fountains of water rush upwards into the air and fall back again foaming.

Where are we going? My uncle lies stretched out at the end of the raft.

The heat increases. I look at the thermometer; it indicates . . . [the figure is obliterated].

Monday, August 24. —It will never end! Why would the state of this very dense atmosphere, now that it has been changed, not be definitive?

We are worn out by exhaustion. Hans as usual. The raft speeds invariably to the south-east. We have run two hundred leagues since we left Axel Island.

At noon the violence of the storm doubles. We must safely stow every piece of cargo. Each of us ties himself down as well. The waves rise above our heads.

Impossible to address a single word to each other for the last three days. We open our mouths, we move our lips, but no perceptible sound comes forth. Even talking into each other's ears we cannot hear each other.

My uncle has approached me. He has uttered a few words. I believe he has told me, "We are lost." But I am not sure.

I decide to write down these words: "Let us lower the sail."

He nods his consent.

Scarcely has he risen up again when a disk of fire appears at the edge of the raft. Mast and sail are swept away together in one stroke, and I see them fly up to a prodigious height, resembling a pterodactyl, that fantastic bird of the first ages.

We are frozen with fear. The half-white, half-blue ball, as large as a ten-inch bombshell, moves about slowly, but revolves with surprising speed under the whiplash of the hurricane. It goes here and there, it climbs up onto one of the raft's crossbeams, jumps onto the sack of provisions, comes back down easily, leaps, and skirts along the box of gunpowder. Horror! We'll blow up! No. The dazzling disk moves away; it approaches Hans, who looks at it steadily; it approaches my uncle, who falls down on his knees to avoid it; it approaches me, pale and trembling in the glare of the light and heat; it spins close to my foot, which I try to pull back. I cannot do it.

A smell of laughing-gas fills the air; it enters the throat, the lungs. We suffocate.

Why am I unable to pull back my foot? It must be riveted to the planks! Ah! the descent of this electric sphere has magnetized all the iron on board; the instruments, the tools, the weapons, move about and clash with a sharp jangle; the nails in my shoes cling tenaciously to a plate of iron set into the wood. I cannot pull my foot away!

At last, I tear it away with a violent effort just when the ball was about to seize it in its gyration and drag me along with it. . . .

Ah! what glaring light! the sphere bursts! we are covered with tongues of fire!

Then all the light goes out. I had the time to see my uncle stretched out on the raft. Hans still at the helm and "spitting fire" under the impact of the electricity that penetrates him.

Where are we going? Where are we going?

....

Tuesday, August 25. —I come out of a long spell of unconsciousness. The thunderstorm continues; the lightning flashes tear loose like a brood of snakes released in the atmosphere.

Are we still on the sea? Yes, we are driven at incalculable speed. We have passed under England, under the channel, under France, under the whole of Europe perhaps!

....

A new noise can be heard! Obviously waves breaking on rocks! . . . But then . . . .

....

XXXVI

HERE ENDS WHAT I have called my "ship log," happily saved from the wreckage. I resume my narrative as before.

What happened when the raft was dashed on the reefs of the shore I cannot tell. I felt myself being hurled into the waves, and if I escaped from death, if my body was not torn on the sharp rocks, it was because Hans' powerful arm pulled me back from the abyss.

The courageous Icelander carried me out of reach of the waves to a burning sand where I found myself side by side with my uncle.

Then he returned to the rocks, against which the furious waves were beating, to save a few pieces from the shipwreck. I was unable to speak; I was shattered by emotion and fatigue; it took me a long hour to recover.

Meanwhile, a deluge of rain was still falling, but with the increased intensity that precedes the end of a thunderstorm. A few overhanging rocks afforded us shelter from the torrents falling from the sky. Hans prepared some food that I could not touch, and each of us, exhausted by three sleepless nights, fell into a painful sleep.

The next day the weather was splendid. The sky and the ocean had calmed down in perfect synchrony. Any trace of the tempest had disappeared. The professor's joyful words greeted my awakening. His good cheer was terrible.

"Well, my boy," he exclaimed, "have you slept well?"

Would not one have thought that we were still in the house on the Königstrasse, that I was coming down peacefully for breakfast, that I was to be married to poor Graüben the very same day?

Alas! if the tempest had only driven the raft to the east, we would have passed under Germany, under my beloved city of Hamburg, under the very street where all that I loved in the world dwelled. Then just under forty leagues would have separated us! But they were forty vertical leagues of granite wall, and in reality we were a thousand leagues apart!

All these painful reflections rapidly crossed my mind before I answered my uncle's question.

"Well, now," he repeated, "won't you tell me whether you slept well?"

"Very well," I said. "I still feel shattered, but it'll soon turn to nothing."

"Absolutely nothing, a bit of fatigue, that's all."

"But you seem very cheerful this morning, Uncle."

"Delighted, my boy, delighted! We've arrived!"

"At the goal of our expedition?"

"No, but at the end of that unending ocean. Now we'll travel by land again, and really go down into the bowels of the globe."

"Uncle, allow me to ask you a question."

"Of course, Axel."

"How do we return?"

"Return? Ah! You think about returning before we've arrived."

"No, I only want to know how we'll do it."

"In the simplest way in the world. Once we've reached the center of the globe, we'll either find a new route to go back to the surface, or we'll just return the way we came like ordinary folks. I'd like to think that it won't be closed off behind us."

"But then we'll have to repair the raft."

"Of course."

"As for food supplies, do we have enough left to accomplish all these great things?"

"Yes, certainly. Hans is a skillful fellow, and I'm sure that he's saved a large part of our cargo. Let's go and make sure, at any rate."

We left this grotto which was open to every wind. I cherished a hope that was a fear as well; it seemed impossible to me that the terrible wreckage of the raft would not have destroyed everything on board. I was wrong. When I arrived on the shore, I found Hans in the midst of a multitude of items, all arranged in order. My uncle shook hands with him in an expression of deep gratitude. This man, with a superhuman devotion that perhaps had no equal, had worked while we were sleeping and had saved the most precious items at the risk of his life.

It's not that we had not suffered appreciable losses; our firearms, for instance; but we could do without them. Our stock of powder had remained intact after having almost blown us up during the tempest.

"Well," exclaimed the professor, "since we have no guns we won't have to bother hunting."

"All right; but the instruments?"

"Here's the manometer, the most useful of them all, for which I'd have exchanged all the others! With this I can calculate the depth so as to know when we've reached the center. Without it we risk going beyond it and re-emerging at the antipodes!"

This cheerfulness was ferocious.

"But the compass?" I asked.

"Here it is, on this rock, in perfect condition, as well as the thermometers and the chronometer. Ah! The hunter is an invaluable man!"

There was no denying it. As far as instruments, nothing was missing. As for tools and devices, I saw ladders, ropes, picks, pickaxes, etc. lying strewn about in the sand.

Still there was the question of food supplies to investigate.

"And the food?" I said.

The boxes that contained them were lined up on the gravel, perfectly preserved; for the most part the sea had spared them, and what with biscuits, salted meat, gin and dried fish, we still had a four-month food supply.

"Four months!" exclaimed the professor. "We have time to go and return, and with what's left I'll give a grand dinner for all my colleagues at the Johanneum!"

I should have been used to my uncle's temperament for a long time, and yet he never ceased to amaze me.

"Now," he said, "we'll replenish our supply of fresh water with the rain that the storm has left in all these granite basins; that way we'll have no reason to fear being overcome by thirst. As for the raft, I'll recommend to Hans to do his best to repair it, although I don't expect it'll be of any further use to us!"

"How so?" I exclaimed.

"An idea of my own, my boy. I don't think we'll go out where we came in."

I looked at the professor with a certain mistrust. I wondered whether he had not gone mad. And yet he would turn out to be right.

"Let's go and have breakfast," he resumed.

I followed him to an elevated promontory after he had given his instructions to the hunter. Dried meat, biscuits, and tea made us an excellent meal there, one of the best, I'll admit, that I have ever had in my life. Hunger, fresh air, calm weather after the trouble, all contributed to give me an appetite.

During breakfast, I asked my uncle where we were now.

"That," I said, "seems to me difficult to calculate."

"Difficult to calculate exactly, yes," he replied; "impossible, actually, since during these three days of tempest I've not been able to keep track of the speed or direction of the raft; but we can still make an approximate estimate."

"In fact, we made the last observation on the island with the geyser . . ."

"On Axel Island, my boy. Don't reject the honor of having given your name to the first island ever discovered in the interior of the earth."

"All right. On Axel Island, we had covered two hundred and seventy leagues of ocean, and we were six hundred leagues away from Iceland."

"Good! Let's start from that point, then, and count four days of storm, during which our speed could not have been less than eighty leagues per twenty-four hours."

"That's right. So that would be three hundred leagues in addition."

"Yes, and so the Lidenbrock Sea would be about six hundred leagues from shore to shore! Do you realize, Axel, that it competes in size with the Mediterranean?"

"Yes, especially if we've not crossed all of it!"

"Which is quite possible!"

"And curiously," I added, "if our calculations are accurate, we now have the Mediterranean right above our heads."

"Really!"

"Really, since we are nine hundred leagues away from Reykjavik!"

"That's a nice long way, my boy; but whether we're under the Mediterranean rather than under Turkey or the Atlantic, depends on whether our direction hasn't changed."

"No, the wind seemed steady; so I think this shore should be south-east of Port Graüben."

"Well, it's easy to make sure of that by consulting the compass. Let's go and see what it says!"

The professor went toward the rock where Hans had put the

instruments. He was cheerful, lively, he rubbed his hands, he posed! A real young man! I followed him, rather curious to know if I was not mistaken in my estimate.

When we reached the rock, my uncle took the compass, placed it horizontally and observed the needle, which after a few oscillations stopped in a fixed position due to the magnetic attraction.

My uncle looked, and rubbed his eyes, and looked again. Finally he turned to me, thunderstruck.

"What's the matter?" I asked.

He motioned to me to look at the instrument. An exclamation of surprise burst from me. The tip of the needle indicated north where we assumed the south to be! It pointed to the shore instead of the open sea!

I shook the compass, I examined it; it was in perfect condition. No matter in what position we placed the needle, it obstinately returned to this unexpected direction.

Therefore, there could be no doubt: during the storm, the wind had changed without our noticing, and had taken our raft back to the shore that my uncle thought he had left behind.

XXXVII

It is impossible to describe the succession of emotions that shook Professor Lidenbrock, amazement, incredulity, and finally rage. Never had I seen a man so disoriented at first, and then so furious. The exhaustion of our journey across the ocean, the dangers we had incurred, all that had to be started over again! We had gone backwards instead of forwards!

But my uncle quickly regained control of himself.

"Ah! Fate plays these tricks on me!" he exclaimed. "The elements conspire against me! Air, fire and water join their efforts to oppose my journey! Well then! They'll find out what my will power is made of. I will not yield, I will not take a single step backwards, and we'll see whether man or nature wins out!"

Standing on the rock, enraged, threatening, Otto Lidenbrock seemed to challenge the gods like the fierce Ajax.* But I thought it appropriate to intervene and restrain this irrational energy.

"Listen to me," I said to him in a firm voice. "There's a limit to ambition down here; we can't struggle against the impossible. We're ill-equipped for another sea voyage; one can't travel five hundred leagues on a paltry assemblage of wood beams, with a blanket for a sail, a stick for a mast, and the winds unleashed against us. We cannot steer, we're a plaything for the storms, and it's madness to attempt this impossible crossing for a second time!"

I was able to unfold this series of irrefutable reasons for ten minutes without being interrupted, but only because of the inattention of the professor, who did not hear a word of my arguments.

"To the raft!" he shouted.

That was his reply. It was no use begging him or flying into a rage, I was up against a will harder than granite.

Hans was finishing up the repairs of the raft at that moment. One would have thought that this strange being guessed my uncle's plans. He had reinforced the vessel with a few pieces of

---

*One of the protagonists of the Trojan War; as described in Homer's *Iliad*. Ajax was second only to Achilles himself. But when a prize for courage, Achilles' armor, was given to Odysseus rather than to him, his pride led him to treachery and suicide.

surturbrand. He had already hoisted a sail in whose folds the wind was playing.

The professor said a few words to the guide, and immediately he put everything on board and arranged everything for our departure. The air was rather clear, and the north-west wind blew steadily.

What could I do? Stand alone against the two of them? Impossible. If only Hans had taken my side. But no! The Icelander seemed to have given up any will of his own and to have made a vow of self-denial. I could not get anything out of a servant so beholden to his master. I had to go along.

I was therefore about to take my usual place on the raft when my uncle stopped me with his hand.

"We won't leave until tomorrow," he said.

I made the gesture of a man who is resigned to anything.

"I must not neglect anything," he resumed; "and since fate has driven me to this part of the coast, I won't leave it until I've explored it."

To understand this remark, one must know that we had come back to the north shore, but not to the exact point of our first departure. Port Graüben must have been further to the west. Therefore, nothing more reasonable than to explore carefully the surroundings of this new landing spot.

"Let's go on discovery!" I said.

And leaving Hans to his activities, we started off together. The space between the water and the foot of the cliffs was considerable. It took us half an hour to get to the wall of rock. Our feet crushed innumerable shells of all shapes and sizes in which the animals of the earliest ages had lived. I also saw enormous turtle shells that were more than fifteen feet in diameter. They had belonged to those gigantic glyptodonts of the Pliocene period,* of which the modern turtle is but a small reduction. The ground was in addition strewn with a lot of stone fragments, shingles of a sort that had been rounded by the waves and arranged in successive lines. This led me to the remark that at one time the sea must have covered this ground.

---

*Extinct animal that resembled an armadillo but was the size of a cow. The Pliocene epoch (5–1.8 million years ago) is the most recent part of the Tertiary period (65 to 1.8 million years ago).

On the scattered rocks, now out of their reach, the waves had left manifest traces of their passage.

This might up to a point explain the existence of this ocean forty leagues beneath the surface of the globe. But in my opinion this liquid mass had to be gradually disappearing into the bowels of the earth, and it obviously had its origin in the waters of the ocean overhead, which had made their way here through some fissure. Yet it had to be conceded that this fissure was now stopped up, because this entire cavern, or better, this immense reservoir had filled up in a relatively short time. Maybe the water, struggling against the subterranean fire, had even partly evaporated. That would explain the clouds suspended over our heads and the discharge of the electricity that gave rise to tempests in the interior of the earth.

This theory of the phenomena we had witnessed seemed satisfactory to me; for however great the wonders of nature may be, they can always be explained by physical causes.

We were therefore walking on a kind of sedimentary terrain, deposited by water like all the soils of that period, of which there are so many across the globe. The professor examined every fissure in the rock carefully. Wherever an opening showed, it was important to him to probe its depth.*

We had walked along the shores of the Lidenbrock Sea for a mile when soil suddenly changed in appearance. It seemed turned upside down, convulsed by a violent upheaval of the lower strata. In many places depressions or elevations testified to a powerful displacement of the earth's substance.

We were moving with difficulty across these cracks of granite mixed with flint, quartz, and alluvial deposits, when a field, more than a field, a plain of bones appeared before our eyes. One would have thought it was an immense graveyard, where the generations of twenty centuries mingled their eternal dust. Tall mounds of residue stretched away into the distance. They undulated to the limits of the horizon and vanished into a hazy mist. Here, in perhaps three square miles, the complete history of animal life was piled up, a history that has

---

*Beginning of the text Verne added in the edition of 1867 to reflect discoveries about Stone Age humans that the French archaeologist Jacques Boucher de Perthes made; see the introduction, p. xxi.

hardly yet been written in the too recent strata of the inhabited world.

But an impatient curiosity drove us on. With a dry noise, our feet crushed the remains of these prehistoric animals, fossils over whose rare and interesting residues the museums of great cities fight. A thousand Cuviers would not have been enough to reconstruct the skeletons of the organic beings lying in this magnificent boneyard.

I was stunned. My uncle had lifted his long arms to the massive vault that served us as sky. His mouth gaping wide, his eyes flashing behind the glass of his spectacles, his head moving up and down, from left to right, his whole posture indicated infinite amazement. He stood facing an invaluable collection of leptotheria, mericotheria, lophiodons, anoplotheria, megatheria, mastodons, protopithecae, pterodactyls, of all the prehistoric monsters, piled up for his personal satisfaction. Imagine an enthusiastic bibliophile suddenly transported to the famous library of Alexandria that was burned by Omar, and which by a miracle had been reborn from its ashes! That was my uncle, Professor Lidenbrock.

But it was a very different amazement when, running across this organic dust, he seized a bare skull and shouted with a trembling voice:

"Axel! Axel! a human head!"

"A human head!" I exclaimed, no less astonished.

"Yes, nephew. Ah! Mr. Milne-Edwards! Ah! Mr. de Quatrefages,* I wish you were standing here where I, Otto Lidenbrock, am standing!"

---

*Jean-Louis-Armand de Quatrefages de Bréau (1810–1892), a friend of Milne-Edwards (see endnote 1) and also a noted zoologist and anthropologist.

The complete history of animal life was piled up.

XXXVIII

To UNDERSTAND MY UNCLE's invocation of these illustrious French scholars, one must know that an event of great importance for paleontology had occurred some time before our departure.

On March 28, 1863, some excavators working under the direction of Mr. Boucher de Perthes, in the stone quarries of Moulin Quignon, near Abbeville, in the department of the Somme in France, found a human jawbone fourteen feet beneath the surface. It was the first fossil of its kind that had ever been unearthed. Nearby stone hatchets and flint arrow-heads were found, stained and coated with a uniform patina by the ages.[8]

The repercussions of this discovery were great, not in France alone, but in England and in Germany. Several scholars of the French Institute, among others Messrs. Milne-Edwards and de Quatrefages, took the affair very seriously, proved the irrefutable authenticity of the bone in question, and became the most ardent advocates in this 'trial of the jawbone,' as it was called in English.

Geologists of the United Kingdom who considered the fact as certain—Messrs. Falconer, Busk, Carpenter,[9] and others—were soon joined by scholars from Germany, and among them, in the first rank, the most energetic, the most enthusiastic, was my uncle Lidenbrock.

The authenticity of a human fossil from the Quaternary epoch* therefore seemed to be irrefutably proven and admitted.

This theory, to be sure, encountered a most obstinate opponent in Mr. Élie de Beaumont.† This scholar, a great authority, maintained that the soil of Moulin Quignon did not belong to the "diluvium"‡ but to a more recent layer and, agreeing with Cuvier, he refused to admit that the human species had been contemporary

---

*The shortest and most recent geological period, which followed the Tertiary and began 1.8 million years ago.
†Prominent French geologist (1798–1874), one of the principal proponents of catastrophism—the theory that the Earth was shaped not by continuous development but by cataclysmic upheavals—and maker of a geological map of France.
‡Geological deposits formed by sudden floods of water, in contrast with alluvial deposits, which are built up through slower, more continuous water flows.

with the animals of the Quaternary epoch. My uncle Lidenbrock, in agreement with the great majority of geologists, had stood his ground, disputed, and argued, until Mr. Élie de Beaumont had remained almost alone on his side.

We knew all the details of this affair, but we were not aware that since our departure the question had made further progress. Other identical jawbones, though they belonged to individuals of various types and different nations, were found in the loose grey soil of certain caves in France, Switzerland, and Belgium, along with weapons, utensils, tools, bones of children, adolescents, adults and old people. The existence of Quaternary man was therefore receiving more confirmation every day.

And that was not all. New remains exhumed from Tertiary Pliocene soil had allowed even bolder geologists to attribute an even greater age to the human race. These remains, to be sure, were not human bones, but products of his industry that carried the mark of human work, such as shin and thigh bones of fossil animals with regular grooves, sculpted as it were.

Thus, with one leap, man moved back on the time scale by many centuries. He preceded the mastodon; he was a contemporary of *elephas meridionalis*;* he lived a hundred thousand years ago, since that is the date that the most famous geologists give for the formation of Pliocene soil.

Such, then, was the state of paleontological science, and what we knew of it was enough to explain our attitude toward this boneyard on the Lidenbrock Sea. It is therefore easy to understand my uncle's amazement and joy when, twenty yards further on, he found himself in the presence of, one might say face to face with, a specimen of Quaternary man.

It was a perfectly recognizable human body. Had some special kind of soil, like that of the St. Michel cemetery in Bordeaux, preserved it like this over the centuries? I do not know. But this corpse, with its tight, parchment-like skin, its limbs still soft—at least on sight—intact teeth, abundant hair, frighteningly long finger and toe

---

*Mammoth that lived in Western Europe at the end of the Pliocene epoch, some 5 million years ago.

nails, presented itself to our eyes just as it was when it had been alive.

I was speechless when faced with this apparition of another age. My uncle, usually a talkative and impetuous speaker, also kept silent. We had lifted the body. We had raised it up. It looked at us with its empty eye-sockets. We touched its resonant torso.

After a few moments of silence, the uncle was overcome by Professor Otto Lidenbrock again who, carried away by his temperament, forgot the circumstances of our journey, the place where we were, the enormous cave that surrounded us. No doubt he thought he was at the Johanneum, lecturing to his students, for he assumed a learned voice and addressed an imaginary audience:

"Gentlemen," he said, "I have the honor of introducing a man of the Quaternary period to you. Eminent scholars have denied his existence, others no less eminent have affirmed it. The St. Thomases of paleontology, if they were here, would touch him with their fingers, and would be forced to acknowledge their error. I am quite aware that science has to be on its guard with discoveries of this kind. I know how Barnum and other charlatans of the same ilk have exploited fossil men.* I know the story of Ajax' kneecap, the alleged body of Orestes found by the Spartans, and of the ten-cubit tall body of Asterius mentioned by Pausanias. I've read the reports on the skeleton of Trapani, discovered in the fourteenth century, which was at the time identified as that of Polyphemus, and the history of the giant unearthed in the sixteenth century near Palermo. You know as well as I do, gentlemen, the analysis of large bones carried out at Lucerne in 1577, which the famous Dr. Felix Plater declared to be those of a nineteen-foot tall giant. I have devoured the treatises of Cassanion, and all those dissertations, pamphlets, speeches, and rejoinders published respecting the skeleton of Teutobochus, king of the Cimbrians and invader of Gaul, dug out of a sandpit in the Dauphiné in 1613! In the eighteenth century I would have fought with Pierre Campet against the pre-adamites of Scheuchzer.[10] In my hands I have a text called *Gigan*—"

---

*American showman Phineas Taylor Barnum (1810–1891) founded a museum famous for its freakish and abnormal specimens; he participated in the 1869 hoax surrounding "Cardiff Man," an alleged fossil man of gigantic height. Barnum created a fake reproduction of the already fake original fossil to exhibit in his museum.

Here my uncle's natural weakness re-emerged, that of being unable to pronounce difficult words in public.

"The text called *Gigan*—"

He could go no further.

"Giganteo—"

Impossible! The unfortunate word would not come out!

They would have had a good laugh at the Johanneum!

"*Gigantosteology*," the professor finally managed to say, between two swearwords.

Then he continued with renewed energy and spirits:

"Yes, gentlemen, I know all these things! I also know that Cuvier and Blumenbach have identified these bones as simple bones of mammoths and other animals of the Quaternary period. But in this case doubt would be an insult to science! The corpse is here! You can see it, touch it. It's not a skeleton, it's an intact body, preserved for a purely anthropological purpose!"

I took care not to contradict this assertion.

"If I could wash it in a solution of sulphuric acid," pursued my uncle, "I would be able to remove all the bits of soil and the splendid shells that are embedded in it. But I do not have this precious solvent at hand. Yet, such as it is, the body will tell us its own story."

Here the professor took the fossil corpse and handled it with the skill of a showman.

"You see," he resumed, "that it's not even six feet tall, and we are far removed from the alleged giants. As for the race to which it belongs, it is obviously Caucasian. It's the white race, our own! The skull of this fossil is a regular oval, with no prominent cheekbones, no projecting jaws. It shows no sign of the prognathism that diminishes the facial angle.* Measure that angle, it's nearly ninety degrees. But I'll go even further in my deductions, and I dare say that this human specimen belongs to the Japhetic family, which extends from India to the boundaries of western Europe. Don't smile, gentlemen."

---

*The facial angle is shaped by two planes, one more or less vertical that touches the brow and the front teeth, the other one horizontal, going through the opening of the ear canal to the lower nasal cavity. In anthropological language, *prognathism* is defined as the projection of the jaw-bone that modifies the facial angle (author's note).

Nobody was smiling, but the professor was used to seeing faces spread in smiles during his learned lectures.

"Yes," he pursued with new energy, "this is a fossil man, a contemporary of the mastodons whose bones fill this amphitheatre. But if you ask me how he came here, how the layers in which he was buried slid into this enormous cavern in the earth, I will not allow myself to answer. No doubt in the Quaternary period considerable upheavals still took place in the earth's crust. The gradual cooling of the globe created cracks, fissures and faults, into which some of the upper soil probably fell. I want to make no assertions, but after all the man is here, surrounded by the work of his hands, by the hatchets and the flint arrow-heads that made the Stone Age possible, and unless he came here as a tourist and a pioneer of science like myself, I cannot doubt the authenticity of his ancient origin."

The professor fell silent, and I broke into unanimous applause. In any case my uncle was right, and more learned men than his nephew would have had trouble arguing with him.

Another clue. This fossilized body was not the only one in the immense boneyard. We found other corpses at every step we took in this dust, and my uncle could choose the most wonderful of these specimens to convince the skeptics.

Indeed it was an amazing spectacle, these generations of men and animals commingled in this cemetery. But one serious question arose that we dared not answer. Had these beings slid down to the shore of the Lidenbrock Sea through an upheaval in the ground when they were already reduced to dust? Or did they rather dwell in this underground world, under this artificial sky, living and dying like the inhabitants of the earth? Until now, only sea monsters and fishes had appeared to us alive! Did some man of the abyss still wander on this desert strand?

XXXIX

FOR ANOTHER HALF HOUR our feet trod on these layers of bones. We pushed on, driven by a burning curiosity. What other marvels, what new treasures for science did this cavern hold? My eyes were prepared for any surprise, my imagination for any amazement.

The shore had long disappeared behind the hills of bones. The rash professor, unconcerned about losing his way, took me along. We advanced in silence, bathed in electric waves. Due to some phenomenon that I cannot explain, and due to its by then complete diffusion, the light illuminated all the sides of an object equally. Its source no longer resided at a particular point in space and cast no shadows. One could have believed that it was midday in the middle of the summer, in the equatorial regions under the vertical rays of the sun. All steam had disappeared.

The rocks, the distant mountains, a few indistinct clumps of distant forests came to look strange in this equal distribution of the light waves. We resembled Hoffmann's fantastic character who has lost his shadow.[11]

After a mile's walk the edge of an immense forest appeared, but no longer one of the mushroom forests near Port Graüben.

It was the vegetation of the Tertiary period in all its magnificence. Tall palm trees of species that have now disappeared, superb palmaceae, pines, yews, cypress, and thujas represented the conifer family, and were linked to each other through a network of inextricable lianas. A lush carpet of moss and hepaticas covered the soil. Some creeks murmured in the shade, which did not deserve the name since the trees cast no shadow. On their banks grew tree-ferns similar to those grown in hothouses on the inhabited earth. Only color was missing from all those trees, shrubs, and plants that were deprived of the life-giving heat of the sun. Everything blended together in a uniform brownish and faded-looking hue. The leaves showed no green, and even the flowers, which were so numerous in the Tertiary period in which they first originated, now had no color or scent and looked under the impact of the atmosphere as if they were made out of faded paper.

My uncle Lidenbrock ventured into this gigantic thicket. I followed him, not without a certain fear. Since nature had here provided plant food, why would there not also be fearsome mammals? In the large clearings left by fallen and decayed trees, I saw leguminous plants, acerineae, rubiceae and many other edible shrubs that are liked by ruminants of all periods. Then trees from vastly different regions on the surface of the globe appeared, blended and mixed in together: the oak grew next to the palm tree, the Australian eucalyptus leaned against the Norwegian fir, the Northern birch-tree interlaced its branches with those of the New Zealand kauri. It was enough to drive the most ingenious classifiers of terrestrial botany mad.

Suddenly I stopped. With my hand I held my uncle back.

The diffuse light allowed us to perceive the most minute objects in the depth of the thicket. I thought I had seen . . . No! really, with my own eyes, I did see vast shapes moving under the trees! Indeed, these were gigantic animals, a whole herd of mastodons, not fossil ones, but live ones, similar to those whose remains were found in the swamps of Ohio in 1801! I saw these large elephants whose trunks were writhing under the trees like a legion of snakes. I heard the noise of their long tusks whose ivory bore into the old tree trunks. The branches cracked, and the leaves, torn off in considerable quantities, were swept into the huge maws of these monsters.

So the dream in which I had seen all this prehistoric world of the Tertiary and Quaternary periods rise again finally became reality! And we were there, alone, in the bowels of the earth, at the mercy of its fierce inhabitants!

My uncle stared.

"Let's go!" he said suddenly, gripping my arm. "Onward! Onward!"

"No!" I cried. "No! We have no weapons! What would we do in the midst of this herd of giant quadrupeds? Come, Uncle, come! No human can safely challenge the rage of these monsters."

"No human being!" replied my uncle, lowering his voice. "You're wrong, Axel. Look, look down there! It seems to me I see a living being! a being similar to ourselves! a man!"

I looked, shrugging my shoulders, and resolved to push skepticism to its furthest limits. But although I was reluctant, I had to yield to the evidence.

Indeed, less than a quarter of a mile away, leaning against the trunk of an enormous kauri, a human being, the Proteus of these underground regions, a new son of Neptune,* watched over this countless herd of mastodons!

Immanis pecoris custos, immanior ipse.†

Yes! *Immanior ipse*! This was no longer the fossil being whose corpse we had raised up in the boneyard, this was a giant, able to control these monsters. He was more than twelve feet tall. His head, huge like a buffalo's, disappeared in the underbrush of his unkempt hair. It seemed like a real mane similar to that of the elephant of the first ages. In his hand he wielded an enormous branch with ease, a crook worthy of this prehistoric shepherd.

We stood immobile, stunned. But we might be seen. We had to flee.

"Come, come!" I exclaimed, pulling my uncle away, who for the first time let it happen.

A quarter of an hour later we were out of sight of this formidable enemy.

And now that I think about it calmly, now that my spirit has found peace again, now that months have gone by since this strange and supernatural encounter, what to think, what to believe? No! It is impossible! Our senses were deceived, our eyes did not see what they saw! No human being exists in that subterranean world! No generation of men dwells in those lower caverns of the globe, unconcerned about the inhabitants of its surface, without contact with them! It is crazy, profoundly crazy!

I prefer to admit the existence of some animal whose structure resembles the human structure, some ape of the early geological ages, some protopithecus, some mesopithecus, like the one discovered by Mr. Lartet in the bone deposit of Sansan!‡ But in its size, this one exceeded all the measurements known in modern paleontology.

---

*In Greek mythology the god Proteus could change his shape at will. Neptune was the god of the oceans in Roman mythology.

†The shepherd of huge herds, and huger still himself (Latin). The language plays on a passage in Virgil's *Bucolica*: "a shepherd of fine herds, and finer still himself." Victor Hugo adapted the form that Verne quotes here for his novel *Notre-Dame de Paris* (*The Hunchback of Notre Dame*).

‡Edouard Lartet (1801–1871), French paleontologist who discovered a fossil anthropoid at Sansan in 1834 that he named pliopithecus.

A human being watched over this countless
herd of mastodons!

No matter! An ape, yes, an ape, no matter how unlikely! But a man, a living man, and with him a whole generation buried in the bowels of the earth! Never!

In the meantime, we had left the clear and luminous forest, speechless with amazement, overwhelmed by a stupefaction that bordered on mindlessness. We ran in spite of ourselves. It was a real flight, similar to those terrible impulses that one is subject to in certain nightmares. Instinctively we ran back to the Lidenbrock Sea, and I do not know in what vagaries my mind would have lost itself if it had not been for a concern that brought me back to practical matters.*

Although I was certain that we were walking on soil where we had never set foot before, I often noticed rock formations whose shape reminded me of those at Port Graüben. This confirmed, in any case, the indications of the compass and our involuntary return to the north of the Lidenbrock Sea. Sometimes one could have mistaken one for the other. Brooks and waterfalls were tumbling everywhere from hundreds of projections in the rocks. I thought I recognized the layer of surturbrand, our faithful Hansbach and the cave in which I had come back to life. Then a few paces farther on, the arrangement of the cliffs, the appearance of a stream, the surprising outline of a rock threw me back in doubt.

I told my uncle about my indecision. Like myself, he hesitated. He could not find his way in this uniform scenery.

"Obviously," I said to him, "we have not landed at our point of departure again, but the storm has carried us a little lower, and if we follow the shore we'll find Port Graüben."

"In that case," replied my uncle, "it's useless to continue this exploration, and the best is to return to our raft. But Axel, aren't you mistaken?"

"It's difficult to say for sure, Uncle, because all these rocks look alike. Yet I think I recognize the promontory at whose foot Hans built our vessel. We must be close to the little port, if indeed it isn't right here," I added, examining an inlet that I thought I recognized.

"No, Axel, we would at least find our own traces, and I see nothing . . ."

---

*End of the text that Verne added in the 1867 edition.

"But I do," I exclaimed, rushing toward an object that glittered in the sand.

"What is it?"

"This," I answered.

And I showed my uncle a rust-covered dagger which I had just picked up.

"Well!" he said, "did you bring this weapon with you?"

"Me? Not at all! But you . . ."

"No, not that I know," said the professor. "I've never had this object in my possession."

"Well, this is strange!"

"No, Axel, it's very simple. Icelanders often have weapons of this kind, and Hans, to whom this belongs, must have lost it . . ."

I shook my head. Hans had never had this dagger in his possession.

"So is this the weapon of some prehistoric warrior?" I exclaimed, "of a living man, of a contemporary of that gigantic shepherd's? But no! This is not a tool of the Stone Age! Not even of the Bronze Age! This blade is made of steel . . ."

My uncle stopped me abruptly on this path into another ramble, and told me in his cold voice:

"Calm down, Axel, and be reasonable. This dagger is a weapon of the sixteenth century, a real dagger, like the ones gentlemen carried in their belts to give the *coup de grace*. It's of Spanish origin. It belongs neither to you, nor to me, nor to the hunter, nor even to the human beings who live perhaps in the bowels of the globe!"

"What are you saying . . . ?"

"Look, it never got chipped like this by cutting men's throats; its blade is coated with a layer of rust that's neither a day, nor a year, nor a hundred years old!"

The professor was getting excited according to his habit, and was getting carried away by his imagination.

"Axel," he resumed, "we're on the way toward a great discovery! This blade has been lying on the sand for a hundred, two hundred, three hundred years, and it got chipped on the rocks of this underground ocean!"

"But it hasn't come on its own," I cried. "It hasn't twisted itself out of shape! Someone has been here before us!"

"Yes! a man."

"And who was that man?"

"A man who has engraved his name somewhere with this dagger. That man wanted once more to indicate the way to the center of the earth with his own hand. Let's search! Let's search!"

And with meticulous attention we walked along the high wall, peeping into the most minute fissures that might open out into a tunnel.

So we came to a place where the shore got narrower. The sea almost came to lap the foot of the cliffs, leaving a passage of at most a fathom. Between two boldly projecting rocks one could see the mouth of a dark tunnel.

There, on a granite slab, appeared two mysterious graven and half-eroded letters, the initials of the daring and fantastic traveler:

$$\cdot \; \dashv \; \cdot \; \natural \; \cdot$$

"A. S.!" shouted my uncle. "Arne Saknussemm! Always Arne Saknussemm!"

XL

Since the beginning of the journey, I had been amazed so many times that I would have believed myself inured to surprises and blasé about any astonishment. Yet at the sight of these two letters engraved three hundred years ago, I fell into an amazement akin to stupidity. Not only was the learned alchemist's signature readable on the rock, but I even held the stylus which had engraved it in my hands. Unless I wanted to demonstrate glaring bad faith, I could no longer doubt the existence of the traveler and the reality of his journey.

While these reflections whirled around in my head, Professor Lidenbrock indulged in a fit of eulogy for Arne Saknussemm.

"Wonderful genius!" he exclaimed, "you did not forget anything to open up the path through the terrestrial crust to other mortals, and your fellow humans can find the traces that your feet left three centuries ago at the bottom of this dark underground! You reserved the contemplation of these wonders for other eyes besides your own! Your name, engraved at every stage, leads the traveler who is bold enough to follow you straight to his destination, and at the very center of our planet, we will once again find it inscribed with your own hand. I too will inscribe my name on that last page of granite! But for ever henceforth let this promontory that you saw, next to the ocean you discovered, be known by the name of Cape Saknussemm!"

That is what I heard, more or less, and I could not resist the enthusiasm that these words exuded. An inner fire flamed up again in my breast! I forgot everything, the dangers of the journey, and the perils of the return. What another had done I also wanted to do, and nothing human seemed impossible to me!

"Onward! Onward!" I shouted.

I was already rushing toward the dark tunnel when the professor stopped me, and he, the man of impulse, advised me to keep patience and calm.

"Let's first return to Hans," he said, "and let's bring the raft to this spot."

I obeyed this order, not without displeasure, and slid rapidly among the rocks on the shore.

"You know, Uncle," I said during the walk, "that circumstances have served us extraordinarily well so far?"

"Ah! You think so, Axel?"

"No doubt; even the tempest has put us back on the right path. Blessed be that storm! It has brought us back to this coast from which good weather would have removed us. Suppose for a moment that we had touched the southern shore of the Lidenbrock Sea with our prow (the prow of a raft!), what would have become of us? We wouldn't have seen the name Saknussemm, and we would now be abandoned on some beach without exit."

"Yes, Axel, there is something providential in the fact that while we were sailing south, we were precisely going back north and toward Cape Saknussemm. I must say that this is more than astonishing, and it's a fact whose explanation eludes me."

"Ah, no matter! The point is not to explain facts, but to benefit from them!"

"Undoubtedly, my boy, but . . ."

"But we'll resume the northern route, pass under the northern regions of Europe, Sweden, Siberia, who knows! instead of burrowing under the deserts of Africa or the waves of the ocean, and that's all I want to know!"

"Yes, Axel, you're right, and it's all for the best, since we're leaving behind that horizontal ocean which leads nowhere. Now we'll go down, down again, and always down! Do you know there are only 1,500 leagues left to the center of the globe?"

"Bah!" I shouted. "That's not even worth talking about! Let's go! Let's go!"

This crazy talk was still going on when we rejoined the hunter. Everything was made ready for an instant departure. Every package was put on board. We took our places on the raft, and with our sail hoisted, Hans steered us along the coast to Cape Saknussemm.

The wind was not well-suited for a kind of vessel that was unable to maneuver against it. So in many places we were forced to push ahead with the iron-tipped sticks. Often the rocks, lying just beneath the surface, forced us to take rather long detours. At last, after three hours' sailing, that is to say at about six in the evening, we reached a place that was suitable for landing.

I jumped ashore, followed by my uncle and the Icelander. This passage had not calmed me down. On the contrary. I even proposed to burn 'our ships' so as to cut off any retreat. But my uncle opposed it. I thought him strangely lukewarm.

"At least," I said, "let's take off without wasting a minute."

"Yes, my boy," he replied; "but first let's examine this new tunnel, to see if we should prepare our ladders."

My uncle turned on his Ruhmkorff device; the raft, moored to the shore, was left behind; at any rate, the mouth of the tunnel was less than twenty steps away, and our little party, with myself at the head, walked toward it without delay.

The aperture, more or less round, was about five feet in diameter; the dark tunnel was cut into the live rock and coated with the eruptive matter that had formerly passed through it; the interior was level with the ground outside, so that we were able to enter without any difficulty.

We followed an almost horizontal plane, when only six paces in, our progress was interrupted by an enormous block across our way.

"Damned rock!" I shouted in a rage when I suddenly saw myself stopped by an insurmountable obstacle.

We searched right and left, up and down, but there was no passage, no bifurcation. I felt deeply disappointed, and I did not want to admit the reality of the obstacle. I bent down. I looked underneath the block. No opening. Above. Same granite barrier. Hans shone his lamp at every part of the rock, but it offered no possibility for continuing. We had to give up all hope of getting past it.

I sat down on the ground; my uncle strode up and down the tunnel.

"But what about Saknussemm?" I exclaimed.

"Yes," said my uncle, "was he stopped by this gate of stone?"

"No! no!" I replied eagerly. "This piece of rock has suddenly blocked the passage after some tremor or one of those magnetic phenomena which move the earth's crust. Many years have gone by since Saknussemm's return and the fall of this block. Isn't it obvious that this tunnel was once a passageway for lava, and that the eruptive material flowed freely at that time? Look, there are recent fissures that groove this granite roof; it's made of pieces that were brought here, enormous stones, as if some giant's hand had worked on this foundation; but one day there was a more powerful push, and this block, like the keystone of a falling arch, slid down to the ground, blocking the passage completely. It's only an accidental obstruction that Saknussemm did not encounter, and if we don't overturn it, we're not worthy of reaching the center of the earth!"

That is how I spoke! The professor's soul had completely passed into me. The spirit of discovery inspired me. I forgot the past, I scorned the future. Nothing existed for me anymore at the surface of this globe into whose interior I had burrowed, neither the cities nor the fields, nor Hamburg, nor the Königstrasse, nor my poor Graüben, who must have given us up as lost forever in the bowels of the earth!

"Well!" resumed my uncle, "with our picks, with our pickaxes, let's make a way! Let's overturn the wall!"

"It's too hard for the pick," I cried.

"Well, then, the pickaxe!"

"It's too long for the pickaxe!"

"But . . . !"

"All right! Gunpowder! A mine! Let's make a mine and blow up the obstacle!"

"Gunpowder!"

"Yes, it's only a piece of rock to break apart!"

"Hans, to work!" shouted my uncle.

The Icelander returned to the raft and soon came back with a pick that he used to bore a hole for the charge. This was no easy work. We needed to make a hole large enough to hold fifty pounds of guncotton, whose explosive force is four times that of gunpowder.

My mind was in a state of tremendous overexcitement. While Hans was at work I helped my uncle eagerly in preparing a long fuse of wet powder inside a cotton tube.

"We'll make it!" I said.

"We'll make it," repeated my uncle.

By midnight our mining work was finished; the charge of gun-cotton was pushed into the hole, and the long fuse ran along the tunnel and ended outside.

A spark would now suffice to start up this formidable device.

"Tomorrow," said the professor.

I had to resign myself and wait another six long hours!

XLI

THE NEXT DAY, THURSDAY, August 27, is a famous date in our underground journey. It never comes back to my mind without terror making my heart beat faster. From that moment on, our reason, our judgment, our inventiveness no longer play any role, and we are about to become playthings of the earth's phenomena.

At six we were up. The moment approached when we would blast a passage through the granite crust with the powder.

I asked for the honor of lighting the fuse. That task accomplished, I was supposed to join my companions at the raft, which had not yet been unloaded; we would then move away in order to avoid the dangers of the explosion, whose effects might not remain confined to the interior of the rock.

The fuse would burn for ten minutes, according to our calculations, before setting fire to the powder hole. So I had enough time to get back to the raft.

I got ready to fulfill my task, not without some anxiety.

After a hasty meal, my uncle and the hunter embarked while I remained on shore. I was equipped with a lighted lantern that I would use to set fire to the fuse.

"Go, my boy," my uncle told me, "and come back immediately to join us."

"Don't worry," I replied. "I'll not entertain myself along the way."

I immediately walked toward the mouth of the tunnel. I opened my lantern, and I took hold of the end of the fuse.

The Professor had the chronometer in his hand.

"Are you ready?" he called to me.

"I'm ready."

"Well then! Fire, my boy!"

I rapidly plunged the fuse into the lantern, which crackled on contact, and returned running to the shore.

"Come on board quickly," said my uncle, "and let's push off."

Hans pushed us back into the ocean with a powerful thrust. The raft shot twenty fathoms out to sea.

It was a thrilling moment. The professor watched the hand of the chronometer.

"Five more minutes!" he said. "Four! Three!"

My pulse beat half-seconds.

"Two! One! . . . Crumble, granite mountains!"

What happened then? I think I did not hear the noise of the explosion. But the shape of the rocks suddenly changed under my eyes; they opened up like a curtain. I saw a bottomless pit open up on the shore. The ocean, overcome by vertigo, turned into nothing but a huge wave on whose back the raft was lifted up vertically.

We all three fell down. In less than a second, the light turned into unfathomable darkness. Then I felt solid support give way, not under my feet, but under the raft. I thought it was sinking. But it was not so. I would have liked to speak to my uncle, but the roaring of the waves would have prevented him from hearing me.

In spite of darkness, noise, surprise, and anxiety, I understood what had happened.

Beyond the rock that had exploded, there was an abyss. The explosion had triggered a kind of earthquake in this ground riven by fissures, the abyss had opened up, and the ocean turned current was taking us down into it.

I gave myself up for lost.

An hour, two hours passed, what do I know! We gripped each other's elbows, clutched each other's hands so as not to be thrown off the raft. Extremely violent shocks occurred whenever it hit against the wall. Yet these shocks were rare, from which I concluded that the tunnel was widening considerably. It was no doubt the path that Saknussemm had taken; but instead of taking it by ourselves, we had through our carelessness brought a whole ocean along with us.

These ideas, it will be understood, came to my mind in a vague and obscure form. I had difficulty putting them together during this headlong race that resembled a fall. Judging by the air that was lashing my face, its speed was faster than an express train. Lighting a torch in these conditions was therefore impossible, and our last electric device had broken at the moment of the explosion.

I was therefore very surprised when I suddenly saw a light shining near me. It lit up Hans' calm face. The skillful hunter had managed to light the lantern, and even though it flickered and seemed about to go out, it threw some light into the awful darkness.

The tunnel was large. I was right in that. The dim light did not allow us to see both its walls at once. The slope of the water that was carrying us along exceeded that of the most difficult rapids in America. Its surface seemed made up of a sheaf of arrows shot with extreme force. I cannot convey my impression with a better comparison. The raft, sometimes seized by an eddy, spun round as it moved along. When it approached the walls of the tunnel I shone the light of the lantern on them, and I could judge its speed by seeing rock projections turn into continuous shapes, so that we seemed caught in a net of moving lines. I estimated that our speed was close to thirty leagues an hour.

My uncle and I looked at each other with frantic eyes, clinging to the stump of the mast which had snapped at the moment of the catastrophe. We turned our backs to the air current so as not to be choked by the speed of a movement that no human power could check.

In the meantime, hours passed. Our situation did not change, but an incident complicated matters.

When I tried to put our cargo into somewhat better order, I found that the greater part of the items onboard had disappeared at the moment of the explosion, when the sea broke in on us so violently! I wanted to know exactly what to count on as far as resources, and with the lantern in my hand I began my investigation. Of our instruments nothing was left except the compass and the chronometer. Our stock of ropes and ladders was reduced to a bit of cord coiled around the stump of the mast. No pickaxe, no pick, no hammer and, irreversible misfortune, we had only one day's food supplies left!

I searched every nook and cranny on the raft, the smallest spaces between the wood beams, the joints and the planks. Nothing! Our food supplies were reduced to one bit of dried meat and a few biscuits.

I stared stupidly! I did not want to understand! And yet, why worry about this danger? Even if we had had food supplies for months, for years, how could we get out of the depths where the irresistible torrent was taking us? Why fear the tortures of hunger when death threatened us in so many other forms? Would there be enough time to die of starvation?

Nevertheless, due to an inexplicable vagary of the imagination, I forgot the immediate peril next to the dangers of the future, which appeared to me in all their horror. At any rate, perhaps we would be able to escape from the fury of the torrent and return to the surface of the globe. How? I do not know. Where? No matter. One chance in a thousand is still a chance, while death from starvation left us no hope, however remote.

It occurred to me that I should tell my uncle everything, show him the straits to which we were reduced, and calculate exactly how much time we had left to live. But I had the courage to keep silent. I wanted to leave him all his calm.

At that moment the light from our lantern became dimmer and dimmer, and then went out completely. The wick had burnt itself out. The darkness became absolute again. We could no longer hope to chase away the impenetrable blackness. We still had one torch left, but we could not have kept it lighted. So, like a child, I closed my eyes firmly so as not to see all that darkness.

After a rather long interval of time, our speed increased. I noticed it by the sensation of the air on my face. The slope of the water torrent became extremely steep. I really believe we were no longer gliding along. We were falling. I had the inner impression of an almost vertical fall. My uncle's and Hans' hands, clutching my arms, held on to me forcefully.

Suddenly, after an interval of time I could not estimate, I felt something like a shock; the raft had not struck against any hard object, but had suddenly stopped in its fall. An enormous spout of water, an immense liquid column crashed down on us. I was choking. I was drowning . . .

But this sudden flood did not last. In a few seconds I found myself in the open air again, which I inhaled with all the force of my lungs. My uncle and Hans squeezed my arm to the point of almost breaking it, and the raft was still carrying all three of us.

XLII

I THINK IT MUST then have been about ten at night. The first of my senses which began to function again after this last bout was that of hearing. Almost immediately I heard, and it was a genuine act of hearing, I heard silence fall in the tunnel after the roars had filled my ears for long hours. At last these words of my uncle's reached me like a murmur:

"We're going up!"

"What do you mean?" I exclaimed.

"Yes, we're going up! Up!"

I stretched out my arm; I touched the wall, and drew back my hand bleeding. We were going up with extreme rapidity.

"The torch! The torch!" shouted the professor.

Hans managed to light it, not without difficulty, and the flame, staying upright in spite of the rising movement, threw enough light to illuminate the scene.

"Just as I thought," said my uncle. "We are in a narrow tunnel, less than four fathoms in diameter. The water has reached the bottom of the chasm, rises back up to its level and carries us with it."

"Where to?"

"I don't know, but we must be ready for anything. We're rising at a speed that I'd estimate at two fathoms per second, that's 120 fathoms per minute or more than three and a half leagues an hour. At that rate, one makes progress."

"Yes, if nothing stops us, if this well has an exit! But what if it's blocked, what if the air is compressed through the pressure of this water column, what if we're crushed!"

"Axel," replied the professor with great calm, "our situation is almost desperate, but there are some chances of escape, and it's these that I'm considering. If we might perish at any moment, we might also be saved at any moment. So let's be ready to take advantage of the most minute circumstance."

"But what should we do?"

"Recover our strength by eating."

At these words, I looked at my uncle with a frantic eye. What I had been unwilling to reveal had to be said at last:

"Eat?" I repeated.

"Yes, without delay."

The professor added a few words in Danish. Hans shook his head.

"What!" exclaimed my uncle. "Our food supplies are lost?"

"Yes, this is all the food we have left! One piece of dried meat for the three of us!"

My uncle looked at me without wanting to grasp my words.

"Well then!" I said, "do you still think we might be saved?"

My question received no answer.

An hour passed. I began to feel the pangs of a violent hunger. My companions were also suffering, and none of us dared touch this miserable rest of food.

In the meantime, we were still rising at extreme speed. Sometimes the air cut our breath short, like aeronauts who ascend too rapidly. But while they feel the cold in proportion to their rise into the atmospheric strata, we were subject to the diametrically opposite effect. The heat was increasing at a disturbing rate and certainly must have reached 40°C at that moment.

What did that kind of change mean? So far, the facts had confirmed Davy's and Lidenbrock's theories; so far the special conditions of non-conducting rocks, electricity and magnetism had modified the general laws of nature and given us a moderate temperature, for the theory of fire at the core remained in my view the only true and explainable one. Were we going back to an environment where these phenomena applied in all their rigor, and where the heat was completely melting rocks down? I feared so and said to the professor:

"If we're neither drowned nor shattered to pieces, nor starved to death, there's still a chance that we might be burned alive."

He confined himself to shrugging his shoulders and returned to his reflections.

Another hour passed and, except a slight increase in temperature, no incident changed the situation.

"Let's see," he said, "we must make a decision."

"Make a decision?" I replied.

"Yes. We must recover our forces. If we try to prolong our existence by a few hours by rationing this rest of food, we'll be weak until the end."

"Yes, the end, which is not far off."

"Well then! If a chance of escape appears, if a moment of action is necessary, where are we going to find the strength to act if we allow ourselves to be weakened by starvation?"

"Ah, Uncle, when this piece of meat has been eaten, what do we have left?"

"Nothing, Axel, nothing. But will it do you any more good to devour it with your eyes? Your reasoning is that of man without willpower, a being without energy!"

"Then you don't despair?" I exclaimed irritably.

"No!" replied the professor firmly.

"What! You still think there's a chance of escape?"

"Yes! Yes, certainly! As long as the heart beats, as long as the flesh pulsates, I can't admit that any creature endowed with willpower needs to be overwhelmed by despair."

What words! A man who pronounced them under such circumstances was certainly of no ordinary cast of mind.

"Well," I said, "what do you plan to do?"

"Eat what food is left down to the last crumb and recover our lost strength. If this meal is our last, so be it! But at least we'll once more be men and not exhausted."

"Well then! Let's eat it up!" I exclaimed.

My uncle took the piece of meat and the few biscuits which had escaped the shipwreck; he divided them into three equal portions and distributed them. That resulted in about a pound of nourishment for each. The professor ate greedily, with a kind of feverish eagerness; myself, without pleasure, in spite of my hunger almost with disgust; Hans quietly, moderately, chewing small mouthfuls without any noise, relishing them with the calm of a man untouched by any anxiety about the future. By digging around he had found a flask of gin; he offered it to us, and this beneficial liquor succeeded in cheering me up a little.

"Forträfflig," said Hans, drinking in his turn.

"Excellent!" replied my uncle.

I had regained some hope. But our last meal was over. It was at that time five in the morning.

Man is constituted in such a way that health is a purely negative state; once hunger is satisfied, it is difficult to imagine the horrors of starvation; one must feel them to understand them. For that reason, a few mouthfuls of meat and biscuit after our long fast helped us overcome our past suffering.

But after the meal, we each of us fell deep into thought. What was Hans thinking of, that man of the far West who seemed dominated by the fatalist resignation of the East? As for me, my thoughts consisted only of memories, and those took me back to the surface of the globe which I should never have left. The house in the Königstrasse, my poor Graüben, the good Martha flitted like visions before my eyes, and in the gloomy rumblings that shook the rock I thought I could distinguish the noise of the cities of the earth.

My uncle, always "doing business," carefully examined the nature of our surroundings with the torch in his hand; he tried to determine his location from the examination of the layered strata. This calculation, or more precisely this estimate, could be no more than approximate; but a scholar is always a scholar if he manages to remain calm, and certainly Professor Lidenbrock had this quality to an uncommon degree.

I heard him murmur geological terms; I understood them, and in spite of myself I got interested in this last study.

"Eruptive granite," he was saying. "We're still in the primitive period; but we're going up, up! Who knows?"

Who knows? He kept on hoping. With his hand he explored the vertical wall, and a few moments later he resumed:

"Here's gneiss! Here's mica schist! Good! Soon the Transition period, and then . . ."

What did the professor mean? Could he measure the thickness of the terrestrial crust above our heads? Had he any means of making this calculation? No. He did not have the manometer, and no estimate could replace it.

In the meantime the temperature kept rising at a fast rate, and I felt immersed into a burning atmosphere. I could only compare it to the heat emanating from the furnaces of a foundry at the moment when the molten metal is being poured. Gradually, Hans, my uncle and I had been forced to take off our jackets and vests; the lightest piece of clothing turned into a source of discomfort, even suffering.

"Are we rising toward a fiery furnace?" I exclaimed, at a moment when the heat increased.

"No," replied my uncle, "that's impossible! That's impossible!"

"Yet," I said, touching the wall, "this wall is burning hot."

At the moment I said these words, my hand had brushed against the water, and I had to pull it back as fast as possible.

"The water is boiling!" I shouted.

This time the professor only answered with an angry gesture.

Then an unconquerable terror overwhelmed my brain and did not go away. I had a presentiment of an approaching catastrophe that even the boldest imagination could not have conceived. An idea, first vague, uncertain, turned into certainty in my mind. I tried to chase it away, but it returned stubbornly. I did not dare to express it. Yet some involuntary observations confirmed my conviction. By the dim light of the torch I noticed irregular movements in the granite layers; a phenomenon was about to take place in which electricity would play a role; then this excessive heat, this boiling water! . . . I wanted to check the compass.

It was running wild!

XLIII

Yes, wild! The needle jumped from one pole to the other with abrupt jolts, ran around the entire dial, and spun as if it had been overcome by vertigo.

I knew quite well that according to the most accepted theories, the mineral crust of the globe is never at absolute rest; the changes brought about by the decay of the interior substances, the movement deriving from the great liquid currents, and the impact of magnetism tend to shake it up continually, even if the beings scattered on its surface suspect nothing of this commotion. This phenomenon would therefore not have particularly frightened me, or at least it would not have provoked the dreadful idea in my mind.

But other facts, other unique details could not deceive me for much longer. The detonations multiplied with frightening intensity. I could only compare them to the noise of a great number of carriages driven rapidly across pavement. It was continuous thunder.

Then the compass gone wild, shaken up by electric phenomena, confirmed me in my view. The mineral crust was about to burst, the granite masses were about to fuse, the fissure was about to clog, the void was about to fill up, and we, poor atoms, we would be crushed in this tremendous embrace.

"Uncle, Uncle!" I shouted, "we are lost!"

"What are you in a fright about now?" was the calm rejoinder. "What's the matter with you?"

"The matter! Look at these walls moving, this mass of rock disintegrating, this burning heat, this boiling water, the thickening steam, the wild needle, all indicators of an earthquake!"

My uncle gently shook his head.

"An earthquake?" he said.

"Yes!"

"My lad, I think you're mistaken."

"What! Don't you recognize the symptoms . . . ?"

"Of an earthquake? No! I expect something better than that!"

"What do you mean?"

"An eruption, Axel."

"An eruption!" I said. "We're in the chimney of an active volcano?"

218

"I think so," said the professor smiling, "and that's the best thing that could happen to us!"

The best thing! Had my uncle gone mad? What did these words mean? Why this calmness and this smile?

"What!" I roared. "We're caught in an eruption! Fate has thrown us in the way of white-hot lava, burning rocks, boiling water, and all kinds of volcanic substances! We're going to be thrown out, expelled, ejected, vomited, coughed up high into the air, along with pieces of rock, showers of ashes and scoria, in a whirlwind of flames, and that's the best thing that could happen to us!"

"Yes," replied the professor, looking at me over his spectacles, "because that's the only chance we have of returning to the surface of the earth!"

I pass rapidly over the thousand ideas which crisscrossed in my brain. My uncle was right, absolutely right, and he had never seemed bolder and more convinced to me than at this moment when he expected and calmly calculated the chances of an eruption!

In the meantime we still went up; the night went by in this movement of ascent; the surrounding noises increased; I was almost choking, I thought my last hour had come, and yet imagination is so strange that I gave myself over to a really childish investigation. But I was the victim, not the master of my thoughts!

It was obvious that we were being driven upwards by an eruptive surge; beneath the raft, there was boiling water, and underneath the water a lava paste, an assortment of rocks that would be hurled in all directions at the summit of the crater. So we were in the vent of a volcano. No doubt in that regard.

But this time, instead of Snaefells, an extinct volcano, we were inside a fully active one. I wondered, therefore, what mountain this might be, and in what part of the world we would be ejected.

In the northern regions, no doubt. Before it went wild, our compass had never deviated from that direction. From Cape Saknussemm we had been carried due north for hundreds of leagues. So had we returned underneath Iceland? Would we be ejected out of the crater of Mt. Hekla or one of the seven other volcanoes on the island? Within a radius of five hundred leagues to the west, I saw at that latitude only the scarcely known volcanoes of the north-west coast of America. To the east there was only a single one at 80° northern

latitude, the Esk in Jan Mayen Island, not far from Spitzbergen!*
Certainly there was no lack of craters, and they were spacious enough
to vomit up a whole army! But I was trying to guess which one of
them would serve as our exit.

Toward morning the ascent accelerated. If the heat increased instead of diminishing as we approached the surface of the globe, this
was because it was completely local and due to volcanic influence.
Our type of movement could no longer leave any doubt in my mind.
An enormous force, a pressure of several hundred atmospheres generated by the accumulated steam was pushing us irresistibly. But to
what innumerable dangers it exposed us!

Soon tawny reflections penetrated into the widening vertical tunnel; on the right and on the left I noticed deep openings that resembled enormous tunnels, from which thick steam escaped; tongues of
fire lapped the walls and crackled.

"Look, look, Uncle!" I shouted.

"Well, those are sulfurous flames. Nothing more natural during
an eruption."

"But if they engulf us?"

"They won't engulf us."

"But if we choke?"

"We won't choke. The tunnel is widening, and if necessary, we'll
abandon the raft and take shelter in a crevice."

"But the water! The rising water!"

"There's no more water, Axel, only a sort of lava paste, which is
carrying us up to the outlet of the crater."

The liquid column had indeed disappeared and given way to
rather dense but still boiling eruptive matter. The temperature was
becoming unbearable, and a thermometer exposed to this atmosphere would have marked over 70°C! I was streaming with sweat.
Without the speed of the ascent, we would certainly have suffocated.

But the professor did not carry out his proposal of abandoning
the raft, and he was right. Those few ill-fitted wood beams offered us

---

*Verne mixes up the geographical information here. Jan Mayen Island, which be-
longs to Norway administratively, lies in the Arctic Ocean between Greenland and
Norway, several hundred miles southeast of Spitzbergen, a group of islands on the
Arctic Circle; its volcano is called Beerenberg, not Esk.

a solid surface, a support that we could not have found anywhere else.

At about eight in the morning, another incident occurred for the first time. The upward movement stopped suddenly. The raft lay absolutely motionless.

"What's the matter?" I asked, shaken by this sudden stoppage as if by a shock.

"A halt," replied my uncle.

"Is the eruption stopping?"

"I hope not."

I rose. I tried to look around me. Perhaps the raft itself, held up by a projection in the rock, was offering a temporary resistance to the volcanic mass. In that case we had to hurry up and release it as quickly as possible.

But it was not so. The column of ashes, scoriae, and rock fragments itself had ceased to rise.

"Might the eruption be coming to a halt?" I exclaimed.

"Ah!" said my uncle between clenched teeth, "that's what you fear, my boy. But don't worry, this moment of calm can't last long; it has already lasted five minutes, and we'll shortly resume our journey to the mouth of the crater."

As he spoke, the professor continued to check his chronometer, and he would again be right in his prediction. Soon the raft was seized again by a rapid but irregular movement that lasted about two minutes, and then stopped again.

"Good," said my uncle, checking the time; "in ten minutes it'll start again."

"Ten minutes?"

"Yes. We're dealing with an intermittent volcano. It lets us breathe along with it."

Nothing could be more true. At the predicted time we were again hurled along at extreme speed. We were forced to grip the wood beams tight so as not to be thrown off the raft. Then the surge stopped.

I have since reflected on this strange phenomenon without finding a satisfactory explanation for it. At any rate it was obvious that we were not in the main vent of the volcano, but in a secondary tunnel that was subject to a reflux effect.

How often this maneuver repeated itself I cannot say. All I can say is that at each new start we were hurled forward with increasing force and as if carried along by a real projectile. During the short halts, we choked; during the moments of upward rush, the hot air cut off my breath. I thought for a moment how delightful it would be to find myself suddenly transported to the arctic regions and a cold of 30°C below freezing. My overstimulated imagination went for a stroll on the snowy plains of arctic lands, and I longed for the moment where I would roll on the icy carpets of the pole! Little by little, at any rate, I lost my head, shattered by the repeated shocks. If it had not been for Hans' strong arm, I would have more than once broken my skull against the granite wall.

I have therefore no exact memory of what happened during the following hours. I have a confused recollection of continuous detonations, the movement of the rock, and a spinning movement that seized the raft. It floated on the flood of lava, amidst a hail of ashes. Roaring flames engulfed it. A hurricane that seemed to come from an enormous ventilator kindled the subterranean fires. One last time, Hans' face appeared to me in a reflection of fire, and then I no longer had any feeling other than the dark terror of the condemned tied to the mouth of a cannon, at the moment when the shot is fired and scatters their limbs into the air.

It floated on the flood of lava, amidst a hail of ashes.

XLIV

WHEN I OPENED MY eyes again, I felt the guide's strong hand hold me by the belt. With the other hand he supported my uncle. I was not seriously injured, but rather bruised by a general aching. I found myself lying on the slope of a mountain, two steps away from a chasm into which I would have fallen with the slightest movement. Hans had saved me from death while I was rolling down the side of the crater.

"Where are we?" asked my uncle, who seemed to me very angry that we had come back to earth.

The hunter shrugged his shoulders as a token of ignorance.

"In Iceland," I said.

"Nej," replied Hans.

"What! Not Iceland?" exclaimed the professor.

"Hans is mistaken," I said, raising myself up.

After the innumerable surprises of this journey, yet another amazing turn was in store for us. I expected to see a mountain cone covered with eternal snow, in the midst of the barren deserts of the northern regions, under the pale rays of an arctic sky, beyond the highest latitudes; but contrary to all these expectations, my uncle, the Icelander, and I were mid-slope on a mountain charred by the heat of a sun that consumed us with its fire.

I could not believe my eyes; but the all-too-real broiling of my body left no room for doubt. We had come half naked out of the crater, and the radiant star, to which we had owed nothing for two months, was generous to us with light and heat, and poured floods of splendid radiation on us.

When my eyes adjusted to this brightness of which they had lost the habit, I used them to correct the errors of my imagination. At least I wanted to be in Spitzbergen, and I was in no mood to give up this idea easily.

The professor was the first to speak and said:

"Indeed, this doesn't look much like Iceland."

"But Jan Mayen Island?" I replied.

"Not that either. This is no northern volcano with granite peaks and a snow cap."

"Nonetheless . . ."

"Look, Axel, look!"

Above our heads, at a height of at most five hundred feet, we saw the crater of a volcano, from which a tall pillar of fire mixed with pumice stones, ash and lava shot out every fifteen minutes with a loud explosion. I could feel the heaving of the mountain, which breathed like a whale and from time to time ejected fire and wind from its enormous blow-holes. Beneath us, down a rather steep slope, sheets of eruptive matter stretched over eight or nine hundred feet, which meant that the volcano's total height was less than three hundred fathoms. Its base disappeared in a real abundance of green trees, among which I noticed olive trees, fig trees, and vines covered with purple grapes.

This did not have the appearance of an arctic region, admittedly.

When the eye moved beyond this green enclosure, it quickly lost itself on the waters of an admirable ocean or lake, which meant that this enchanted place was an island, scarcely a few leagues wide. To the east one could see a little harbor with a few houses scattered around it, where boats of a peculiar shape floated on the waves of the azure water. Beyond, groups of islets emerged from the watery plain, so numerous that they resembled a big anthill. To the west, distant coasts lined the horizon; on some, blue mountains were outlined in a harmonious arrangement; on others, more distant, there appeared an extremely tall mountain with a plume of smoke at its summit. In the north, an immense expanse of water glittered in the sunlight, with the top of masts or the convex shape of wind-blown sails showing here and there.

The unexpectedness of this spectacle increased its marvelous beauty a hundredfold.

"Where are we? Where are we?" I repeated in a low voice.

Hans closed his eyes with indifference, and my uncle stared without understanding.

"Whatever mountain this may be," he said at last, "it's very hot here. The explosions are still going on, and it really wouldn't be worth escaping from an eruption only to be hit on the head by a piece of rock. Let's go down, and we'll find out what's going on. Besides, I'm dying from hunger and thirst."

The professor was definitely not of a contemplative disposition. I for my part would have stayed in this place for many hours still, forgetting need and exhaustion, but I had to follow my companions.

The side of the volcano had very steep slopes; we slid into real potholes full of ashes, and avoided the lava streams that flowed down like serpents of fire. While we climbed down, I chattered volubly, for my imagination was too full not to overflow into words.

"We're in Asia," I exclaimed, "on the coasts of India, on the islands of Malaysia, or in the middle of the Pacific Islands! We have passed through half the globe and ended up almost at the antipodes of Europe."

"But the compass?" replied my uncle.

"Yes! The compass!" I said with a confused look. "According to the compass we've always gone north."

"So has it lied?"

"Lied!"

"Unless this is the North Pole!"

"The Pole! No, but . . ."

This was a fact I could not explain. I did not know what to think.

But now we were approaching the greenery, which was a pleasure to look at. Hunger tormented me, and thirst as well. Fortunately, after two hours of walking, a pretty countryside appeared before our eyes, completely covered with olive trees, pomegranate trees, and vines that looked as if they belonged to everybody. At any rate, in our destitute state we were not likely to be particular. What pleasure it was to press these tasty fruits to our lips, and to eat grapes by the mouthful from the purple vines! Not far off, I discovered a spring of fresh water in the grass, under the delicious shade of the trees, into which we plunged our faces and hands voluptuously.

While each of us surrendered to all the sweetness of rest, a child appeared between two clusters of olive trees.

"Ah!" I exclaimed, "an inhabitant of this happy land!"

It was a poor little wretch, miserably clothed, rather sickly, and apparently very frightened at our appearance; indeed, half-naked, with unkempt beards, we looked very bad, and unless this was a land of thieves, we were likely to frighten its inhabitants.

Just as the child was about to run away, Hans went after him and brought him back, in spite of his cries and kicks.

I could feel the heaving of the mountain.

My uncle began by reassuring him as well as he could, and asked in good German:

"What is this mountain called, my little friend?"

The child did not answer.

"Well," said my uncle. "We are not in Germany."

And he repeated the same question in English.

Again, the child did not answer. I was very curious.

"Is he mute?" exclaimed the professor who, proud of his polyglottism, now reiterated the same question in French.

The same silence.

"Now let us try Italian," resumed my uncle, and he said in that language:

"*Dove noi siamo?*"*

"Yes, where are we?" I impatiently repeated.

The child still did not answer.

"Now then! Will you speak?" shouted my uncle, who began to lose his temper, and shook the child by the ears. "*Come si noma questa isola?*"

"*Stromboli*,"† replied the little shepherd, who slipped out of Hans' hands and headed for the plain through the olive trees.

We had not thought of that! Stromboli! What effect this unexpected name had on my imagination! We were right in the Mediterranean, in the middle of the mythological Aeolian archipelago, on ancient Strongyle, where Aeolus‡ kept the winds and the storms chained up. And those blue mountains curving up in the east were the mountains of Calabria! And that volcano rising up on the southern horizon was Mt. Etna, the fierce Mt. Etna!

"Stromboli! Stromboli!" I repeated.

My uncle accompanied me with his gestures and words. We seemed to be singing like a choir!

Ah! What a journey! What a wonderful journey! Having entered through one volcano, we had exited through another, and that other

---

*Where are we? (Italian). The question below translates as "What is this island called?"

†Stromboli (Strongyle in Latin) is a volcanically active island off the northeastern coast of Sicily.

‡God of the winds in Greek mythology.

one was more than twelve hundred leagues away from Snaefells, and from that barren landscape of Iceland at the edge of the world! The coincidences of the expedition had taken us into the heart of the most harmonious areas of the earth. We had exchanged the regions of perpetual snow for those of infinite green, and had left the grayish fog of the icy regions over our heads only to come back to the azure sky of Sicily!

After a delicious meal of fruits and fresh water, we set off again to reach the port of Stromboli. Revealing how we had arrived on the island did not seem advisable to us: Italians with their superstitious tendency would inevitably have cast us as demons vomited up from the pit of hell; so we had to resign ourselves to pretending we were only victims of a shipwreck. It was less glorious, but safer.

On the way I heard my uncle murmuring:

"But the compass! The compass that pointed due north! How to explain that?"

"Indeed!" I said with an air of great disdain, "it's easier not to explain!"

"Absolutely not! A professor of the Johanneum unable to find the reason for a cosmic phenomenon, that would be a disgrace!"

As he spoke these words, my uncle, half-naked, with his leather purse around his waist and adjusting his glasses on his nose, became once more the fearsome professor of mineralogy.

One hour after we had left the olive grove, we arrived at the port of San Vicenzo, where Hans claimed the price of his thirteenth week of service, which was paid out to him with warm handshakes.

At that moment, even if he did not share our natural emotion, he at least allowed himself an unusual expression of feeling.

He lightly squeezed our hands with the tips of his fingers, and began to smile.

XLV

THIS IS THE END of a story that even people who are not usually amazed at anything may refuse to believe. But I am armed in advance against human incredulity.

The Stromboli fishermen received us with the care that is due to victims of shipwreck. They gave us clothing and food. After forty-eight hours of waiting, a small rowboat took us to Messina* on August 31, where a few days of rest helped us recover from all our exhaustion.

On Friday, September 4, we embarked on the steamer *Volturne*, one of the steamships used by the imperial French postal services, and three days later we landed in Marseilles, with only one worry left on our minds, that of the accursed compass. This inexplicable fact kept bothering me very seriously. On the evening of September 9, we arrived in Hamburg.

Martha's amazement and Graüben's joy I will not even try to describe.

"Now that you're a hero, Axel," said my dear fiancée to me, "you won't need to leave me ever again!"

I looked at her. She cried and smiled at the same time.

I will leave it to you to guess whether Professor Lidenbrock's return to Hamburg caused a sensation. Thanks to Martha's indiscretion, the news of his departure for the center of the earth had spread around the whole world. People refused to believe it, and when they saw him again, they refused to believe even more.

But Hans' presence and various pieces of information that had come from Iceland gradually changed public opinion.

Then my uncle became a great man, and myself the nephew of a great man, which is at least something. Hamburg gave a party in our honor. A public lecture took place at the Johanneum, where the professor told the story of his expedition and omitted only the facts relating to the compass. On the same day, he deposited Saknussemm's document in the municipal archives and expressed his deep regret that circumstances more powerful than his will had prevented him

---

*City in northeastern Sicily.

from following the traces of the Icelandic traveler to the center of the earth. He was humble in his glory, and his reputation increased even more.

So much honor inevitably had to create envy. It did, and since his theories, supported by solid facts, contradicted existing scientific theories on the question of core heat, he had remarkable discussions with scholars of all countries, in writing and in person.

For my part, I cannot agree with his theory of cooling: in spite of what I have seen, I believe and will always believe in core heat; but I admit that certain as yet ill-defined circumstances can modify this law under the impact of natural phenomena.

At the moment when these questions were most exciting, my uncle experienced a real distress. Hans, in spite of his entreaties, had left Hamburg; the man to whom we owed everything did not want to let us pay him our debt. He was overcome by nostalgia for Iceland.

"Farval," he said one day, and with that simple word of farewell he left for Reykjavik, where he arrived safely.

We were extremely attached to our brave eider-down hunter; in spite of his absence, he will never be forgotten by those whose lives he has saved, and certainly I will not die before I have seen him again one last time.

To conclude, I should add that this *Journey to the Center of the Earth* caused an enormous sensation in the world. It was printed and translated into all languages; the leading newspapers snatched the main episodes from each other, which were commented on, debated, attacked and defended with equal conviction in the camp of the believers as in that of the skeptics. A rare thing! My uncle was able to enjoy in his lifetime all the fame he had attained, and even Mr. Barnum himself proposed to "exhibit" him in the States of the Union for a very high price.

But one concern, one might even say a torment, remained in the middle of this glory. One fact remained inexplicable, the one involving the compass; now, for a scholar, such an unexplained phenomenon becomes torture for the intelligence. Well! Heaven had destined my uncle to become completely happy.

One day, when I was arranging a collection of minerals in his study, I noticed that famous compass in a corner, and I began to examine it.

It had been there for six months, unaware of the trouble it was causing.

Suddenly, what amazement! I gave a shout. The professor came running.

"What's the matter?" he asked.

"That compass!"

"Well?"

"But its needle is pointing south and not north!"

"What are you saying?"

"Look! Its poles are reversed."

"Reversed!"

My uncle looked, compared, and made the house shake with a gigantic leap.

What light broke in on his spirit and mine at the same time!

"So then," he exclaimed, as soon as he was able to speak again, "after we arrived at Cape Saknussemm, the needle of this damned compass pointed south instead of north?"

"Obviously."

"That's the explanation for our mistake. But what phenomenon could have caused this reversal of the poles?"

"Nothing easier."

"Tell me, Axel."

"During the storm on the Lidenbrock Sea, that ball of fire which magnetized the iron on the raft had very simply disoriented our compass!"

"Ah!" shouted the professor and broke out in laughter. "So it was an electric trick?"

From that day on, the professor was the happiest of scholars, and I was the happiest of men, for my pretty Virland girl, resigning her place as ward, took up position in the house on the Königstrasse in the double capacity of niece and wife. No need to add that her uncle was the illustrious Otto Lidenbrock, corresponding member of all the scientific, geographical, and mineralogical societies on the five continents of the earth.

Endnotes

1. (p. 5) *Humphry Davy ... Saint Claire-Deville:* British chemist Sir Humphry Davy (1778–1829) discovered several chemical elements. German naturalist and explorer Alexander von Humboldt (1769–1859) contributed crucially to the Earth sciences. British explorer of the Arctic Sir John Franklin (1786–1847) discovered the Northwest Passage. British astronomer Sir Edward Sabine (1788–1883) traveled to the Arctic and was a pioneer in magnetism. Antoine-César Becquerel (1788–1878) and his son, Alexandre-Edmond Becquerel (1820–1891), were both physicists. Jacques-Joseph Ebelmen (misspelled "Ebelman" by Verne) (1814–1852) was a French chemist. Scottish physicist Sir David Brewster (1781–1868) invented the kaleidoscope. Jean-Baptiste-André Dumas (1800–1884) was a French chemist. French zoologist Henri Milne-Edwards (1800–1885), professor at the Sorbonne and director of the Muséum d'Histoire Naturelle in Paris, researched crustaceans, mollusks, and corals. Henri-Étienne Sainte-Claire Deville (1818–1881) was a French chemist; his brother Charles Sainte-Claire Deville (1814–1876) was a French geologist who published a book on the Stromboli volcano.

2. (p. 6) *Graüben:* Verne uses a spelling for the goddaughter's name that could not exist in German. Some translators have therefore chosen to normalize the name to "Gräuben," but this variation still does not render a name that would be likely to be used in German. For this reason, Verne's original spelling is preserved here.

3. (p. 14) *"Arne Saknussemm ... a famous alchemist!":* Verne may have based this character on the Icelandic philologist Árni Magnússon (1663–1730), who specialized in the early history and literature of Scandinavia and built up an extensive collection of books and manuscripts from Norway, Sweden, and Iceland. He was not an alchemist, however.

4. (p. 14) *"Avicenna ... Paracelsus":* The Iranian doctor and philosopher Avicenna (980–1037) exerted enormous influence, especially in the areas of philosophy and medicine. British philosopher and scientist Roger Bacon (1220–1292) studied alchemy as well as mathematics, astronomy, and optics; he was the first European to give a detailed account of the manufacture of gunpowder. Catalan writer and mystic Ramon Llull

(1232/33–1315/16) proposed a general theory of knowledge in his *Ars magna* (1305–1308). The German-Swiss doctor and alchemist known as Paracelsus, whose real name was Philippus Aureolus Theophrastus Bombast von Hohenheim (1493–1541), was responsible for giving chemistry a crucial role in medicine.

5. (p. 34) *"a visit that the celebrated chemist . . . born nineteen years later":* By this accounting, Axel was born in 1844 and he would be nineteen at the time of the expedition in 1863; Uncle Lidenbrock, who Verne has said was fifty in 1863, would have been only twelve years old in 1825—a rather young age to be receiving visits from famous scientists!

6. (p. 57) *"Olafsen . . . scholars aboard the* Reine Hortense":* Icelandic poet and natural historian Eggert Ólafsson (1726–1768) carried out a substantial scientific and cultural survey of his country from 1752 to 1757 and recorded the results in his *Travels in Iceland* (1772); together with Bjarni Pálsson (pseudonym Povelsen), he undertook the first ascent of the Snaefells volcano in 1757. Uno von Troil (1746–1803), archbishop of Uppsala, Sweden, traveled to Iceland in 1772 and published a report on his journey in 1777. French naturalist Joseph Paul Gaimard (1796–1858) undertook expeditions to Iceland in 1835 and 1836 and published a nine-volume study as a result of this journey, with the collaboration of Eugène Robert (1806–1879). French navigator Jules Alphonse René Poret de Blosseville and members of an expedition team, to whom Verne refers simply as the "scholars," sailed to Iceland and Greenland aboard the *Reine Hortense* in 1833 and disappeared in the Arctic.

7. (p. 162) *leptotherium . . . mericotherium:* Verne seems to have invented these names. There is an orchid genus but no animal called *leptotherium*, which combines the Greek words for "slender" and "wild beast." The name *mericotherium* is similar to those of such other prehistoric species as the *hyracotherium*, a small ancestor of the horse, but has no specific zoological referent.

8. (p. 192) *Boucher de Perthes . . . by the ages:* Verne moves events that actually took place in the 1830s and 1840s to the 1860s. Jacques Boucher de Perthes, an archaeologist, was director of the custom house at Abbeville in France and made important discoveries of Stone Age tools in the area that demonstrated the ancient origins of the human species. His research remained controversial until 1859, when it was supported by British scientists.

9. (p. 192) *Falconer, Busk, Carpenter:* Hugh Falconer (1808–1865) was a Scottish naturalist and paleontologist. British surgeon, zoologist, and

paleontologist George Busk (1807–1886) had a specialization in polyzoa, a fossil marine species, and an interest in vertebrate fossils. William Benjamin Carpenter (1813–1885) trained as a medical doctor and published in diverse fields, including mental physiology, microscopy, marine biology, and religion, with particular achievements in marine zoology.

10. (p. 194) *"I know the story . . . the pre-adamites of Scheuchzer":* Pausanias, a Greek scholar and writer from the second century A.D., tells the story of a man who claimed to have found the skeleton of the Greek hero Ajax; he described it as gigantic and said the kneecap was the size of a pentathlon discus, which would make it more than 7 inches wide. Asterius is a mythological giant whose tomb Pausanias claimed to have seen. Herodotus, a Greek historian from the fifth century B.C., reports the story of Orestes' body being found by a Spartan who simply takes the word of a blacksmith for the authenticity of the remains. Polyphemus is a one-eyed giant who imprisons Odysseus in Homer's *Odyssey*; Trapani and Palermo are cities in Sicily. Felix Platter (1536–1614; spelled "Plater" in Verne's text) was a Swiss doctor who identified bones found near Lucerne as those of a giant, but they were actually the remains of a mammoth. Jean de Chassanion (1531–1598) was a French clergyman and author of a book on giants in human history. Georges Cuvier (1769–1832) was a French naturalist who examined bones said to be those of Teutobochus, king of the Cimbrians, and found them to belong to the elephant relative deinotherium; the Cimbrians were a Germanic tribe. Peter Camper (1722–1789; spelled "Campet" in Verne's text) was a Dutch anatomist best known for his work on anatomy and human races. In 1725 Johann Jakob Scheuchzer (1672–1733), a Swiss naturalist, claimed to have discovered the fossil remains of one of the victims of the biblical flood; in the nineteenth century, Georges Cuvier identified these fossils to be those of a giant salamander.

11. (p. 197) *Hoffmann's fantastic character who has lost his shadow:* In the short story "The Wonderful Tale of Peter Schlemihl" (1814), by German Romantic author Adelbert von Chamisso (1781–1838), the protagonist sells his shadow. E. T. A. Hoffmann (1776–1822), another German writer of the period and friend of Chamisso's, mentions the story in his own "Adventures of New Year's Eve" (1815).

Inspired by
Journey to the Center of the Earth

Science-Fiction

Oscar Wilde supposedly once remarked that H. G. Wells was a "scientific Jules Verne." It is hard to determine which author Wilde wished to slight more, but it doesn't really matter: Verne and Wells are *the* two progenitors of modern science fiction. Without these authors, science fantasy writing—a category that includes such notables as Kingsley Amis, Isaac Asimov, Anthony Burgess, Arthur C. Clarke, Philip K. Dick, Aldous Huxley, C. S. Lewis, George Orwell, Ray Bradbury, and J. R. R. Tolkien—would not exist as we know it today.

Herbert George Wells supported himself with teaching, textbook writing, and journalism until 1895, when he made his literary debut with *The Time Machine*, which was followed before the end of the century by *The Island of Dr. Moreau*, *The Invisible Man*, and *The War of the Worlds*—books that established him as the first original voice in the realm of scientific fantasy since Verne. Where Verne dealt with scientific probabilities—for example, the *Nautilus* from *Twenty Thousand Leagues Under the Sea* serves as the forerunner to the modern submarine—time travel, interplanetary warfare, and invisibility and other fantasies are the subjects of Wells's conceptual fiction.

Perhaps because of this fundamental difference in their artistic aims, Wells was famously loath to be compared to his literary ancestor. In a letter to J. L. Garvin, the editor of *Outlook*, Wells refused to attack Verne publicly, though he had openly denied having been influenced by the latter: "A good deal of injustice has been done the old man [Verne] in comparison with me. I don't like the idea of muscling into the circle of attention about him with officious comments or opinions eulogy. I've let the time when I might have punished him decently go by." Although the prolific Wells delved into social philosophy and criticism, history, utopian and comic novels, literary parodies, and even feminism, he was always best remembered for his auspicious beginnings as a science fiction writer.

The Underground Novel

Underground worlds have fascinated mankind for millennia—consider the Hades of the Greeks and the subterranean inferno of Dante—but Verne's story is an important nineteenth-century manifestation. With Verne as a thematic predecessor, so-called Lost World and Lost Race novels took strong hold in the English-speaking world. In fact, Verne himself took inspiration from *Journey to the Center of the Earth* to write another underground tale, the little-known *Les Indes Noires* (1877), which chronicles a family living in a coal mine beneath the surface of Scotland. In English, the novel has been published under titles as various as *Underground City, The Child of the Cavern, Strange Doings Underground, Black Diamonds*, and the literal *The Black Indies*. The African adventure tales of British author H. Rider Haggard, including the treasure-hunt classic *King Solomon's Mines* (1885) and the mystical *She: A History of Adventure* (1887), utilize the underground as a key setting and metaphor. Two of the best-selling fictions of their time, Haggard's novels are still read today and also are known for helping inspire the Indiana Jones movie franchise of the 1980s. Lost World and Lost Race themes appear in works as wide-ranging as the science fiction of H. G. Wells, the anti-imperialism works of Joseph Conrad, the Professor Challenger novels by Sir Arthur Conan Doyle, and the Tarzan and Pellucidar series of Edgar Rice Burroughs.

Film

The first adaptation of Verne's novel, *Voyage au centre de la terre* (1909; *A Journey to the Middle of the Earth*), was by Spanish director Segundo de Chomón; no copies are known to exist today. By the middle of the twentieth century, though, film audiences were quite familiar with Verne. The Czech *Cesta do Praveku* (1955; *Journey to the Beginning of Time*), directed by Karel Zeman, was inspired by Verne's novel, though this story of traveling to past epochs is not really an adaptation. That came in 1959 with *Journey to the Center of the Earth*. James Mason plays Professor Oliver Lindenbrook and a frequently shirtless Pat Boone sings musical numbers in his role as

Alec McEwen, Lindenbrook's student. Arlene Dahl is the strong-willed Carla Goetaborg, a role created for the movie. Director Henry Liven portrays realistic-looking dinosaurs with footage of lizards blown up to monstrous proportions, and the magnificent settings include crystal gardens, forests of giant mushrooms, and footage of Carlsbad Caverns in New Mexico. Bernard Herrmann's excellent score completes this classic. America also saw a wave of other Verne adaptations in the 1950s: *20,000 Leagues Under the Sea* (1954) and *Around the World in 80 Days* (1956) were popular hits, the latter winning an Academy Award for Best Picture.

An admirable Spanish adaptation, *Viaje al centro de la Tierra*, by director Georges Méliès (1976), appeared in the United States in 1978; it is sometimes known as *Where Time Began* and *Fabulous Journey to the Center of the Earth*. The creative opening sequence shows a pastiche of early, silent Verne films from prolific director Georges Méliès. *Journey to the Center of the Earth* (1989), featuring model-actress Kathy Ireland, takes little from Verne's novel but the name; the same holds true for a 1993 television movie. A loosely adapted miniseries starring Treat Williams, *Journey to the Center of the Earth* (1999), moves the action to New Zealand and focuses on a dinosaur plot and a missing-person saga.

Director Gavin Scott's *Journey to the Center of the Earth* (2005) depicts four young people who discover the original manuscript for Verne's novel. When they find a map of Verne's travels under the Earth's surface, they realize that the author based the book on his real-life adventures and agree to go underground and follow Verne's path. Part of this story rings true to actual events: Verne's original manuscript for the novel, lost for decades, came to light in 1994.

Comments & Questions

In this section, we aim to provide the reader with an array of perspectives on the text, as well as questions that challenge those perspectives. The commentary has been culled from sources as diverse as reviews contemporaneous with the work, letters written by the author, literary criticism of later generations, and appreciations written throughout the work's history. Following the commentary, a series of questions seeks to filter Jules Verne's Journey to the Center of the Earth *through a variety of points of view and bring about a richer understanding of this enduring work.*

Comments

JULES VERNE

My object has been to depict the earth, and not the earth alone, but the universe, for I have sometimes taken my readers away from the earth, in the novel. And I have tried at the same time to realize a very high ideal of beauty of style. It is said that there can't be any style in a novel of adventure, but that isn't true; though I admit that it is very much more difficult to write such a novel in a good literary form than the studies of character which are so in vogue to-day.

—as reported to R. H. Sherard and printed in
McClure's Magazine (January 1894)

THE NATION

The death of Jules Verne should strike with a sense of personal bereavement all boys who read and all men in whom the romantic imagination of boyhood has not yet perished. He was a prophet with honor in his own country, for he and the famous Cathedral of Amiens were the twin marvels of that provincial city. Their two pictures, in all sizes and styles, stare from hundreds of shop windows. But this tribute is only a faint echo of that which came to him from every corner of the globe. Wherever love of adventure, coupled with curiosity as to the mechanism of the universe, exists, there Jules Verne finds his disciples. 'Around the World in Eighty Days,' 'Twenty Thousand Leagues Under the Sea,' 'The Mysterious Island,' 'A Voyage to the Centre of the Earth,' 'From the Earth to the Moon'—here is a rollcall that should stir the pulses of graybeards, and almost summon back their irrevocable youth. . . .

The books of Jules Verne are the 'Arabian Nights' elaborately fitted with all modern improvements. The genii and the sorcerers of a few centuries ago have their lineal descendants in the accomplished gentlemen who are sometimes described as "the wizards of science." A submarine boat, a fast express, an automobile, a dirigible balloon, or a hollow shell shot at the moon, is a comfortable and highly plausible substitute for a travelling carpet or a roc. Given the problem of annihilating space and time, the unknown authors of the 'Arabian Nights' and Jules Verne both solve it according to formulas popular in their own day.

The charm of mystery is evident in the very title of Verne's works. No lad of twelve can resist the challenge of 'Twenty Thousand Leagues Under the Sea,' 'Voyage to the Centre of the Earth,' and 'The Mysterious Island.' Had the subject-matter belied the captions, many eager readers would still have pegged away, lured by the mere magic of the words stamped on the binding. But the stories are worthy of their delicious names. . . .

On the scientific side of Verne's writings one may easily lay undue stress. He is not the first to embed scientific knowledge in stories for boys, though he is uncommonly successful in sugar-coating the pill. The method of Abbott and his imitators is to let Rollo draw Uncle George into endless and often futile discussions of the wonders of earth and sky. There is too much talk and too little action. Verne, on the contrary—and he has had many followers, notably H. G. Wells—vitalizes the dead fact by employing it in some striking feat in mastery of man or nature. —March 30, 1905

CHARLES F. HORNE

Jules Verne was the establisher of a new species of story-telling, that which interweaves the most stupendous wonders of science with the simplest facts of human life. Our own Edgar Allan Poe had pointed the way; and Verne was ever eager to acknowledge his indebtedness to the earlier master. But Poe died; and it was Verne who went on in book after book, fascinating his readers with cleverly devised mysteries, instructing and astonishing them with the new discoveries of science, inspiring them with the splendor of man's destiny. When, as far back as 1872, his early works were "crowned" by the French Academy, its Perpetual Secretary, M. Patin, said in his official address, "The well-worn wonders of fairyland are here replaced by a new and more marvelous world, created from the most recent ideas of science."

More noteworthy still is Verne's position as the true, the astonishingly true, prophet of the discoveries and inventions that were to come. He was far more than the mere creator of that sort of scientific fairyland of which Secretary Patin spoke, and with which so many later writers, Wells, Haggard and Sir Conan Doyle, have since delighted us. He himself once keenly contrasted his own methods with those of Wells, the man he most admired among his many followers. Wells, he pointed out, looked centuries ahead and out of pure imagination embodied the unknowable that some day might perchance appear. "While I," said Verne, "base my inventions on a groundwork of actual fact."

—from his introduction to the *Works of Jules Verne* (1911)

GEORGE ORWELL
Like most writers, Jules Verne was one of those people to whom nothing ever happens.

—from the *New Statesman* (January 18, 1941)

KINGSLEY AMIS
With Verne we reach the first great progenitor of modern science fiction. In its literary aspect his work is, of course, of poor quality, a feature certainly reproduced with great fidelity by most of his successors.

—from *New Maps of Hell: A Survey of Science Fiction* (1960)

WILLIAM GOLDING
Verne's verbal surface lacks the slickness of the professional; it is turgid and slack by turns. Only the brio of his enthusiasm carries us forward from one adventure to another.

—from *The Hot Gates* (1961)

JORGE LUIS BORGES

Before Wells resigned himself to the role of sociological spectator, he was an admirable storyteller, an heir to the concise style of Swift and Edgar Allan Poe; Verne was a pleasant and industrious journeyman. Verne wrote for adolescents; Wells, for all ages.

—as translated by Ruth L. C. Simms, from
Other Inquisitions 1937–1952 (1964)

ISAAC ASIMOV

[Verne] gives careful detail, when detail is advisable, and makes omissions when it is safe. He carefully overcomes a known difficulty by reference to some authentic scientific hypothesis which, for the purposes of the story, turns out to be true. He uses currently impressive words and phrases at key points.

Done well enough, as Verne does, a story, however fantastic it may seem, becomes acceptable not only in its own time but also a century later when its science is as outmoded as Dante's descriptions of the Inferno.   —from his introduction to *A Journey to the Center of the Earth* (1966)

Questions

1. What is the appeal of fiction, movies, and paintings that depict events that could never occur or things that could never exist? Is it pure escapism? Or is there something more fulfilling about these fantasies? Do they somehow reflect on the world around us?

2. Think of the metaphoric implications of digging deeper and deeper until you come to a hidden world within the world, a world in which monsters roam. In part, is Verne's story about what lies at the hidden center of the human mind? Or does it concern the monstrous at the heart of the day-to-day workings of human society?

3. In what ways is *Journey to the Center of the Earth* tied to its own time, and in what ways does it represent universal, timeless concerns?

4. How does *Journey to the Center of the Earth* compare to other works of science fiction? Is it as compelling as, say, *Star Trek* or *Jurassic Park*?

5. How does the novel foreground the contrast between animate beings and the inanimate world? How do Verne's metaphors complicate or blur this opposition?

6. Are the characters intended as realistic figures, or are they symbolic representations of certain mindsets? How do their relations to one another affect the outcome of the story?

For Further Reading

Biographical Materials

Allotte de la Fuÿe, Marguérite. *Jules Verne*. Translated by Erik de Mauny. New York: Coward-McCann, 1956.

Jules-Verne, Jean. *Jules Verne: A Biography*. Translated by Roger Greaves. New York: Taplinger, 1976. Written by the author's grandson.

Lottmann, Herbert R. *Jules Verne: An Exploratory Biography*. New York: St. Martin's Press, 1996.

Critical Materials

Barthes, Roland. "The *Nautilus* and the Drunken Boat." In *Mythologies*, translated by Annette Lavers. New York: Noonday, 1972, pp. 65–67.

Butcher, William. *Verne's Journey to the Centre of the Self: Space and Time in the* Voyages Extraordinaires. New York: St. Martin's Press, 1990.

Chesneaux, Jean. *The Political and Social Ideas of Jules Verne*. Translated by Thomas Wikeley. London: Thames and Hudson, 1972.

Costello, Peter. *Jules Verne: Inventor of Science Fiction*. London: Hodder and Stoughton, 1978.

Evans, Arthur B. *Jules Verne Rediscovered: Didacticism and the Scientific Novel*. New York: Greenwood, 1988.

Lynch, Lawrence W. *Jules Verne*. New York: Twayne Publishers, 1992.

Macherey, Pierre. *A Theory of Literary Production*. Translated by Geoffrey Wall. London: Routledge, 1978, pp. 159–248.

Martin, Andrew. *The Knowledge of Ignorance: From Genesis to Jules Verne*. Cambridge and New York: Cambridge University Press, 1985.

Martin, Andrew. *The Mask of the Prophet: The Extraordinary Fictions of Jules Verne*. Oxford and New York: Oxford University Press, 1992.

Smyth, Edmund, ed. *Jules Verne: Narratives of Modernity*. Liverpool, UK: Liverpool University Press, 2000.

Materials in French

Bessière, Jean. *Modernités de Jules Verne.* Paris: Presses Universitaires de France, 1988.

Butor, Michel. *Essais sur les modernes.* Paris: Gallimard, 1960. Contains the important essay "Le point suprême et l'âge d'or à travers quelques oeuvres de Jules Verne."

Chesneaux, Jean. *Jules Verne, un regard sur le monde: Nouvelles lectures politiques.* Paris: Bayard, 2001.

Compère, Daniel. *Un voyage imaginaire de Jules Verne: Voyage au centre de la terre.* Paris: Lettres Modernes, 1977.

Fabre, Michel. *Le problème et l'épreuve: Formation et modernité chez Jules Verne.* Paris: Harmattan, 2004.

Raymond, François, ed. *La science en question.* Paris: Minard, 1992.

Serres, Michel. *Jouvences sur Jules Verne.* Paris: Minuit, 1974.

———. *Jules Verne, la science et l'homme contemporain.* Paris: Pommier, 2003.

Vierne, Simone. *Jules Verne.* Paris: Balland, 1986.

Look for the following titles, available now and forthcoming from
BARNES & NOBLE CLASSICS.

Visit your local bookstore for these fine titles.

Adventures of Huckleberry Finn	Mark Twain	1-59308-000-X	$4.95
The Adventures of Tom Sawyer	Mark Twain	1-59308-068-9	$4.95
Aesop's Fables		1-59308-062-X	$5.95
The Age of Innocence	Edith Wharton	1-59308-143-X	$5.95
Alice's Adventures in Wonderland and Through the Looking-Glass	Lewis Carroll	1-59308-015-8	$5.95
Anna Karenina	Leo Tolstoy	1-59308-027-1	$8.95
The Art of War	Sun Tzu	1-59308-017-4	$7.95
The Awakening and Selected Short Fiction	Kate Chopin	1-59308-001-8	$4.95
The Brothers Karamazov	Fyodor Dostoevsky	1-59308-045-X	$9.95
The Call of the Wild and White Fang	Jack London	1-59308-200-2	$5.95
Candide	Voltaire	1-59308-028-X	$4.95
A Christmas Carol, The Chimes and The Cricket on the Hearth	Charles Dickens	1-59308-033-6	$5.95
The Collected Poems of Emily Dickinson		1-59308-050-6	$5.95
The Complete Sherlock Holmes, Vol. I	Sir Arthur Conan Doyle	1-59308-034-4	$7.95
The Complete Sherlock Holmes, Vol. II	Sir Arthur Conan Doyle	1-59308-040-9	$7.95
The Count of Monte Cristo	Alexandre Dumas	1-59308-151-0	$7.95
Cyrano de Bergerac	Edmond Rostand	1-59308-075-1	$3.95
Daisy Miller and Washington Square	Henry James	1-59308-105-7	$4.95
Daniel Deronda	George Eliot	1-59308-290-8	$8.95
David Copperfield	Charles Dickens	1-59308-063-8	$7.95
The Death of Ivan Ilych and Other Stories	Leo Tolstoy	1-59308-069-7	$7.95
Don Quixote	Miguel de Cervantes	1-59308-046-8	$9.95
Dracula	Bram Stoker	1-59308-114-6	$6.95
Emma	Jane Austen	1-59308-089-1	$4.95
Essays and Poems by Ralph Waldo Emerson		1-59308-076-X	$6.95
The Essential Tales and Poems of Edgar Allan Poe		1-59308-064-6	$7.95
Ethan Frome and Selected Stories	Edith Wharton	1-59308-090-5	$5.95
Frankenstein	Mary Shelley	1-59308-115-4	$4.95
Great American Short Stories: from Hawthorne to Hemingway		1-59308-086-7	$7.95
Great Expectations	Charles Dickens	1-59308-006-9	$4.95
Grimm's Fairy Tales	Jacob and Wilhelm Grimm	1-59308-056-5	$7.95
Gulliver's Travels	Jonathan Swift	1-59308-132-4	$5.95
Hard Times	Charles Dickens	1-59308-156-1	$5.95
Heart of Darkness and Selected Short Fiction	Joseph Conrad	1-59308-021-2	$4.95
The Histories	Herodotus	1-59308-102-2	$6.95
The House of Mirth	Edith Wharton	1-59308-153-7	$6.95

(continued)

The House of the Dead and Poor Folk	Fyodor Dostoevsky	1-59308-194-4	$7.95
Howards End	E. M. Forster	1-59308-022-0	$6.95
The Hunchback of Notre Dame	Victor Hugo	1-59308-047-6	$5.95
The Idiot	Fyodor Dostoevsky	1-59308-058-1	$7.95
The Importance of Being Earnest and Four Other Plays	Oscar Wilde	1-59308-059-X	$6.95
The Inferno	Dante Alighieri	1-59308-051-4	$6.95
Jane Eyre	Charlotte Brontë	1-59308-007-7	$4.95
Jude the Obscure	Thomas Hardy	1-59308-035-2	$6.95
The Jungle Books	Rudyard Kipling	1-59308-109-X	$5.95
The Jungle	Upton Sinclair	1-59308-008-5	$4.95
Kim	Rudyard Kipling	1-59308-192-8	$4.95
King Solomon's Mines	H. Rider Haggard	1-59308-275-4	$4.95
The Last of the Mohicans	James Fenimore Cooper	1-59308-137-5	$5.95
Leaves of Grass: First and "Death-bed" Editions	Walt Whitman	1-59308-083-2	$9.95
Les Misérables	Victor Hugo	1-59308-066-2	$9.95
Little Women	Louisa May Alcott	1-59308-108-1	$6.95
Lord Jim	Joseph Conrad	1-59308-084-0	$4.95
Main Street	Sinclair Lewis	1-59308-036-0	$5.95
Man and Superman and Three Other Plays	George Bernard Shaw	1-59308-067-0	$7.95
Mansfield Park	Jane Austen	1-59308-154-5	$5.95
The Mayor of Casterbridge	Thomas Hardy	1-59308-309-2	$5.95
The Metamorphosis and Other Stories	Franz Kafka	1-59308-029-8	$6.95
Middlemarch	George Eliot	1-59308-023-9	$8.95
Moby-Dick	Herman Melville	1-59308-018-2	$9.95
Moll Flanders	Daniel Defoe	1-59308-216-9	$5.95
My Ántonia	Willa Cather	1-59308-202-9	$5.95
My Bondage and My Freedom	Frederick Douglass	1-59308-301-7	$6.95
Narrative of the Life of Frederick Douglass, an American Slave		1-59308-041-7	$4.95
Nicholas Nickleby	Charles Dickens	1-59308-300-9	$8.95
Night and Day	Virginia Woolf	1-59308-212-6	$7.95
Northanger Abbey	Jane Austen	1-59308-264-9	$5.95
Nostromo	Joseph Conrad	1-59308-193-6	$7.95
Notes From Underground, The Double and Other Stories	Fyodor Dostoevsky	1-59308-037-9	$4.95
O Pioneers!	Willa Cather	1-59308-205-3	$5.95
The Odyssey	Homer	1-59308-009-3	$5.95
Oliver Twist	Charles Dickens	1-59308-206-1	$6.95
The Origin of Species	Charles Darwin	1-59308-077-8	$7.95
Paradise Lost	John Milton	1-59308-095-6	$7.95
Persuasion	Jane Austen	1-59308-130-8	$5.95
The Picture of Dorian Gray	Oscar Wilde	1-59308-025-5	$4.95
The Portrait of a Lady	Henry James	1-59308-096-4	$7.95
A Portrait of the Artist as a Young Man and Dubliners	James Joyce	1-59308-031-X	$6.95
The Possessed	Fyodor Dostoevsky	1-59308-250-9	$9.95
Pride and Prejudice	Jane Austen	1-59308-201-0	$5.95
The Prince and Other Writings	Niccolò Machiavelli	1-59308-060-3	$5.95

(continued)

The Prince and the Pauper	Mark Twain	1-59308-218-5	$4.95
Pygmalion and Three Other Plays	George Bernard Shaw	1-59308-078-6	$7.95
The Red Badge of Courage and Selected Short Fiction	Stephen Crane	1-59308-119-7	$4.95
Republic	Plato	1-59308-097-2	$6.95
Robinson Crusoe	Daniel Defoe	1-59308-360-2	$5.95
The Scarlet Letter	Nathaniel Hawthorne	1-59308-207-X	$4.95
Selected Stories of O. Henry		1-59308-042-5	$5.95
Sense and Sensibility	Jane Austen	1-59308-125-1	$5.95
Six Plays by Henrik Ibsen		1-59308-061-1	$8.95
Sons and Lovers	D. H. Lawrence	1-59308-013-1	$7.95
The Souls of Black Folk	W. E. B. Du Bois	1-59308-014-X	$5.95
The Strange Case of Dr. Jekyll and Mr. Hyde and Other Stories	Robert Louis Stevenson	1-59308-131-6	$4.95
A Tale of Two Cities	Charles Dickens	1-59308-138-3	$5.95
Tao Te Ching	Lao Tzu	1-59308-256-8	$5.95
The Three Musketeers	Alexandre Dumas	1-59308-148-0	$8.95
The Time Machine and The Invisible Man	H. G. Wells	1-59308-032-8	$4.95
Tom Jones	Henry Fielding	1-59308-070-0	$8.95
Treasure Island	Robert Louis Stevenson	1-59308-247-9	$4.95
The Turn of the Screw, The Aspern Papers and Two Stories	Henry James	1-59308-043-3	$5.95
Twenty Thousand Leagues Under the Sea	Jules Verne	1-59308-302-5	$5.95
Uncle Tom's Cabin	Harriet Beecher Stowe	1-59308-121-9	$7.95
Vanity Fair	William Makepeace Thackeray	1-59308-071-9	$7.95
The Varieties of Religious Experience	William James	1-59308-072-7	$7.95
Villette	Charlotte Brontë	1-59308-316-5	$7.95
The Voyage Out	Virginia Woolf	1-59308-229-0	$6.95
Walden and Civil Disobedience	Henry David Thoreau	1-59308-208-8	$5.95
The War of the Worlds	H. G. Wells	1-59308-085-9	$3.95
Ward No. 6 and Other Stories	Anton Chekhov	1-59308-003-4	$7.95
The Waste Land and Other Poems	T. S. Eliot	1-59308-279-7	$4.95
The Wings of the Dove	Henry James	1-59308-296-7	$7.95
Wives and Daughters	Elizabeth Gaskell	1-59308-257-6	$7.95
Wuthering Heights	Emily Brontë	1-59308-044-1	$4.95